Murderer In The Mikdash

To order additional copies, please contact us.
BookSurge, LLC
www.booksurge.com
1-866-308-6235
orders@booksurge.com

GIDON ROTHSTEIN

MURDERER IN THE MIKDASH

2005

Murderer In The Mikdash

To Elizabeth, Who Encouraged Me All The Way

PREFACE AND ACKNOWLEDGEMENTS

I wrote *Murderer in the Mikdash* to see whether I could flesh out a world much like our own, with only the additional fact that the Messiah had arrived and Israel had become a benevolent dictatorship operating under the rules of traditional Judaism. Since how that time will look is a mystery—how could a benevolent theocratic dictatorship work in modern times?—I couched it in a mystery novel. I hope you will enjoy coming to know Rachel Tucker, Elijah Zeale, and Reuven HaOzer as much as I have these past years. I also hope that readers will see this book as a beginning and not an end, will use it as a jumping-off point for their considerations of what the Messianic future will look like, and will share their own thoughts and ideas with me, at gidonr@att.net.

As I put the finishing touches on this book, I have to thank the too-many-people-to-name who read and commented on earlier drafts. In particular, I want to thank Rabbi Barry Kornblau, who treated this as a real book way before I had committed to making it one; Rabbi Barry Dov Katz, who saw my voice expressed in the earliest kernel of this work; the Riverdale Jewish Center, where I delivered the sermon that began this process; and John Rieck, who helped me bring it to press.

Most of all, I need and want to thank my family for their support throughout the years, in forms related and unrelated to this book. My children, Tamar—whose enjoyment of the book suggested I was on the right track in writing it—Aryeh, and Adin are a source of pleasure and a goad to do whatever I can to leave them with a better world than we have now. And Elizabeth, already mentioned in the dedication, deserves more thanks and greater praise than the page can hold. To her, in a different way, silence is the best praise.

CHAPTER ONE

Rachel's first thought was that only dumb luck had made her look up when she did. She immediately added, as she often did these days, if, after the *Arrival*, we're still allowed to believe in such things. A second later, she knew, she wouldn't have seen him full face, and wouldn't have recognized him from any other angle.

She had to divide her focus between her thoughts and keeping up with the man, whose quick pace matched the permanently harried expression on his face, as if he was always forced to endure a world that asked too much of him. His red hair, so oily that it instantly explained his pockmarked face, had given Rachel a nickname for him, always her first concern when looking at unknown people on the street.

The face offered a painful reminder of her own high school years, dominated by hyperawareness of the many pimples that dotted her complexion. Only the worry of looking like Oily Haired Man had helped her resist the urge to pick at them, so that she had avoided his kinds of blemishes. Still, prom week had been a blur of worry about whether the copious amounts of Oxy Clean she applied would perform the desired magic.

The sound of her lungs raggedly drawing in air brought her back to the present, reminding her that it had been several months since she had walked quickly. She couldn't remember when in the pregnancy she had lost the ability to move faster than a stroll, but it hadn't been much beyond that first trimester. With chagrin, she thought of her former fanaticism about exercise, her arrogant disdain for all the women who failed to suck it up and keep themselves in shape despite their morning sickness. Somewhere in the middle of the sixth month, what with all the drama in her life and her alarmingly large stomach, it had just seemed pointless, and she was paying for it now.

After the second time she almost lost him flattening herself against the wall to avoid an oncoming car, she picked up her pace, to close some of the gap between them. The narrow alleyway he was leading her through brought back memories of the afternoons she and Elijah had spent watching construction crews trying to widen the streets, slowly moving the walls of entire buildings. They would sit for hours, picnic basket in front of them, hands interwoven, watching what Elijah—Lije to all my friends, he would always say— thought of as progress and she as wanton destruction of charming byways. Now, she wished the government had moved faster.

As she edged closer, she fervently hoped she had not made as deep an impression on him as he had on her. She'd never been particularly good at trailing people, and needed as much slack as she could create. Her inadequacy at a fundamental skill of investigative reporting always fueled her fear that over the years she had become just a pretty-face anchorwoman. Complicating her life, Oily-Haired Man had a nervous habit of glancing around every few yards, forcing her to repeatedly duck into doorways.

She clung desperately to the trail, losing him around one curve only to catch a glimpse of him turning back onto Jaffa Road as the semicircular side road intersected once again with the larger street.

Too bad that policeman with all the questions wasn't here now! He had wanted to know all about Liat's marital history, her drug problems, the history of their friendship, he'd been real interested in all of that, but when she finally came up with a piece of information she thought was important, *that* he had shrugged away.

Most of what happened that night was just a haze. She remembered the medics frantically working to save her dying friend, the police asking questions, the flashing lights. In the middle of the chaos that was Liat's deathbed, she could still see him, tugging at a jacket that identified him as a volunteer medic.

He stood out because he was one of the only people not rushing from one task to another. Once he caught her attention, she noticed his facial expression and body language, which testified that he was not an actual medic, and that his presence here had little to do with trying to help Liat. Somebody needed to investigate this man, she had said to herself.

She turned to call the police officer who had asked that she contact him with anything that seemed relevant. At that exact moment, in a memory that still made her gnash her teeth in frustration at some people's stupidity, some idiot had asked for her autograph; by the time she got rid of him, Oily Haired Man was gone. Of course she had told the cop, but, with no actual person to interrogate, he had just shrugged in that quintessentially Israeli way, saying he couldn't do anything without a better description.

Anyway, he had said, the guy was probably just a harmless kook, one of the many slightly off people who own police-band radios so they can show up at scenes like this—makes them feel like they participated in important events or some such thing. It needn't affect our investigation, he said, since Liat died of sudden respiratory distress. Especially given her drug use, such a death, while rare, is not completely unexpected.

The distraught family had had to decide whether to push for an investigation, delaying the funeral and almost inevitably making a public spectacle of the divorce and Liat's subsequent downward descent, or to accept the coroner's offer to rule it death by natural causes. Rachel understood their opting for a quick, quiet end, but had felt guilty that she had not done more. Now that the opportunity had presented itself, she was doubly determined not to let him get away.

Staying close enough to keep him in sight while not actually walking into him took so much of her attention that she didn't notice when they entered the Old City or the direction they were walking. As she hurried after him through the gates that had sprung up since the Arrival, she considered her next move. Call a police officer? Why would he care? She would love to rummage in her purse for that officer's card, but knew she'd never be able to find anything in there while also trailing someone.

At the third gate, the crowds were noticeably denser. Rachel picked up her pace to avoid losing him, only to be stopped.

"*Selihah, geveret, mazal tov `al ledet benekh,* excuse me, miss, congratulations on your son's birth." The Hebrew of the guard's words startled her out of her focus on the red-haired man. Realizing he had seen the badge on her arm, like so many people in the last three weeks, she thanked him and began to move on.

"I'm sorry, ma'am, but I won't be able to allow you beyond here for another few weeks," he persisted.

"But you don't understand, that man…" Rachel sputtered, as her target melted into the crowd. "Look, it's very urgent that I get in touch with that man right there. It's a matter of catching a murderer!" She hadn't meant to sound so melodramatic, especially since she wasn't sure of the penalties for lying to a security guard. She needn't have worried, since he was singularly unimpressed.

"Ma'am, if you'd like, I can take a description, but I cannot let a woman in your condition onto the Mount."

His customer service tone of voice, calm and level, ready to deal with whatever she would throw his way, brought her fully away from the now-lost oily-haired man and moved it to the jet-black-haired one standing before her. He wasn't a security guard, she realized, he was a Levi, and he wasn't manning a security gate, he was working the entrance to the Temple Mount. Why had Oily-Haired Man gone *there*, where she couldn't? Come to think of it, why couldn't she go?

Automatically, Rachel read the name off his tag, to be a little friendly, at least at the beginning of the conversation. Levi. *Kishmo ken hu,* Lije used to say, he was as his name. Levi the Levi. If it were me, she thought, I'd change it to something else; I guess it's his life.

"I'm sorry, Mr. Levi. What did you say?"

He corrected her automatically, as if he were used to the mistake. "No, ma'am, Levi's my first name; it's actually Levi Yoetz. We put the first name on to put people at ease, to ease the sting of telling them what they don't want to hear. Like you might be annoyed that I won't let you in, you might think that I'm helping a murderer get away, but knowing my first name, well, it's always sounded strange to me, but the studies show that people find it harder to blow up at someone else when they're on a first name basis." He paused, expecting further questions, and even as she opened her mouth to ask them, she noticed how much of her inner anger he had managed to defuse.

As she tried to formulate her questions, her mind launched into the speech she had delivered countless times in the last several years. Well, Mr. Yoetz, I've never interested myself much in the Temple...Actually, that was the diplomatic way of phrasing her repeated semi-conscious decision to avoid, ignore, and hide from information about the Temple or the new rules. A twenty-first century theocracy, however benevolent, gave her what a younger Rachel Tucker would have called the heebie-jeebies.

Ignoring it, her strategy of choice, was particularly difficult considering that it was these very changes that had drawn Lije here. She had had to agree to shuttle between Jerusalem and New York, but had gotten her revenge by giving her "I've never interested myself..." speech as often as she could. Lije hadn't liked it, but, well, we all have to compromise in life, right? Flying in her first trimester had been so unpleasant that he had cut back their social engagements, for fear of hearing nothing but that speech for three months, and had also agreed to do most of the commuting.

As she tried to pick up the thread of her conversation with Levi, the back of her mind dragged her back to high school, to one of those classes where old rabbis had tried to force-feed Bible lessons. She had long ago learned to trust such mental wanderings, which now were replaying a day in the class of, what was his name, Rabbi Faithful? droning on about being barred from the Temple, the Mount, or the City.

The badge! Flashing forward to her hospital bed, she remembered the obstetrician explaining it as the government's way of mandating a friendlier society. Exhausted from the delivery, wishing for more Percoset and more time before she had to go home, she hadn't been about to protest. She'd actually been kind of touched when Dr. Vlad did the sewing herself, saying she wanted to be part of the effort to connect Jews to each other.

To be honest, she'd thoroughly enjoyed the flood of congratulations coming her way at all times and places. It eased, ever so slightly, the fatigue of caring for a three-week-old without another parent, and had made her feel significantly more connected to the people around her, "I'm not really interested" speech or not. She'd even gotten into the habit of talking to total strangers, offering *them* congratulations or condolences, depending on their badge.

A gentle smile lingering on her face from the memories of her experiences in stranger-kindness, her mind finally deposited her back into the present, where Levi was waiting. His message, that the badge was also a way of spying on her for the benefit of those charged with guarding the Temple, wiped the smile off her face, replacing it with the beginnings of her theocracy-headache. When that throbbing appeared, she usually went home to rest in bed until she could get herself back to paying no attention to Israel's new religious concerns. Right now, though, some stubborn part of her insisted on pushing the conversation.

"You mean you're going to stop me from following a man who could be a murderer, or hold the key to a murder, just because I gave birth last month?" She had wanted to vent all her anger, over this latest incident, over Liat, over Lije, over, well, *everything*, but his patience in waiting for her to formulate her thoughts had disarmed her, so that the words came out sounding like she was just curious.

Patient as he was, Levi the Levi answered quickly, clearly seeking to move the conversation towards its conclusion. After all, the line at the gate was growing rapidly; there had to be some rules for how long he could spend with her. "Ma'am, first of all, I have no evidence that that man was "possibly a murderer" or holds the "key" to anything; more important, my job is protecting the Mount from improper entry, and I don't have any leeway to override that concern.

I can give you the number of a more senior Levi if you'd like, or we can arrange to discuss this further when I'm not quite so busy..."

Rachel looked up at him, probably in his late 30's, absolutely certain of the righteousness of his cause. Part of her wanted to ask him to detain all red-haired men (did they have a loudspeaker? could they announce "Would all men with oily red hair please come to the information booth?").

The thought was actually a blessing, because outrageously crazy ideas were her internal signal that she had run out of real options, that it was time to pack it in. The trail was cold, there were at least six other exits he could use, and she couldn't watch them all. Arguing with Levi—whom she had already dismissed as either a deeply committed religious fanatic or a petty bureaucrat committed only to following rules—would be futile. She hated futility.

She briefly considered touching him, since Lije had often complained about how few people realized that contact with those who hadn't specially prepared to go into the Temple forced a Levi off the Mount for the rest of the day. She settled for a look rich with disdain for him and his religious system, got no reaction, turned on her heel, and stalked away.

It was only now that she paid enough attention to notice that Oily-Haired Man had done her the favor of depositing her on the side of the Mount she knew. What had once been called the Kotel, the Western Wall courtyard and prayer venue, had now been cut in thirds. One still hosted prayer services, for people who either could not or did not want to enter the Mount. The other two accommodated subsidiary aspects of the service, offering animals, birds, flour, and wine for purchasing, changing money into the special coinage of the Temple, and, of course, ritual baths for a last-minute cleansing.

She ordinarily would have left through the old Arab marketplace, the quickest route home, but her headache demanded aspirin ASAP, so she took the steps up to what had once been called the Jewish Quarter, where she assumed she'd find a pharmacy. When she got to the top of the stairs, having now officially walked more than at any time in the last four months (and perhaps than in all of them combined), she turned right and walked down the row of stores.

When she saw a coffee bar, she thought caffeine might do just as well. A bell tinkled, announcing her arrival, and the perky girl behind the counter chirped "Welcome to the Temple Grounds, best fresh-brewed coffee in the city of Jerusalem. What can I get you?" Still engrossed in thoughts about Levi and Oily-Haired Man, it took a while for the question to penetrate.

The counter girl was opening her mouth to repeat the greeting, which probably would have come out exactly the same as the first time, but Rachel mustered up a quick "Um, cappuccino, thanks." While she waited and then as she took her coffee to a table, half-noticed incidents from the past year flooded her memory, taking on new meaning.

Avshalom, her ABC News contact in Israel, mentioning his having to postpone a meeting in Jerusalem because of a skin problem. She remembered his chagrined laugh when she had expressed her concern, assuring her that his doctor had been positive it wasn't a physical problem, and that his priest thought that with the right behavior, it would disappear fairly soon. He hadn't seemed concerned, shifting his meetings to Tel Aviv, so she had let the incident slip from her mind.

Or Renee, who had had to burn her favorite dress because of a stubborn red stain. Or the neighbor Rachel had seen taking all the furniture out of her apartment because a priest was coming to check out a spread of mold on her wall. Only in retrospect did she see how odd it was that she had managed to not notice these, not to see how they hung together. What a wall she had placed around herself!

"You a reject, too?" Her train of thought already having put her on edge, she looked up furiously. The gentle smile of the giant standing over her, who introduced himself as Reuven, staunched the flow of invective at the edge of her mouth. Not fully mollified, she controlled herself enough to say, "Only on the Temple Mount."

"Yeah, that's what I meant; there's lots of rejects here, that's why I got this location. I figured when people got told they couldn't go in, they'd need a pick me up right away. See that guy over there? He helped at a car accident with a fatality; he's waiting out his week by hanging out here. And see her? She..."

He was about to go on, but she stepped into the opening.

"It doesn't bother you?" she blurted out.

"What?"

"That these people are being excluded from a place they think is holy for reasons beyond their control? That that guy is being punished for helping give dignity to the dead?" She was happy she could sound so principled, when her real beef was being excluded from a place she wanted to enter.

The question startled him. He looked at her for a moment, and then said, "You know what, I'm sorry, I misunderstood your situation."

Puzzled, she said, "What do you mean?"

"Well, two kinds of people come in here. Most go to the Mikdash regularly, and are bummed at being out of it for a while. But we also get people who are not so used to the way the system works. I've had people in here who'd come to Israel for a week especially to see the Temple and its workings, hadn't consulted with anybody and then got told they couldn't get in for at least a week! They are *not* happy, let me tell you, and in a whole different way from that first group. Anyway, something about your look or dress made me think you were in the first group, usually called a *haver, haverah* for a woman, and that led me to misspeak. My apologies."

He was about to go on, but she was way ahead of him. A two-level society, with Ins and Outs, was beginning to sound like a news story, so she bit back her urge to sarcasm and asked, "So these *haverim* are okay with being excluded for silly reasons? And for those who aren't, is it right that they be excluded from an important place—it's a central place of worship, right?"

He hesitated, weighing how to respond. "Well, let me say this. I bought this coffee shop because I was interested in meeting anyone who comes away from the Mikdash unhappy. What with the conversation and maybe the drugs we slip in the coffee, they often go away happier than when they came in, which means I'm helping, which is all I really want."

His mischievous smile as he finished speaking conveniently coincided with another customer calling for his attention. Rachel liked him, his sincerity, his obvious belief in what he said, and his good-natured acceptance of the people around him. They were many of the same qualities that had drawn her to Elijah and that she still found attractive, despite the nightmare loving him had eventually become. But meeting a nice and sincere man wasn't enough to dispel her dark cloud of resentment about what had happened earlier, nor to distract her from the question she had asked him. When he worked his way back to her table, she pounced.

"You didn't answer my question, you avoided the issue!"

He put on a horrible Irish accent. "Ah, chickadee, did I say we answer questions here? I just said people go away happier." Without the accent, he continued, "I actually consciously avoid answering questions about how to reconcile oneself to the new society, because I have had too many long, deep conversations about issues raised in objective, intellectual terms when the real concern is emotional. I suspect your own reaction—you can't go in because of your son, right? Mazal Tov, by the way—was also emotional, but you would know better than I."

As she smiled politely at his congratulation wishes, she was both insulted by the insinuation that she was letting her emotions rule her intellect, and annoyed that he was right. In the months after Lije disappeared, Liat had become her closest companion. The trauma of losing her right after the baby was born was hard enough; her unresolved guilt over not having looked into her death more thoroughly had been there, just beneath the surface, ever since.

She woke up nights wondering what her friend would say if they could have one last conversation; she wandered the streets with the baby in the stroller, listening for some clue. She thought about the diary Liat had become obsessed with in the month before her death, over and over begging her to swear to read it if something happened to her. She had tried to find it, pestered the police about it, without success. Seeing the red-haired man had, if only for a few minutes, raised the hope that she might find the answers. Levi Yoetz had forced the painful mystery to continue.

Something about Reuven gave the impression that he was not only willing to hear about Liat, but that he would deem it a personal favor if she would share her story with him. As she launched into her tale, her suspicious side expected him to take perverse pleasure in her confirming his guess that her righteous anger was really just personal frustration. She had underestimated him again; he dropped that completely and thrust himself into Liat's story.

"What makes you think she didn't die naturally, like the Medical Examiner said?"

"I don't have any real reason, I guess. It's just, she was so young, and seemed so healthy, and I know that those aren't reasons, but along with how she had been acting…I mean, you had to know her. Sometimes she was such a joy to be around, not a care in the world, always concerned that everybody around her have a good time. And then, other times, something would change, and she'd start to ramble, in conversation, on the phone, whenever. And when I'd mention it, she'd get all defensive, and clam up."

"Ramble?"

"Yeah, going off on tangents that didn't seem related to her point…the only consistent thing was her diary. For a while she'd be worrying that maybe it wasn't safe, maybe something would happen to it, but a few weeks before she…died, that changed, too, and she started talking about how at least that was safe, and if that was safe, it would all come out in the end. She wouldn't tell me what she meant, but it was strange, because even though you'd think she'd be happy that it was safe, whatever that meant, she actually seemed more resigned than anything else…"

Her voice trailed off as she saw a red-headed man through the coffee shop window. For a minute, she thought it was him; as he got closer, she saw her mistake.

"What is it? Is something wrong?"

"No, I'm fine, thanks. I think I've got men with oily red hair on the brain." She was suddenly very tired. The Liat emotions, the headache from before, she wasn't ready for this. She stood to leave.

"Thank you for the coffee, Mr....." He had introduced himself by his first name.

"It's HaOzer, but please, everyone calls me Reuven."

She smiled, but it was her polite social smile; she was too tired for a real one. "All right, thank you, Reuven, what do I owe you for the coffee?

He ignored her question, focusing on the change in their conversation. "Did I upset you?"

"No, why do you ask?"

"Well, you seemed to end our conversation abruptly, as if something happened."

"I'm just tired; seeing that red-haired man, losing him, thinking about Liat. I still have a tension headache from the excitement at the Temple, and I feel another coming on, and the coffee, good as it was, didn't stop it. Also, if I get home quickly, I can get in a 20 minute power nap before the babysitter leaves. Without being rude, I'd like to pay for my coffee, say how nice it was to meet you, and be on my way." She could always sense when a man was working up to asking her out, and was hoping to avoid that particular awkwardness.

"The coffee's always on the house for first-time rejects—we are the Temple Grounds after all—but I had also wanted to ask you whether..."

"Look, I'm sorry, I think you're a very nice man, but I'm just not ready to begin dating yet..."

"Dating?" Horrified, she saw that that was absolutely not what he had been thinking about. He looked befuddled, his face showing that her words had come out of nowhere. "Aren't you a new mother? Where's your husband?"

CHAPTER TWO

There, he had said the word, and the sting was strong as ever. It took her back to the first night Lije had failed to come home; she had just arrived for a four day weekend, and had made dinner, able to stand the smell of food long enough to cook for the first time in the pregnancy.

When he was late, she had gotten annoyed. He was wonderful in many ways, but when he got sidetracked, which happened both easily and often, he would forget to call. Then, as the hours wore on, and she tried various numbers and places, she began to worry. What if something had happened?

She called the police the next morning, and then had to deal with what they called customer service. The worst had been the knowing looks. They had seen it all too many times before: a young, attractive man, particularly an immigrant who could wow women with his worldly sophistication, with a wife in the first stage of pregnancy, maybe not satisfying him as often as he'd like, doesn't show up at home, it means he's found a better field to plant. It sounded more natural in Hebrew, but that's what they said, adding that he'd be back, shamefaced, in a few days.

She couldn't believe they'd think that. She also couldn't believe they had said it to her straight out like that, but that was a whole different issue. Lije run off on her? And yet, as neither he nor his car showed up, she had begun to doubt.

Of course there was no way she was telling any of that to this stranger, who seemed not to have met the question he wouldn't ask. Looking up at Reuven, she informed him, in her most clipped tones, that she did not choose to discuss her private life with people she had only just met, and in a coffee shop, of all places.

He apologized. "I know, I get carried away. It's only…I meet so many people desperate for someone, anyone, to listen to them, that I get used to asking any questions that come up, as a way of showing concern. I go too far sometimes; my fault. Forgive me?" It was a smile of such remorse that she couldn't help relent a little.

"Certainly I forgive you. Was there anything else?"

Thankfully, he ignored her shortness, which she regretted as soon as the words came out, replying that yes, he wanted to mention a group meeting she might like to try out. "I know I didn't get around to explaining much about how I see this new era. I could tell you, and maybe I will if we ever have a lot of time, but I think you might enjoy seeing how other people struggle with it. These meetings, which they call Democrats' Anonymous, gather people who are offended by the new rules in one way or other. If you'd like to see one, I can arrange it, and I think you'd understand a lot better."

"A support group?" She managed to avoid curling her lip in distaste. "With a sixty year old social worker telling us how wonderful we are for having feelings?"

He smiled. "You've heard of them, I see. Actually, this one is different; it's more of a discussion among the people than an attempt to get to any conclusion. They talk about infuriating things that happened, like you and Levi Yoetz, and everyone else listens. The fact of having an audience helps many more people than you'd imagine. If nothing else, I think you'd get a kick out of seeing people share some of your indignation over their indifference to your search for A POSSIBLE MURDERER."

His flourish on those last words was so exaggerated that she couldn't help but laugh at her earlier melodrama.

"Are you going to be there?" She couldn't believe the question slipped out of her mouth. Knowing him for maybe half an hour, she already felt safe in a way that had little to do with his physical size or strength.

"I could go, sure, but I think you might gain more if you went alone. Tell you what, I'll drop you off, introduce you around, then leave, so you can make your own way. How does that sound?"

She agreed, and they arranged to meet at the Temple Grounds at 10 the next morning. She left the shop with a lighter step, although she wasn't sure why. She felt...not excited, certainly, but interested in what would happen at the meeting the next day. She wouldn't mind finding some way to accept the country and system Lije loved so much, yet she had few hopes or expectations that that would happen, either.

Of course, the night she wanted to get a good rest, the baby decided to be a monster. She took him from the sitter at 6:30, he complained until 10 with only brief breaks when she switched to a new game or song, and then woke up every hour and a half until 5:30. When he finally fell asleep for four hours straight, the sitter was already back.

Rachel barely slept, and in the one long sleep she did get, she dreamt that Liat was floating above her, frantically dialing the phone but never getting connected. She woke up sweaty and, if possible, less rested than when she had fallen into bed exhausted the night before.

To match the rest of her life, on her way to the coffee shop she saw him, twenty feet ahead of her, sitting in the open area of the Jewish Quarter, the courtyard near the Old Hurva synagogue. Surprised at seeing him again so soon, she debated her next step. She had promised to meet Reuven at 10, but didn't want to lose the red-haired man.

Then she realized she didn't have to choose yet. If he was going to the Mount as he had yesterday, he would pass the coffee shop, and she could quickly explain to Reuven what was going on.

No such luck. He ended up heading out of the Old City and going to the Hilton Hotel, which, Rachel dimly knew, had some other name now. For her, Jerusalem should have stayed as it was when she had visited Israel for the first time, as a teenager.

Knowing she'd have to make it up to Reuven later, she called Information for the number of the Temple Grounds, but got an operator who insisted she couldn't want to call a coffee shop of that poor caliber. No, she should call this other, more authentic coffee shop.

Seeing the humor in the moment, knowing she could use the story at parties for years, she didn't even get annoyed. She had found that if she insisted long enough while maintaining her composure, she would get what she wanted. When she finally got it, Reuven wasn't at the shop, easing her guilt tremendously. Leaving a message that she had to reschedule, she hung up, feeling virtuous and even annoyed that he wasn't immediately accessible.

Entering the hotel, she paused for a moment to breathe in the atmosphere, as she always did. She hadn't been poor in a long time, but the opulence of hotel lobbies—the marble floors, the smell of money, the waterfalls of various shapes and sizes that were part of the décor in Israeli hotels—were irresistible draws. Business travel was one of the perks she missed most, especially accommodations like this one.

A member of the staff walked up to her. "Excuse me,..."

She had been down this road often, although less so in Israel than in America. "Yes, I'm Rachel Tucker, thank you."

The words left her mouth, she realized her error, and flushed. He had only been trying to help her find her way; like almost everyone in this stupid country, he did not watch American news, did not know or care who she was. Close your mouth, Rachel, she gritted to herself, and then, out loud, "I'm sorry, I thought you were asking me something else. Could you tell me, did you notice a man with red hair come through this lobby in the last few minutes?"

The bellboy turned to the receptionist behind the desk, about thirty feet from where they were standing.

"Hey, Limor, did you see a *gingi* come through here in the last five minutes?"

Limor started to shake her head no, then called, "Wait, he went to the meeting?"

She could hardly believe it. "Meeting?"

The bellboy answered with practiced professional pride, "Oh, yes, ma'am, we host the most popular Democrats' Anonymous meeting in the country. Fifth floor, to your left as you get off the elevator."

The meeting! What was he doing there? Was *he* learning to adjust to the New Israel? Not killing Liat would have been a big step in the right direction, she thought as she hurried to the fifth floor, wondering what she would find.

She shared the elevator with two couples, both in their mid-forties and stylishly dressed, although different styles. One couple was Israeli-stylish, the man in slacks and a white shirt, the woman wearing clothing that emphasized each curve of her fit body. The other woman, no less attractive, wore an outfit that lured the eye in, giving a hint of what lay underneath, drawing attention more subtly but no less effectively. That was the outfit Rachel would have to find and buy.

The American couple was staring at her. Finally, the woman said, "Excuse me," she wasn't falling for that one again, "but are you Rachel Tucker, the anchorwoman?

After the embarrassment in the lobby, it was actually nice to be recognized. She acknowledged she was, signed an autograph, which, now that she signed maybe three a week, she enjoyed more than when she had been asked for fifty a day. Elegant clothes informed her, "This is my husband Bob, and I'm Elaine Gordon. We've only just moved here from Teaneck, NJ. So nice to meet you."

If they were going to become acquaintances, Rachel would do them the courtesy of looking at them a little more carefully. Bob Gordon was nearing fifty, still able to hide a few years, but rapidly approaching the time when his age would be clear to all. His waistline, probably a little thicker than in college, looked reasonably fit, and his hairline, flecked with gray, had held up admirably. Elaine, a few years short of Bob, had done a remarkable job of staving off signs of aging. From her perfect makeup to her well-toned arms, she was clearly a woman who had the time and means to insure that middle age was in her mind, not on her person.

She put out her hand, not sure that these were her kind of people. "We've lived here for several years, about five years after the

Arrival," Rachel started, deciding to reward friendliness in kind. Too late to take it back, she noticed the plural pronoun and how it invited questions she did not want to answer. "I mean, I…my son came along three weeks ago; I'm used to speaking of us as a unit." Not a bad recovery, they'll assume I'm divorced or had a child out of wedlock or something. Which is better than having to tell the truth.

Luckily, they were more interested in talking about themselves than noticing her. "It's funny, you know, the whole time we lived in New Jersey, everyone we knew and were friendly with was Orthodox—totally observant. When the Arrival happened, we were so excited. We thought, this is it! This is what we've always wanted, what we've waited for thousands of years, what we've prayed for! So we closed up shop, sold everything as fast as we could, and, well, we're just having the hardest time! We find these meetings *really* helpful, though, meeting people like ourselves and talk about the little frustrations, well, it *really* helps."

Rachel knew it was her problem and not theirs, but thought she would need to shoot herself in the head if she had to spend more than another two minutes with the Gordons. The sugar coating on every word that came out of Elaine Gordon's mouth felt like enough to rot three sets of teeth. She managed to nod politely when required—her silence did not hinder Elaine's stream of words—and then separate from them as soon as they got into the room.

Which was a shock. She had assumed there would be maybe fifteen social misfits gathered around a conference table moaning and groaning about the good old days before the Arrival. But the Gordons had walked her into a ballroom that easily could seat two hundred people, and was around three-quarters full. People were milling around, many of them obviously already catching up with friends they had not seen since the previous week's meeting. Not sure of the procedure, she checked that Red-Haired Man was there and found an empty seat next to a woman who looked inoffensive if uninteresting.

"Excuse me, is this seat taken?"

"No, my husband's not going to make it this week, feel free to sit down. My name is Hulda Weiner, nice to meet you."

"I see we don't work too hard for anonymity at Democrats' Anonymous."

"There's no need. The government has made it clear that they won't punish us for coming, so we just use our names."

"But if no one's anonymous, why call the meetings Anonymous?"

Hulda looked puzzled, as if she had never thought of the question. "I don't know." Nor did she seem to care now that it had been brought to her attention. Not a good start. She tried again.

"Why does the government value these meetings so much?"

"I don't know, but I think they were nervous about seeming like they were coercing religion. Which, of course, they are, because public behavior, at least, has to conform to some religious standards. On the other hand, they give us as much time to adjust as we need as long as we attend meetings regularly and behave reasonably well in public. Truthfully, I mostly only still come so I can occasionally indulge my cravings for a meal at one of the non-kosher restaurants. When I feel guilty enough, I'll stop coming."

Raised in a strict law-and-order family, Rachel had always assumed laws were to be followed by all, like it or not. A government that set laws, communal standards, and future goals was one she'd want to think about again later, but she was afraid of losing her momentum with Hulda, whom she expected to pump for enough information to maybe convert into a story for one of ABC's newsmagazines.

Physically unremarkable, Hulda's short mousy-brown hair unattractively drew attention to the length of her neck, oddly thin on a body probably thirty pounds beyond pleasing. Rachel felt like she had met her type before, too shy to initiate relationships, but happy to ramble on to anyone who expressed an interest.

"So, I'm a first-timer. Can you explain to me what happens?"

"It's pretty simple. We sit on these red chairs and watch

other people bare their souls; or, if the mood strikes, do it ourselves. Anything said in here is completely confidential and unpunishable."

"Sorry to seem dense, but I lost you right at the beginning. Does the meeting come to order at some point?"

The bang of a gavel on the front podium answered her question. A tall man with a full head of beautiful white hair called them to order, and began reading from the Bible, Hebrew and then English. That week's portion spoke of the laws that Moses had laid down as preparation for a Jewish society, eliciting groans from the assemblage.

When he had finished, he said, "We gather here to share. A reminder about rules: Anything said here remains completely confidential and is inadmissible in any outside proceeding. Violating that confidentiality is itself a punishable offense, so I warn you ahead of time. Also, no talking other than by those recognized by the chair." So much for getting information out of Hulda Weiner, thought Rachel. I may have to buy her coffee afterwards. Meanwhile, the man was finishing up, saying, "and remember, introduce yourself to the extent that you are comfortable, and speak for no more than five minutes."

CHAPTER THREE

In the two hours that followed, Rachel painfully re-learned three lessons she had been taught many times before—an amateur can make five minute seem like hours; intelligence does not necessarily include being articulate; and empathizing with a person does not have to mean that you want to hear them speak about their problem.

An hour into what would otherwise have been an ordeal, one comment stuck in her head enough to make the whole meeting worthwhile. She had been about to overcome her aversion to ruffling others' feathers and walk out when a muscular guy in his late twenties got up to speak. Everything about him, the way he dressed, the way he walked, the way he carried himself, and the way he spoke, made it clear that he was used to dealing with tough situations.

Looking around furtively, as if he could not quite believe that he would not be prosecuted for what he was about to say, he started, "My name is Jacko. My brother got killed last night in a barroom brawl, and I'm going to off the guy who did it. I never thought the system was helpful before, but getting rid of the guy who caused my family this much pain will help a lot. So I guess there's something good about all this. He's running to Hevron, I think, but I'm going straight from here; I'll catch him before he gets close. And then..." He pointed his finger and thumb and made a shooting motion.

Shocked at what seemed like a public announcement of a plan to commit murder, Rachel turned to Hulda and asked, "What is he talking about?" Wrapped up in the meeting, Hulda shushed her.

Trying to figure out how the rest of the group could accept his words without reacting took all of Rachel's attention until fifteen minutes before the end, when the white-haired man announced that there would only be time for three more speakers. The first was another blubberer, who spent his entire allotment talking about how thrilled he was that the government wasn't punishing him for some meaningless crimes he saw as world-shaking. She forgot him right away.

The second one she couldn't forget, because it was Oily Red Haired man. He stood up hesitantly, moved to the microphone, and began speaking, in a surprisingly high-pitched voice for any man, let alone the one Rachel had come to think of as Liat's murderer. "My name is…Harvey, and I am required to come here by my Levi. Coming here was supposed to keep me from forgetting the lessons I learned in prison. I've been coming now for seven months, and I wanted to thank the group for being here."

And he sat down, leaving her so confused that she completely missed the last speaker. All right, so he was a guy with a past, but what did that have to do with Liat? Was he flat-out lying? He sounded sincere, he looked sincere. She bet a lot on her skill at assessing people, yet she couldn't link this Harvey to the one she had seen at Liat's.

Coffee with Hulda no longer seemed particularly appealing, especially when she turned down Rachel's offer. Rachel instead turned to her new default plan, following Harvey. Knowing his name took some of the adventure out of it; now it felt more like she was keeping track of an old friend.

As he headed back to the Old City and towards the Temple Mount—did he know she was following him and use the Mount as a way to shake her?—she assumed she'd pass the shop, and could explain to Reuven what had happened. Instead, Harvey went around, down the steps past the Montefiore Windmill known as Yemin Moshe, across Solomon's Pools, where she and Lije had once heard Bob Dylan, and up to Zion Gate.

Expecting to be stopped, she decided to go as far as she could anyway. A different Levi was here, less off-putting than yesterday's. This one, his name tag said Yedidya, was about 5'11", in his early

30's, with light brown hair cut close to his head. His blue eyes, shockingly bright in an otherwise dark complexion, looked right through her, penetrating and welcoming at the same time.

Less flustered today, Rachel took the time to ask a few questions. "Pardon me, but do you know that red-haired man who went by?"

"I'm sorry, ma'am, I don't." And he turned away to help someone else, whose Mikvah-ticket had gotten stuck in the turnstiles. Rachel waited until he was free, and then asked him what it meant to refer to someone as "my Levi." Yedidya seemed unsure, so she told him about the meeting and Harvey's comment. He interrupted to remind her to change any identifying details, to safeguard the confidentiality of the meeting.

Once she had asked her question, he hesitated, and said, "I can give you a short answer or a long one. First, as you can tell, my name is Yedidya. And you are...? It seems so impersonal to have a conversation like this without at least exchanging names."

Rachel again felt a twinge at not being recognized, but hid it. "I'm Rachel Tucker, I live here in Yerushalayim. May I ask your family name?"

"Gross, Yedidya Gross. I also live here. Here's my card, in case we get interrupted or you have other questions in the future. The short answer is that most parole officers now are Levis and Kohanim, priests, since adding a spiritual side to the rehabilitation process helps reduce recidivism. It's also part of our job in general, which is why people call their parole officer their "Levi" even if he happens to be a priest."

"The long answer would take too much time now, while I'm on duty. I'm finished at 7 this evening, however, if you'd like to meet me somewhere, I'd be glad to explain further. Why don't you check with your husband, maybe he'd like to join us?"

Rachel knew he was simply trying to avoid the appearance of asking her out; like everyone else, he assumed a new mother was married. In some sense she was, although the bastard hadn't had the decency to get in touch in the last six and a half months. Still, she hated having to explain her situation to people she barely knew, and she was in no mood to do it now. She thanked him politely, said she was busy that evening but hoped to call soon, pocketed the card, and left.

With the adrenaline of the chase wearing off, her stomach's insistent growling finally broke into her consciousness. Looking down at her watch, she was surprised to find that it was 2 o'clock, when she hadn't eaten since 7 that morning. She should have offered to take Yedidya for lunch. Did Levis get lunch breaks on days they were working in the Temple? Mindful that TV cameras were in her future, she allowed herself only a Caesar's salad, dressing on the side. Of course, she was so proud of her self-restraint that she had Cookies and Cream frozen yogurt for dessert, wiping out her calorie savings.

Sitting there, her body told her that she was pushing too hard. After yesterday's chase of Harvey Oily Red Hair, she had felt strained, determined not to overdo it again. Luckily, Harvey had been in a relaxed mood after the meeting, so that the walk to the Mount hadn't been too taxing. Even without racing, it was more than she was used to. She would get to her next destination, whatever that was, in a cab.

Destination-- the word brought here back to the meeting. Pulling out her cell phone, she dialed the operator, asking for the police.

"Jerusalem police, shalom. For emergency assistance, please dial 0."

Which was better than the phone mail systems that forced you to listen to a thousand possibilities before you got to a live person, she thought as she pressed zero.

"To report a crime, press 1. For any other emergency, press 2."

1. "Thank you for calling the Jerusalem Police Emergency Crime Detection Phone System. Your call will be answered in the order it was received. Thank you for waiting."

The moment before someone got on the line gave her time to think about how much her life had changed in the past day. Then, she had been struggling with adjusting to the early stages of single motherhood, anxiously wondering when she would be able to get back to work. Liat's death had saddened her, sure, but was a tragedy like so many others, one she mostly managed to keep out of her mind.

She had dealt with Lije's disappearance the same way, taking a week off after he vanished, but compartmentalizing after that. The people at ABC were surprised that she didn't take a longer leave, but that was the way she was; she wasn't going to let Lije, or Liat, or even Atid, derail her entire life.

Not that she felt guilty about it. She had flown back to Israel regularly throughout the pregnancy, even though she didn't have any real reason to come. Each flight had required a doctor's note, drinking enough to drown a horse to make sure she didn't go into early labor, and tolerating the excessive concern of the flight attendants. It had been a way to keep on top of the police, make sure they were actively looking for him.

The police! What an idiot she was! She hung up in the middle of the fourth time hearing the phone tell her that her call was very important and dialed the direct number that the head of the search for Lije, Lieutenant Mehapes, had given her.

"Hello, Ms. Tucker. I'm sorry to tell you that there's no news. Please believe me, I will call as soon as"

She interrupted, relieved to have something else to talk about. "Thank you, but I'm calling on another matter. I wanted to report a crime."

"A crime? What happened?"

"Well, it didn't happen yet, but one man is about to kill another."

Mehapes' voice rose in shock, then lowered again. "Whaat! How do you know?"

Rachel told him about what Jacko had said, leaving out the circumstances where she heard it. Mehapes asked a few questions, she guessed to see whether there was exact enough information to make it worth the police's while to try to stop the murder. She felt like she was accomplishing something truly important, saving someone's life, until his final two questions.

"How did you hear about this?"

Unthinkingly, she mentioned the meeting, and his whole attitude shifted.

"I'm sorry, Ms. Tucker, but you know we can't violate confidentiality. Out of curiosity, though, could you tell me whether he mentioned a motive?"

"Sure, the guy had killed his brother."

Mehapes' tone changed now as well, reverting to the brusque officer of the law she usually dealt with. "Rachel, that's not a *crime*, don't you understand? Think of how you'd have embarrassed me (and yourself) if I had forwarded your report without asking that question! You have to know that something's wrong before you can file a report." Angrily, he hung up.

More bewildered than before, she left the restaurant and began wandering aimlessly, as did her thoughts. Lije, Liat, Atid, Jacko, Harvey, her entire cast of characters took their turns at flashing through her unsettled mind, a flickering theater that left her conscious of inner turmoil she might have managed to mask, at least from herself.

When she dragged her mind away from its ruminations and looked at where she was, her tired body was relieved to find itself a block away from the Temple Grounds. A nice cup would hit the spot; she also had to be home for Atid soon, and owed Reuven an apology for this morning.

Even the word raised bile in her throat. Some therapist would get rich helping her unravel her aversion to apologies, but she'd have to agree to enter therapy first. Meanwhile, she needed a gift to do the heavy lifting. She'd be happy to supply the embarrassed smile, but let the items do the talking. What would be appropriate to give a man she barely knew?

A book. A book about...coffee? No; he might own and operate a coffee shop, but it seemed clear that it wasn't about the coffee. Unlike *some* people she knew, who could spend hours discussing flavors, types, and processes of preparation. No, for Reuven, Rachel sensed, coffee was a way to meet, interact with, and help people. For Rachel, it was a way to stay awake.

Apologize, apologize, apologize. Maybe a book on apologies? Everybody was writing histories of who knows what, somebody must have done that for apologies. Back in the Cardo, the underground shopping mall, there was a Barnes and Noble, one of the few signs Rachel accepted as proof of the arrival of the Redeemer. She'd get an apology book, write a cute little inscription, and have her opening.

True to the recent course of her life, she couldn't find one. The Israeli workers at the store were not up to the standards of B&N's back home, so she settled on a copy of Plato's Apology, and headed to the coffee shop. Mentally, she filed away the idea of a history of apologies, another of the many bestsellers she had already decided to write when she found time.

Reuven was seated at a table, so engrossed in his conversation with a young man that he didn't look up when the door opened and closed. She went to the counter, where a different college student said, as perkily as the day before, "Welcome to the Temple Grounds, how may I serve you?" ordered her coffee, and watched him talk.

She couldn't know from where she was standing, but the scene seemed self-explanatory. The kid had big, sad eyes, a little moist, as if he was talking about a topic that pained him, but held his attention obsessively. Reuven would not solve the problem, she knew from having interviewed similar people over the years. The kid would have to go through whatever he had to go through, and Reuven might ease it, but he wouldn't greatly alter it. She figured he knew that, yet there was no impatience in him, not even the hint of an impression that he was waiting out the end of the monologue.

She watched a little more, curious about this man who had managed to make her feel guilty enough to buy him a book. His size jumped out at you right away, but for all that he was tall and broad and solid, there was no threat. She could not imagine his intentionally initiating harm, physical or otherwise, although she could easily visualize him furiously and physically defending any victim. Rachel had always been one to watch a man's hands at least as much as his eyes; the eyes might be the window on the soul, but the hands revealed how the person actually lived. Reuven's hands were big and meaty, warmly enveloping whatever came into them.

As she watched him work his magic, the conversation seemed to reach its natural end. The kid wiped his eyes on a tissue, drank the last remnants of his coffee, and leaned over to embrace Reuven, who gracefully pushed his chair back and stood up, whispering something she couldn't hear, but managing to avoid the hug without giving any obvious offense. The boy left, promising over his shoulder that he would call and let him know "how it worked out."

Finished, Reuven only now looked around the shop, saw her standing at the counter. Without saying a word, Rachel held up the gift-wrapped book and motioned towards it, as if to say, "You can't yell at me until you see what I have."

He worked his way over towards her, passing coffee-drinkers along the way, greeting each one by name or introducing himself and briefly getting a sense of the patron. Watching him, she realized the shop was more of a community than a business, with Reuven the focal point. Most of the patrons appeared to be regulars, having established relationships of various kinds with him and other people in the store, getting something in these four walls that they could not find out there. She almost expected a cry of "Norm" when a new customer walked in, like in a bar where everybody knew your name.

He was wagging a finger at her reprovingly, though playfully. "I remember seeing 'They're Playing Our Song' on Broadway as a kid," he started, which ranked high on the list of least likely words Rachel would have expected to hear. "It starred Robert Klein and Luci Arnaz. I remember because it was my first Broadway show, because I thought Luci Arnaz was beautiful, and because there's a scene in the play in which she's late for a meeting with him. He is sitting in a studio waiting for her, and he writes in his diary—out loud—'she is now 24 hours and 20 minutes late. And it's not the 24 hours that bother me, it's the 20 minutes. And, then she walks in, and all is right with the world.'"

"And which part of that story applies to me? I'm several hours late, not 24."

"No, the all is right with the world."

She had not been prepared for that direct a compliment. To recover, she assured herself that he was only giving her what he had learned needy people craved, that he was treating her as any other patron. Her face, with a mind of its own, flushed hot red with the embarrassment she had been trying to suppress. Flustered, she gave him the book, and stammered out her apology.

"But I did go to a meeting, at the Old Hilton."

"Did you really? I thought you were too nervous to go by yourself?"

So she told him the story, regaining enough composure to note again how impressive a listener he was. She had seen it yesterday and just now with the college student, but was surprised all over again by how comforting it was to be held in the thrall of his readiness to hear whatever she or anyone else chose to share.

She told him about seeing the red-haired man, leaving the name for the dramatic part of the story, following him to the hotel, where, it turned out, *he* was going to a meeting! She told him some of the highlights of the two hours, including her excitement about putting a name on the red-haired man, Harvey. She was so caught up in finishing her story so that she could ask him the questions that had been bothering her since she left the meeting, that she didn't notice the look on his face when she said the name.

"Reuven, why would Jacko be allowed to kill the man who killed his brother before he got to a city of refuge?"

He looked at her, surprised. "You don't know?"

"Know what?" Now, he was reminding her of Mehapes, who had been too busy to explain. She was used to having to work to get information from people, but not from people who were specifically designated to give out information to those seeking it. Getting a little annoyed, she said "Look, I assume you think I'm supposed to know something here, but I don't. So do you want to tell me what's going on or mock my ignorance a little more?"

But she had lost him, which was more infuriating than it might otherwise have been, since it was in such startling contrast to the attentiveness she had witnessed and experienced moments ago. "Reuven?" No answer; he was looking out the window, staring off into space.

"Reuven?"

He didn't move his eyes, but his mouth formed the words, "You said you followed a red-haired man, right?"

"Yes, why?" Rachel looked out the window now, trying to follow his gaze, but she couldn't see anyone who looked remotely like Harvey.

"And you saw him go to the Temple Mount twice?

"Yes. Reuven, what is it?"

"And today you found out his name is Harvey?"

"Yes. Reuven, is there a reason we're replaying the last five minutes of our conversation?"

He lifted his arm and pointed down the block, at an ice cream store on the other side of the street. She looked over and saw Harvey walk out, licking a cone, and turning in the direction of the Temple Mount. He was out of his chair and at the door before she had a moment to react.

"I'll follow him; leave your phone number with Meltzer behind the counter, and I'll call when I have some news."

She would have wondered whether this was a ruse to get her phone number if she hadn't seen Harvey herself. Puzzled over how often their paths had crossed over the last few days, she went home to Atid.

CHAPTER FOUR

Other priests spoke of the exhaustion of focusing on each detail of complicated rituals for a whole day, but Pinhas Moshel always came away exhilarated. He kept careful track of the statistics and took pride knowing that he consistently served more days in the Temple than any other priest, and went through more sets of garments. Not given to introspection, he rarely paused to consider why he was so attached to this structure and its sacrifices.

Even less often did he remember his days as Pinky Cohen, a dreamy kid from Brooklyn whom his friends described as nerdy and the local bullies called dorky. Even back then, thirty years before the Arrival, he had been so excited by the idea of a future rebuilding that he began growing his right thumbnail to be able to break birds' necks from the back, as required.

With the Temple's sacrificial day over and the sun beginning its downward descent towards the horizon line, he let himself into his office for a few hours' work before heading home. Not home, he thought bitterly, until I have a woman with whom to share it. Although he knew he was a sensitive and loving man, Pinhas had yet to find someone to properly appreciate his many talents.

Truth was, he and Ricky had been wonderfully happy for all those years, but it had soured when he realized she was never moving to Israel. His ever-growing thumbnail would stare up at him each day as he clutched a prayer book, reciting the traditional words of longing to return to Israel. As they began raising their children, and he saw them absorbing the values and attitudes of the Diaspora Jew, he gradually stopped accepting her excuses for not moving to the

Holy Land. Once he knew she wasn't leaving America, and that he *was*, the end wasn't long in coming.

The pull of the Land had been too strong, although he still automatically shook his head in regret when he thought of her. As he turned the key in the lock, his mind already thinking about what the budget figures would look like, he thought, not for the first time, that he had sacrificed a lot for this Land and this structure, hastily adding that it all was worth it, almost as if to convince himself or to forestall other thoughts.

One day, he hoped, their boys would come to get to know him, and then they'd understand why he hadn't been able to be there for them when they were growing up. That Ricky had never allowed them to come here for a visit, that they hadn't bothered to come when they reached the age they didn't need her approval, still irked him every time he thought about it; he pushed it aside and resolutely turned himself back to what was of genuine importance, the computer screen in front of him.

1500 sheep, 800 rams, and 600 bulls sold in the last quarter, a good pace. Donations also moving along nicely, especially that piece of land in the Golan he had been working for weeks to get; Pinhas was proud of having slowly grown into the ability to wine and dine people in the way that would help them live up to their responsibilities to support the Temple with their donations. Still a deficit in gold and silver, but smaller than the comparable period last year, so they seemed to be moving in the right direction.

Satisfied, he decided, not for the first time, that he could probably stop worrying about a return to the early days, when donations and individual sacrifices came in a trickle, when he had been the one who had had to balance the institution's debts and creditors, to avoid the embarrassment of a Temple having to declare bankruptcy. Many a time, he remembered going abroad to beg for a few dollars from some rich Jew too comfortable in his life to be moved by the Arrival.

Compared to that time, when covering expenses had been a significant challenge, he took satisfaction in their economic stability, and looked forward to the time when the Temple would have the kind of wealth always spoken of in the Talmud. His economic accomplishments alone should be enough to put him over the top, to get him chosen High Priest when the position became available.

Humming tunelessly, he put his computer on standby, checked his appointment book to see which donors would be visiting tomorrow—Morris Moskowitz, good, he usually coughed up big money after a personal tour of what they were doing. Pinhas sometimes felt guilty at the correlation between how much Moskowitz gave and how recently he had completed a major swindle back in the States, but comforted himself that the Lord works in mysterious ways.

The knock on the door startled him out of his reverie; closing the appointment book, he said, "Come." He was surprised to see Harvey Keiter walk in, but, as was his practice, did not show any emotion as he waved him to a seat. "What brings you back so soon?"

Harvey perched on the edge of the chair, ever alert for danger, fight, or flight. "A couple of things. First, I went by the hospital— don't worry, I didn't go in, I know the rules. But I saw Dr. Contact, who told me a couple of interesting things. Yirmy Nadiv was diagnosed today with pancreatic cancer, stage IV. The doc thinks it'll be only weeks before the end, so you might want to start getting to know the family, offer your services, or whatever."

Pinhas whistled. "That's a lot of money and no close relatives— will he get out of the hospital, or do I have to go there?" He hated going to the hospital. It used to be that he'd have the hospital provide an escort to seal all the hallways other than the one he was walking. That way, even if someone did die while he was visiting, he would be separated from any corpse-impurity.

It hadn't worked. With all those precautions, he had been in the room when a young guy, in stable condition, suddenly *went*. Sure, he knew it was an awful tragedy for the man's wife, children, and family—and he'd expressed his sympathy skillfully enough to secure years of major donations—but what had stuck with him was the week he had had to stay away from the Temple. Out of touch, losing his lead in hours worked, he felt back to being dopey Pinky Cohen, the weird kid with the long thumbnail. The weeks after he got back had been exhausting, as he threw himself into every aspect of the Mikdash, to reassert his vital role in its running.

The necessity of avoiding that circumstance had been the mother of the sealed golf cart, which warded the person inside from any kinds of impurity. It had been a challenge constructing something that fit the requirements both of the laws of ritual purity and the government's new environmental laws. He'd eventually gone with an electric battery, which meant that priests couldn't use it as their personal car in general, but hospitals had found it lucrative to buy a few and rent them to priests for the duration of their visit.

To his surprise, it had actually become something of a money maker, with priests from all over the world ordering them. Outside of Israel, he had heard, priests would tow their cart to the hospital, hop in for a visit, and then bring it back home. Some hospitals would house a priest's personal cart, like renting a parking spot.

The money had been nice for a couple of reasons. First, giving a fifth of the proceeds to the Temple had lessened the debt load in the early years. Better, though, when he stood for election to the High Priesthood, the other priests wouldn't have to worry about making sure he was wealthy. He had always suspected that he didn't win last time because some priests were reluctant to have to chip in to enrich him so that he would be able to properly hold the office.

Harvey had been talking the whole time, but it was only now that Pinhas pulled himself back to what he was saying. "...but said he'd be in touch. I need some shekels to grease that palm, by the way, I could tell that he was getting tired of giving us this info without getting anything."

"Does keeping the Mikdash afloat not count for anything?"

"It counts, he says, but he's got bills to pay and mouths to feed."

Pinhas sighed. So few appreciated the daily grind of keeping this operation going. And now this doctor, with vacation homes in

Switzerland and New Zealand so that he could be sure of year-round skiing, and Hawaii for beachgoing, wanted money for helping them find their next donors. Chutzpah!

Harvey had another lead. "I'm not positive, but I think Naval Ashir accidentally killed a man in a bar last night."

Pinhas snorted. "That's not a big donor. Not that he couldn't, but we've never seen any sort of interest from him."

"Even if we tell him the blood-avenger's planning on chasing him to Hevron?"

Pinhas was impressed at the creativity of thought; too bad he was going to lose Harvey soon, he had developed a wonderful grasp of the business. "So that he can go north to Shechem instead. Verrrrry nice. But wait, how do we know that?"

Harvey looked a little uncomfortable. "Nobody has to know how we know it; the point is that it's true and can help fill the Mikdash's coffers. That's all that matters now."

Pinhas was surprised. He had known the redheaded man had been changing, but hadn't realized how much. Absolution was a powerful drive for some people, and apparently Harvey was getting in on the act.

His next words were even more important. "On the other thing, I've certainly captured her interest—she followed me to the meeting this morning. Which, before I go on, reminds me that you'd better start giving serious thought to my replacement, because I'm pretty sure I'm almost done, and then I'm moving North, buying a farm and settling down to a quiet life growing grapes, olives, figs, raising sheep, and living off the Land."

Pinhas waved away the warning as he had so many times before; Harvey would leave when he said he would and not before. "Fine, fine. What happened with her?"

"After the meeting, she followed me, which is a hoot. I have to turn around every once in a while, because she'd get suspicious if I didn't. But if I ever turned suddenly, she'd be caught totally flat-footed, believe me. So I have to go through this elaborate turning around ceremony, and she's still usually hasn't finished ducking to the side when I finally look back." He laughed at the thought, thinking he might lure the priest into joining. All he got, though, was the same stone face any news elicited. Better finish up and get out of here. "Anyway, when I followed her to the Temple Grounds, HaOzer picked me up. I lost him before I came here, but he'll know where I went."

Moshel gnashed his teeth. "HaOzer! Meddling fool! All right, that complicates matters a bit, but the basic plan stays the same. When are you going to let her see you going to the apartment?"

"I don't know. Now that *he's* involved, he'll probably tell her about certain events, if you catch my drift, that will make her more cautious, maybe even scare her off totally. On the other hand, he may strengthen her resolve to figure out what happened, and I may not need to do anything. So I figured I'd wait and see what happens."

Pinhas stood up, ending the meeting; Harvey left, as usual astonishing Pinhas with how silently he could move. Time to go home, entertain his guests at a quick dinner, and get some sleep. Services started well before sunrise, and he liked to be at the beginning. With one last look at the column of smoke rising from the altar, a glance at the sky to see how soon the stars would come out and his guests would arrive, Pinhas Moshel turned for home.

CHAPTER FIVE

Rachel had not expected the first weeks of parenthood to be as difficult as Atid was making them. Friends from the States told her she would start getting real smiles out of him at about three weeks, and that six weeks after that, he'd start sleeping through the night and playing more. For now, she had to be satisfied with his quieting down and looking at her when she played games, which she fervently hoped meant that he was actually interested. Since he was often fussy, Rachel tended to fill their time together by taking him for walks in the stroller, bathing him, singing to him, feeding him, changing him, and putting him to sleep for blessed and too-brief times of quiet.

Lije should have been here for this, she thought to herself for the umpteenth time since the birth, right after she got him to go down for his "nighttime" sleep, which would last until 1 am if she was lucky. She mostly assumed Lije had met some terrible accident, and mourned him as if he was dead. But when Atid was difficult or people asked her about her husband, she let him have the full force of her deep anger, at him for disappearing and at the world for letting this happen to her. That made her feel guilty since he was probably dead, which then made her feel angry, a cycle she hated.

Putting Lije away, she tried to plan her night. She knew she should get into bed right now, but she always needed unwinding time. On nights when there was a particularly good movie on TV, she sometimes found herself having stayed up straight until he woke up for a feeding. The days after were blurs of fatigue.

Tonight was better. Her producer helped by calling, ostensibly to chat but actually to remind her that they were expecting her back and fit in six weeks. Full of resolve, she took out her exercise video and worked out for half an hour, which also convinced her not to snack all night. Charged by the workout, she meditated for fifteen minutes; as usual, she got no enlightenment, but did fall into a satisfying sleep.

Which lasted until 10:15, when the phone woke her.

"I'm sorry, I know you're a new mother and it's late, but I had to talk to you."

"Who's this?" Rachel had never been good at phone voices, which insulted some people. No, really, you must know who this is, they would say. Groggy from sleep, there was no way she was going to recognize a voice on the phone. She wasn't even sure whether it was male or female.

"It's Reuven. Are you awake enough to remember what I'm going to tell you?"

"Yes, why? What's wrong?" She did, however, pride herself on picking up undercurrents of other people's speech, a skill she connected to her success in journalism. In his voice, she heard urgency, concern, fear, and determination. She didn't know how those mixed, but assumed she would find out.

"Can I come over? Would your husband mind?"

Why did everybody have to focus on her husband? 10:15 at night was not when she was going to tell him, who managed to exasperate her as often as inspire admiration, any more about Lije.

"I don't think now is a good time. My son is going to wake up in the next couple of hours and then again all night long. Can't this wait until tomorrow? I'll meet you at the coffee shop at 10, unless I find myself forced to follow Harvey again." A weak attempt at humor, but not worthy of the reaction it got.

"NO! Whatever you do, promise me you *will not* follow Harvey again until we've talked."

Aside from her surprise at his strong reaction, she was a little put off. Who was he to tell her who to trail and who not to? The journalist in her bristled, urging her to spite him by dressing and wandering the streets looking for Harvey.

Perhaps sensing her reaction, he continued in a calmer tone.

"Look, I know you have no reason to take my instincts seriously, but I'm asking you to. Come here as early tomorrow as you want—we open at 5, for the crowd going to see sunrise at the Temple. I'll be here all morning, and after speaking to me, I think you'll understand."

"All right. But you'd better have a really convincing story."

"Just wait. And lock all your doors and windows."

She at first thought he was joking, but he brought it up twice more before they got off the phone. She would have ignored him, but images of the conversation she would have to have with the police if something did happen forced her out of bed. She did not want to face questions such as: "Ma'am, is there a reason your windows were unlocked?" "Ma'am, did you have any reason to suspect that something untoward might happen tonight?" "Ma'am, do you know of anyone who would want to hurt you in this way?"

The possibilities ringing in her head, she walked through the apartment, feeling intensely foolish the entire time. She half-expected some friend to jump out and laugh at her for being so gullible. It took until 10:45 to get back into bed, by which time, of course, she had been sufficiently roused that she could not fall asleep. After a few moments of lying there awake, she began to worry that she wouldn't get any sleep before the baby woke up, keeping her up even longer. She drifted a few times, but was certain she saw the clock switch to midnight.

At some point after that, she saw Atid floating over her bed, watching and waiting until she would be ready to hold and feed him. She repeatedly shushed him, telling him she was tired and he shouldn't call until he absolutely needed her. When that dream went away, Liat got her on the phone. Only this time, she thought she heard her say, "I like that Reuven."

Perhaps as a survival skill, Atid miraculously didn't cry until 6:00, when she had gotten in a few hours of restful sleep. After his feeding, feeling high on her unusually long sleep, she decided to take her baby with her to see what kind of crazy people went to the Temple Grounds so early. Sure enough, when she got there at 7:15, a steady stream of people was coming in, grabbing a cup of caffeine, and heading towards the Mount. Curious, she stopped one young woman, asking what time things got started at the Temple.

"It changes with sunrise, but usually by 6 there's something going on. I like to hit the Mikdash for about a half hour before I head to the gym and to work. It sort of charges up my day nicely." And she headed off. Rachel, never a morning person until Atid came along, couldn't even relate to voluntarily rising as early as 5:00 to spend a half hour watching priests get the Temple ready for the day, and then go to a workout and a job. It was a new world, all right.

Which reminded her of why she had come. As she stepped into the store, she was surprised to see people sitting at the tables, but then realized they were simply waiting to get served and get out to the Temple. She waved to Reuven behind the counter. Busy with customers, he waved back, motioned that he'd be with her as soon as he could, and went back to serving.

Coffee appealed to Atid, or at least the shop did, and he went right to sleep. Rachel looked around for someone to interview, pretty much the only way she knew how to find out about the world. When she was little, she drove her parents crazy with her persistent questioning; now they couldn't stop telling people about their daughter the newswoman.

She approached a man in his late twenties wearing a Levi's uniform. "Excuse me, but aren't you a little late?" And then immediately backtracked, since accusing someone was rarely a way to get him to open up and she hadn't meant it that way at all. "Sorry, that came out wrong, let me try again. I'm trying to understand more about the Temp...the Mikdash, and I thought Levis had to be there way before sunrise to set things up."

He smiled engagingly. "No offense taken. Actually, I'm a trainee—I don't get my full certification until I turn thirty. Some days I have to be there for the beginning, but my supervisor told me I could come in a little late today—I had middle of the night guard-shift last night, so he had pity on me. Thanks for asking."

"Do you mind if I ask a couple of other questions, too?"

"Not at all; that's our job, to answer your questions."

"I thought your job was guarding the Temple."

He laughed and then apologized. "I'm sorry, I don't mean to laugh, but I find it...not ha-ha funny, but weird funny, how hard it is for us to get certain messages out to the public. Certainly, guarding the Mikdash is an important element of what we do, but what you and I are doing, that's more important. After my training, you know, I won't be at the Mikdash more than a few days a year; mostly, we wander around the country or the world, answering questions, offering classes, and so on. As a trainee, I actually have a sort of informal quota of questions to answer each month. If I don't meet it, my supervisor will send me for a course on how to be more approachable. So, if anyone should thank anyone, it should be me thanking you."

His words and demeanor reminded her of Yedidya from yesterday, who had also seemed anxious to talk more. She had assumed it was because he was a man and she was an attractive woman, but maybe it was something else. His card was still in her purse, somewhere. She fished it out.

"Would that be why Levis carry cards, to drum up potential business?"

"Exactly. Only business is the wrong word; most of the guys I know enjoy that part of the job as much or more than the Mikdash time. Also, a lot of us start great friendships with people we first meet in that context."

"And it's a great way to pick up women, I bet."

The young Levi flushed. "I won't say it doesn't happen, but it's frowned upon—we're supposed to be doing this for a higher purpose, and letting that get in the way...well, there's no official rule, but it's clearly discouraged. Anyway, that shouldn't matter to you, having a kid and all."

It was getting easier to let it pass. "Do you know this particular Levi..." she looked at the card in her hand, "Yedidya Gross."

"No, sorry, but I've only been here a few months and have been overwhelmed trying to keep up with classes and duties. I can ask and get back to you, if you'd like?"

Rachel knew he wouldn't find out anything she couldn't find out herself, so she thanked him, excused herself, and made a mental note to call Yedidya. Then, since giving birth had fried her mind, she pulled out her new 5x7 spiral notebook—she took a perverse pleasure in having avoided a PDA, but had had to graduate from random scraps of paper—and wrote Yedidya? on it, putting the card in as well.

Still waiting for Reuven, Rachel stared out into the street, watching the people move towards the Temple, trying to guess their life stories in the brief interval they were in her line of vision. There were the tourists of all types—she liked seeing the ultra-Orthodox Americans, who were shocked by how different Temple society was from what they had assumed all their lives. She suspected they saw this Messiah as the first step in everyone eventually becoming just like them.

Then there were the less observant ones, obviously struggling with the attention to detail required to get access to the Temple. These were the ones who walked through the streets clutching their Mikvah tickets high in the air, avoiding touching anything for fear that some guard would tell them they had to wait another day before they could be allowed in.

One blond woman in particular caught Rachel's eye, hair and makeup a little too perfect, clothes probably a little too tight and a little too revealing for public taste in Israel, tripping down the street on heels a tad too high for the stone streets of the Old City and the Temple grounds. She wondered idly whether the Levites at the gates would make an issue of her getup. That would have been her, she thought, if not for Lije.

Lije. How he had blown her away when they first met. His looks certainly helped, since she wouldn't have given a second thought to a man who wasn't well put together. But it was his eyes, sparkling with the intensity with which he approached...everything. Pursuing her, building a life committed to ideals, getting closer to

God. It wasn't, she thought to herself for the thousandth time, that she had shared his passions, it was the passion itself she found so irresistible.

The passion that had drawn him here as soon after the Arrival as possible, without worrying himself over the geographical inconvenience that her career, the one that supported them (including him) in the style to which he had become accustomed, was in America. He had always pooh-poohed her worries, assuming she could find a job in Israel, they could cut back on their spending, change their approach to life. She wasn't willing to do any of that, but love a man for his passion and you have to roll with it, she had told herself, so she had arranged assignments to stories that would bring her here, come for long weekends, brought him home to New York when she couldn't get away.

But it had been a strain, one she had handled by refusing to get to know anyone or anything in Israel. All of which only further complicated their relationship.

"Sorry it took so long, but there was a late-breaking rumor that the High Priest was performing today's service. His mother passed away, and he wants to honor her memory by working this entire month himself."

"And that's a big deal?"

Reuven seemed nonplussed by her ignorance and indifference, a combination she was actually fairly proud of. "Well, yeah, I mean, usually you only get to see him work hard in the weeks before Yom Kippur. To see him in the late winter, that's a real treat."

Rachel was not in the mood to find out more about the Temple right then. Atid was going to want to nurse soon, she wanted a nap, and she was getting back some of her dander at having been summoned so imperiously.

"So, Reuven, tell me what was so urgent that you had to call me after 10 last night?" The words that seemed so logical in her head sounded a little ridiculous coming out of the mouth of ABC News' 11 o'clock anchorwoman. Truth was, since Atid's birth, 10 was a late night. It would be a while before she could return to her usual slot, unless she broke down and got a full-time night nurse, adding to the burden of guilt she already felt for not being the devoted parent her own mother had been. She had been convincing herself the network would let her switch to morning anchor jobs, but was slowly coming around to the idea of a live-in, at least in the short term.

"I followed Harvey to the Mount. It was the end of the day, so there wasn't a big crowd, which made tailing him unseen a little challenging, but I think I managed it. And when I saw who he met, I managed to ask a few questions about him, and didn't like what I heard. So I felt I had to warn you."

"Warn me about what?"

"Harvey went to see a priest, named Pinhas Moshel. Does the name mean anything to you?"

Liat's ex-husband! Immediately, Liat's ramblings began replaying themselves in her head, with the recurring refrain that she shouldn't let Pinhas get his hands on the diary. She had been right, the red-haired man *was* connected to Liat's death. "Actually, it does, but why don't you finish your story?"

"Well, I found out that Harvey meets with Pinhas often, like he's his errand boy. And since I know the kind of stuff Pinhas does, getting too close to his hired hand struck me as particularly dangerous."

"What do you mean? What kind of stuff would Pinhas need to hire people for?"

Reuven paused for a long time before he answered, so long that Rachel asked her question again. Finally, he seemed to make a decision, leaned in a little closer to her, and whispered, "I'm pretty sure that Pinhas Moshel is behind my toe being cut off."

CHAPTER SIX

Rachel sat back so hard she almost knocked her chair backwards. She had always sensed that Liat feared her ex, but never would have guessed that she'd hear a sentence like that out of someone else's mouth. "He what?"

Reuven looked around to make sure no one was listening. When he spoke again, it was so quiet that she almost missed it. "It goes back to the very early days, right after the rebuilding. I made myself a pest, about money and where we would get it, what kind of donations we should accept."

"We?"

"I was—am—a priest, and I wanted us to accept money only from people we knew earned it honestly and respectably. I was particularly upset about an arms dealer who gave us a large donation. This guy made his living supplying insurgencies and counterinsurgencies, governments and rebels, and I protested his right to help put a place of peace on sound financial footing, since he certainly was not a man of peace."

He paused, she thought for air. As it lengthened, she thought perhaps he needed a drink and turned to get him one, but he waved her off. As he got his emotions under control, he continued in the same low, flat tone he had been using since beginning his story. "I convinced the king to let me investigate the sources of the funds keeping the Mikdash afloat. I held public hearings, and was getting a lot of coverage, and it looked like I'd be successful at rooting out some corruption."

"One day, Pinhas appears at my apartment, to warn me. At the time, I thought he was expressing friendly concern; he said I was going to bring a lot of trouble on myself if I kept looking into these things, that some truths were best left undiscovered. But me, the big idealist, I ignored him. I actually thought he was being a nice guy."

"Then, suddenly one day, I'm walking down the street when a red van pulls up, the door opens, two guys in masks grab me and pull me inside before I have a chance to react. They blindfold me, drive me I have no idea where, take off my blindfold only long enough for me to see the knife. When they cut off the toe, the pain was so intense that I vomited, mostly on myself."

"I was still in shock when one of them said, "Next time, you'll listen when you're warned and keep your nose out of other people's business." Listen when you're warned? I sure knew what that meant. Anyway, they blindfolded me again, drove around for a while, knocked me on the back of the head, dumped me out of the van and drove off. By the time I woke up they were long gone, and I was left, a shell of a man. And, obviously, it came from Moshel."

Reuven stopped, as if he had more to say but couldn't bring himself to continue. He has spoken quietly, devoid of any obvious emotion, except that Rachel heard the rivers of anger fueling the intensity of what she assumed was a resolve to settle up with Pinhas. A part of her respected the feelings, but so many parts of the story didn't make sense that she almost didn't know where to start.

"I don't understand, why didn't you go to the police?"

He looked at her like she was crazy, the sensitivity that was so clear when talking about *her* problems overwhelmed by the enormity of his own. "Of course I went to the police, but what could they do? They interviewed Pinhas, who acted offended at the possibility that he was in any way involved. He swore he did not know who had done it, and had been warning me because he had heard that such things happened sometimes. I had no information on the van, although a stolen red van was found abandoned in Tel Aviv the next day, there were no witnesses (or none who could provide any useful evidence), and so it's in the cold case files."

"Besides that, even back then the police had begun to discourage reports about Pinhas. Some of them, I assume, were and are in his debt one way or another, some are on his payroll, but many are just tired of trying to nail a guy who leaves no trail. Nobody's ever caught him doing anything other than serving loyally and righteously, so they put a moratorium on unsubstantiated reports. I guess I understand it—as they see it, it's unpunishable if unprovable, and they can't allow maligning someone who's innocent until proven guilty."

"But still, there was your lost toe!"

"Sure, but I could have lost it in an accident, as far as they knew. Or, if I was crazy, I might have sliced it off myself because I had a grudge against him. He's very powerful, you know, and people like that often arouse resentment, deserved or not. He controls much of the sacrificial economy; he supplies most of the animals and oil, and guards those contracts jealously. What if I was trying to horn my way in on that gravy train? So I don't blame the police; they're in a difficult position."

"But that doesn't change what I know—well, I guess its rumor, but I'm ok with that. I think he saw me as a threat, hired some guys, and got rid of me. So when I hear that name, I know there's real danger, which is why I was so insistent."

Rachel wanted to be sympathetic, but his bitterness turned her off. "I don't mean to minimize this, Reuven, but I'm missing something. Sure, it's a toe, but in the broad scheme…"

He didn't let her finish. As he looked up, his eyes glistening with tears, he spoke more angrily. "You don't get it, do you? Think about this place for a minute. You know what drew me to Temple rejects? *I'm* a reject, have been for eight years now. Being on the Mount, watching others do their bit for God and country is usually too much for me to bear. I make sure to be away for most holidays, so I don't have to go on the Mount, and see him still serving, while I live out my life…."

He saw the bewilderment on her face, and took a deep breath. "All right, let me try this again. I heard what that Levi said to you before, that the teaching is more important than the service. That may be true for him, maybe even for a lot of priests, but for me, it was the Mikdash. It was standing in the courtyard, cleaning the altar, sweeping up, moving used animals, whatever, but being part of that center, that hub of...I used to be in the Mikdash more than 300 days a year...I used to hold the record for consecutive days of service...it was everything to me. It was the reason I couldn't stay married; no woman could put up with my...dedication."

"When they sliced off my toe, it ended. Sure, I can still get gifts as if I was a real priest, but I can't serve. And, people being people, the gifts slow to a trickle when you're not out there, doing something they can see."

Then, as if by pure force of will, he cleared his mind and face of the storm that had raged but a moment before. "But enough of my self-pity; the day will come when he'll go too far, or make a mistake, and I'll be there, a part of it. But you, you stay away. This is a man of no morals, no restraint, other than getting what he wants. He could commit murder and not blink."

Murder and not blink. Liat. "And that wouldn't make him unfit to serve?"

A bitter smile from Reuven. "Sure it would, if he got caught; so far...."

Rachel's head was spinning. One part of her couldn't fully absorb what he had said. A racket in the Temple? One of God's designated priests running it? Of course, she had never been fond of Pinhas, but she always assumed that that was only because he was Liat's ex, and she saw him through her friend's eyes.

Another part of her was surprised at her surprise; a jaded journalist, never much interested in the Mikdash, yet thinking about Pinhas like this had shaken her more than she would have guessed. A third part of her was a little suspicious of Reuven, who had to be exaggerating. Could someone as prominent as Pinhas order somebody's toe cut off and get away undetected?

Most of her, though, was thinking of Liat. Whatever she thought of Reuven's story, it confirmed her feelings about Harvey. Pinhas wouldn't have killed her himself, he'd be the first one the police investigated. No, it was Harvey, the fixer; he slipped her something that made her death look natural, then came back to make sure it had worked.

An idea was nibbling at the back of her head, but her fury at Pinhas and Harvey was blocking almost all other thought. She had to get away from here; Reuven was becoming so involved in her life, she needed space. She'd find the answers to her many other questions elsewhere. Fingering Yedidya Gross' card, she got up and thanked Reuven for all his help.

He rose as well, not recognizing how much he had upset her. "It was my pleasure. I hope you find peace with Liat's death soon. And, let me say, I hope our paths cross again. May it be His Will."

There, Rachel thought. Had he stopped before the "May it be" stuff, it would have been a nice farewell between two acquaintances. Just like Lije, he had to go that one step too far.

Musing why that flipped her switch, she left the store and headed home to feed the baby, but not fast enough. Atid woke up and informed the passersby of how close he was to starvation, at least as he experienced it. She would have stopped to feed him, but she wasn't that adept at it and always felt squeamish about performing such a private act in public. The volume of his cries wore away at her until she almost tried anyway, but she managed to make it home, feed, burp, and make cooing noises at him until it was time for him to go back to sleep. Thank God babies sleep so much, she thought to herself, because otherwise who knows if he (or she) would make it past his infancy?

CHAPTER SEVEN

After a nap and a shower, Rachel felt ready to get back to what was beginning to feel like a quest. She dialed Yedidya Gross' number, hoping she hadn't misjudged him. When he answered, she reintroduced herself and added that she had a particular question.

"Sure, fire away," came the confident voice from the other side.

Rachel hesitated. "I'm sorry, but do you think, I mean, is there any way we could do this in person? We've only met once, I don't know you that well, and..."

"Oh, sure. Look, it's 9:15, have you had breakfast?" Now that she thought about it, she hadn't. "Great; why don't we meet at the Temple Grounds and talk?"

That wasn't quite going to work. Didn't he have an office?

"Um, sort of, but I'd rather meet in some kind of public place; it takes away any chance of misunderstandings, if you know what I mean." Rachel didn't. "I guess you could say it's a way of protecting against claims of sexual harassment. You know, if we're never alone together, it's harder to claim that anything untoward happened."

That made some sense. "What about the old Hilton? They serve a wonderful breakfast." She could catch another meeting after breakfast. Sure, it was long and boring, but it had given her plenty to think about, and was the best bet for finding Harvey again.

Twenty minutes later, as she walked into the hotel, she flashed back to the security they had had when she first came, maybe twenty years ago. The security guard then brusquely examined your purse and bags, and sent you on your way. Now, the man at the door functioned primarily as a greeter, welcoming people to the hotel and directing them to their destination. She suspected he was trained to spot trouble, but the image was remarkably different.

The different approach also meant that she could bring almost anything she wanted into the hotel as long as it fit in her bag, since no one would suspect her. Today, it was Lije's gun, the small .22 he had carried around with him for emergencies; since hearing about Harvey's connection to Pinhas, the gun had worked its way into her purse. It felt good to know she had options on how to handle whatever she learned about him.

She entered the breakfast room, spotted a table that provided the privacy and lack of conspicuousness she sought, and had the maitre d' seat her there. When Yedidya walked in and started across the room towards her, the many people standing for him as he went by made it clear that they would be neither private nor inconspicuous.

Rachel turned to a woman at the next table. "Why's everybody standing?"

"You don't know who that is? That's Yedidya Gross, one of the rising stars of the Jerusalem Levites. They expect he'll be named the head of the tribe one day; he already helps hundreds weekly."

Rachel was surprised, although not nearly as surprised as the other woman was, when Yedidya sat down at her table. Suddenly embarrassed at summoning such an important man to the restaurant of her choice, she tried to babble out an explanation.

"Mr. Gross—or is it Rabbi?—I am so sorry. I had gotten the impression that Levis are available for consultation, and then you had given me your card, and then I didn't want to go to the Temple Grounds because I've been there a lot lately, and, well, anyway, I hope you can forgive me for imposing on you like this."

Yedidya waved away her words with a smile. "In order, Mr., Rabbi, or Levi Yedidya is fine, but I don't care; in fact, for now, plain Yedidya works. Second..."

"'For now'? What would change?"

"Well, a student owes respect to a teacher. I guess that would mean that if we developed a teacher-student relationship, you might need to stop feeling comfortable treating me as a peer. On the other hand, if we become friends there's a different dynamic, since friends always teach and learn from each other. So we'll have to see what happens; maybe we'll never speak again and the whole question will be moot."

"Second, Levis *are* available for consultation, so I was pleased when you called; that is, indeed, why I gave you my card. Third, don't worry about insisting on a different place, it's nice for me to have a change of pace as well. And, finally, you're not imposing; if people know me and like me it's because I truly enjoy discussing their issues. So fire away and don't worry about it."

Rachel hadn't expected such a detailed response, and certainly not so well ordered on the spur of the moment. Pushing aside how intimidated she felt, she pressed on. "Well, I went to this meeting, here at the hotel, I think it's called Democrats' Anonymous..." she paused to see if he knew what she was talking about and continued when he nodded encouragingly, "and this guy, said his name was" but before she could go on, Yedidya put up a hand to stop her.

"Please, no identifying details; the confidentiality of those meetings is sacrosanct. Can you tell the story without any information that would let me know or be able to track down who you're quoting?"

"All right, this guy, we'll call him Stanley" she looked to make sure he had no problem with Stanley, "swore he was going off to get revenge on his brother's killer; what did he mean?"

He answered immediately and automatically, as if she were accessing a prerecorded message. "He's a *go'el hadam*. If someone is killed, their close relatives have the right, maybe the responsibility, to avenge the death by killing the murderer."

"Without a trial or anything?"

"Well, the murderer runs to a city of refuge. If he gets there safely, he gets to have a trial. Until he gets there, though, or if the court decides it was premeditated or close enough to it, the *go'el hadam* can kill him."

His voice had taken on a singsong quality, which she knew

meant he was so involved in his topic that he wasn't wondering why she cared. She had unleashed the lecturer in him; he was answering the question he had been asked, as well and as fully as he could, without thinking about who was asking or why. It felt like she could risk one more question without arousing suspicion.

"What if the murderer doesn't run?"

"Well, that would be an error, because then the *go'el* could kill him at any point."

Which was exactly what she had hoped to hear. She changed the subject, she hoped smoothly, and engaged in aimless chitchat until he looked at his watch, asked her whether she had any more questions, and excused himself to another appointment. Clearly bringing the meeting to a close, he nonetheless ended the discussion so smoothly and graciously that Rachel wasn't even sure whether he was annoyed at being dragged down here to answer questions that could easily have been handled over the phone. She didn't much care, though, since he had shown her how to vent her anger and frustration of the last few months, which was already beginning to bubble over in anticipation of righting at least some of the wrongs she had seen and suffered.

She didn't get up with him, saying that she wanted to linger over her coffee. Which wasn't quite true, since she wanted to embrace her anger over Lije and his unseen killer, Liat and her mysterious end. As the fury grew and fed on itself, she allowed herself to focus not only on what happened to them, but how it happened. Some post-Messianic age, when good people could go to their deaths improperly buried, mourned, or avenged. Someone needed to stand up for the Lijes and Liats of this world, starting today.

She slipped into a state of focused attention she could not remember experiencing before. Outside events, people who walked by her, all seemed to fade into insignificance. All she registered was her next step, then her next, step by step. Hoping she didn't look too nervous, she went up to the reception desk, where the pretty young woman behind the counter—pre-Arrival pretty, long black hair, stark makeup emphasizing her lips and cheekbones, skintight uniform emphasizing a body Rachel knew meant many hours in a gym and many meals resisting tasty foods—asked, "May I help you?"

"Yes, is there a...meeting here today?"

"Democrats' Anonymous? Yes, ma'am, every day at 12 o'clock, fifth floor ballroom, and, ma'am? No need to be nervous, many people attend now and then."

Two hours to kill, Rachel thought, then laughed at her pun. A walk was out of the question; her body continued to protest the abuse of the last days and would get more fuel for its complaints in a little while. The next time she had a baby she would have to remember not to start investigating a murder right afterwards. She ordered a diet Coke, and, with a temporary lull in the action, turned to the usual questions her mind raised when left to its own devices.

Raise Atid alone, or try to find relatives and friends to share the parenting, at least until the Lije situation cleared up and she could marry again? Would she ever find out what happened to Lije? When should she go back to work? She was acutely aware of how hectic her schedule was when she was working, and with no other parent around, she worried about the effects on Atid. Too, going back to work meant moving back to the States, returning here only for holidays and special occasions.

Guilty as she felt about work and motherhood, she knew that she needed an outlet for her energies—her interest in Liat's case was partially fueled by her excitement over finding any intellectual and emotional challenge that had nothing to do with diapers or a baby who had yet to do any of the things that parents celebrate.

Her reverie, mostly re-treading familiar ground with little movement on decision-making, was less entertaining than usual, as most of her mind was focused on whether Harvey would show. She got into the ballroom ten minutes early, pacing the room anxiously until he came in and took a seat at the front. The Gordons were also there; since she had questions for them, she was almost glad they came over.

"You come every day?"

"Well, it depends on our plans, but we come as often as we can. It gives us a boost, gets us in the mindset to face another day of Israeli society. Also, Thursday is Speaker Day, and they're often pretty good. But also, the Government credits our tax bill for each time we come, didn't you know that?"

Rachel didn't much care, since she had little Israeli income to speak of, but it was exactly the kind of knowledge you needed at some point later and had forgotten to pay attention to originally. She made a mental note and then took out her notebook to make a written one. She didn't get a chance to pump them more, since the meeting was called to order. Knowing she'd want the freedom to leave quickly, she carefully found a seat far enough away from them to insure not having to speak to them again.

When the Gordons mentioned it, she had assumed that Speaker Day was an excuse to give regular attendees a day off from hearing other people obsess out loud. Today it turned out to be an extended advertisement for *ulpan,* Hebrew speaking classes. Lije had always pushed her to take one, but she had insisted she would learn Hebrew by walking the streets and forcing herself to function. It had worked, but Lije's way would have been easier. She started to raise her hand to share that insight with the group, then remembered that it was Speaker Day and that she did not want Harvey to notice her.

She distracted herself by putting the pieces of the puzzle together: Liat, a healthy young woman, suddenly dies of respiratory failure. Pinhas, her ex-husband, a priest who wouldn't dare kill someone since then he could never serve in the Temple again (according to Reuven), was known to associate with Harvey, who, as it happens, was at the scene when Liat was discovered and was being treated by EMTs. It all added up for Rachel, who subconsciously slipped her hand in her purse for reassurance.

As the meeting broke up, Rachel slipped as close as she could to Harvey without being obvious. He made conversation with other attendees, had some soda from the refreshments table and, on the whole, gave every impression of being fully comfortable in his surroundings and in his own skin. He must be some kind of psychopath, Rachel thought. Wouldn't killing Liat weigh on his conscience at all?

When he finally left the meeting—really, didn't the bastard know she had other things to do?—she followed, not quite sure of how to proceed. He turned down one street, another, and finally down a little alleyway with few stores or people. With each step, as the moment drew closer, she felt the blood pumping faster in her body, her pulse pounding in her ears, the gun burning a hole in her purse.

She walked up behind him, pulled the gun out of her pocket and cocked it, like Lije had shown her. She would have shot him from behind, but the sound made Harvey turn. When he saw her behind the gun, pointed steadily at his chest, he seemed more puzzled than scared.

"What's with the gun?"

She hadn't prepared for a confrontation. Was there etiquette to being a blood avenger? She had forgotten to ask Yedidya about that. No matter, she'd improvise.

"Harvey the Oily Red-Haired Man, I am here to avenge the death of Liat Moshel." It sounded self-important, but she thought he ought to know why he was about to die. Of all the many ways she had pictured this moment—and she had been thinking about it obsessively since yesterday's meeting—uproarious laughter had never been part of the plan. It made her feel a little foolish, her with a gun and he laughing hysterically.

"If I shoot you in the kneecap, you won't be laughing."

He shook his head and put a hand up, to stop her from doing it. "No, please," he managed to gasp out, "I'm not laughing at you." His laughs subsided a bit, and he got control of himself. "Well, all right, maybe I was laughing at you, but it was the tension of having a gun pointed at me coupled with the ridiculous reason you gave for doing it."

"You deny killing Liat?"

"Ms. Tucker, I won't even dignify that with a response."

"You know me?"

He hesitated, which Rachel thought meant he realized he had slipped up, but then he said, "I don't like to admit it, but I've got a thing for anchorwomen. I download their pictures from the Internet, tape the news whenever I'm in the States, and then watch newscasts for pleasure."

She knew it wasn't the topic, but she couldn't resist. "Why don't you like to admit that?"

"Well, for one thing, I've got a girlfriend, who doesn't appreciate it. But also, in the circles that I, well, used to travel, caring about the news was not so...acceptable. It might get you labeled a...."

"Sissy?"

"Exactly. So I sort of try to keep it quiet. Even if I never hang out with those types of people again, they need to always know that I'm strong enough to beat anyone who might try to settle some old scores, if you know what I mean."

She wasn't sure if she did, but she was tired of being sidetracked. "Liat Moshel? You *were* there when she died, wearing a jacket that identified you as an EMT."

Harvey tried to stonewall, almost a fatal mistake. "Hey, I had nothing to do with that, she died of respiratory failure, the docs said."

"You and I both know that's not true, don't we? Well, as Liat's *go'elet hadam*, as the avenger of her blood, I hereby execute your judgement."

Her mom had always complained about her ability to shut out what she didn't want to notice; over the years it had often served her well, letting her focus on what she needed or wanted to without getting distracted by the dross of life. At this moment, her refusal to notice Israeli society meant that what happened next was a complete shock, which was all the more surprising because she had argued repeatedly with Lije about how a public video/loudspeaker system endangered freedom and civil liberties.

As she began to squeeze the trigger (not jerk, Lije's voice reminded her), a voice rang out from all sides, out of loudspeakers she had long ago stopped noticing, saying, "Rachel Tucker, put your weapon down and wait for the authorities to arrive. Please be aware that if you kill Harvey Keiter, you will be arrested and put to death as a murderer. PUT THE WEAPON DOWN!"

She wavered, unsure of what to do—maybe they didn't know she was acting as Liat's avenger. No, that couldn't be right, if they could see her, they could probably hear her, too. But then why would they stop her? Hadn't Yedidya said she had the right to kill him for Liat? She heard the sirens now, and she and Harvey waited for the police, he relieved, she puzzled.

When the car pulled up, Yedidya stepped out and came towards her. "Rachel, kick the gun over towards me." He seemed more embarrassed than anything else. He picked up the gun, gave it to one of the police officers who had driven him to the alley, turned back to her, raising his arms in a two handed placating gesture.

"Rachel, I am so sorry. I was a little busy this morning, so I didn't pay a lot of attention to our conversation. I am, truth to tell, frequently approached by people who waste my time, so when you set up a whole meeting for no good reason, I was working not to be annoyed without thinking about it from your end. When I took a moment to mull it more fully, and spoke to some people about you, I realized that you might have gotten it into your head to avenge Liat. So really, this is my fault, and I'm sorry."

As the moment receded, along with the pounding in her head and heart, the calm part of her was surprised at what she had almost done. She had never been one to leap to violence, but Liat's killing—she knew it was that, even if Harvey denied it—had affected her more than she realized. She could actually have done it, and without a twinge of regret. Whoever had killed Liat—Harvey had been convincing enough that she wasn't positive it was him anymore—needed to be put in the ground, and she still would want to be the one to do it. She had never known what bloodlust was until now; the urge to kill the man who had done this to Liat had been intensely exciting, for the few hours that she yielded to it.

But there were holes in Yedidya's apology and her interrogatory instincts were taking over. "But how did you know who I would want to kill?"

Yedidya shook his head. "I didn't; I had the police get a warrant, find you on their monitors and track you. When you showed the gun, they turned on the speakers, and then we knew we had to stop you."

"But why did you have to stop me? You told me I could kill this..." the word escaped her, which would have looked terribly inarticulate on camera. She'd have to get back into practice at speaking smoothly and extemporaneously. "...murderer, if he was stupid enough not to run to an..." The term escaped her.

"*Ir miklat*, a city of refuge."

"Yes."

"Actually, what I said was that the blood avenger could kill the murderer, but neither part of that has been established here. For example, the killing you asked me about—I looked up police records, the guy you called Stanley was actually named Jacko, right? a well-known character, by the way, and he didn't catch his murderer; somebody tipped the guy off, so he fled North to another city. But here's the real point—in that case, there were fifty witnesses, all of whom identified the killer. The police haven't classified Liat's death as a murder at all, although I know you think it was."

"More than that, though, I left out the most important characteristic of the avenger, because I thought you were just curious, trying to understand how one guy would be allowed to kill another. Had I known what you were thinking, I would have emphasized that the avenger has to be a *blood relative*. You could never be Liat's avenger, much as you would like to be."

As he finished, leaving her speechless as she realized what she had almost done, the policemen, who had been standing by respectfully, approached and asked her to place her hands behind her back. When she did, they handcuffed her, and placed her in their police car. Yedidya looked in at the window before they pulled off.

"Don't worry, they aren't going to keep you long. I already

explained the situation, and I'm pretty sure they're going to limit themselves to a stern warning. I think you'll be a few hours, though. Is there anybody you'd like me to call?"

"The babysitter. If I'm late without calling, she throws a fit. I had told her I'd be home by 4 today, and I don't know if I'm going to make it. I can't afford to lose her!"

As the car pulled away, Rachel heard Yedidya promise he had it under control, although she had no idea of what that meant. She knew the babysitter, in a pinch, wouldn't leave until she got there, but hated to think of what it would cost her.

What would be would be; right now, she had more significant problems. Were they going to charge her? Jail her? Deem her an unfit mother and put Atid up for foster care and adoption? Would the network fire her?

That last thought saved her, because it was her "tell," her reminder that she had let her thoughts spiral out of control. She closed her eyes and willed herself not to think until they reached the police station and a policewoman told her it was time to get out.

As she walked in, she thought of all the times she had stuck microphones in the faces of people taking the "perp walk." Luckily, her own arrest had not (yet? or had she disappeared from the world's radar?) brought out the hordes of reporters an attempted murder charge normally would. She walked into the station unnoticed, was ushered into a large bare room, an interrogation room in the old style. Good to know not every thing changed with the Arrival, she thought to herself as a captain (or something; the man in charge) walked in.

"Well, Ms. Tucker, we meet again." He smiled pleasantly.

CHAPTER EIGHT

Ok, again. Again meant they had met before, usually a good sign. If she could remember where, she might get out of this intact, or at least soon. Think, Rachel, think. Where would she have met a police captain? That fraud investigation? No, that was in the States; her Israel pieces were mostly fluff on the new peace agreement and how it was holding up—had she spoken to him about the quiet borders, a drop in crime?

She looked at him more carefully. Tall, he probably looked good twenty years ago, but had aged—she figured late forties—poorly. Balding (bald really, but journalistic niceties had wormed their way into the fiber of her being), probably fifteen pounds overweight, although he looked like he exercised, so that could be a little high or low. Most importantly, not at all familiar, when remembering him would have helped immensely.

He noted her confusion, although he could not have known how frantically she was grasping for memory, and smiled. "I'm sorry, Ms. Tucker, I was playing with your mind a little; it's a game of mine I indulge far too often. There's no reason you should have remembered our meeting; I was once in the guard detail for the King at an embassy party you covered, and he decided to introduce us all to the reporters from the American media. My name is Shomer Kapdan." His smile said that he had enjoyed her discomfiture, but not maliciously; Rachel heaved an inward sigh.

"So what brings you back to regular police work, Captain Kapdan?" She wasn't sure he was a captain, but better to guess up than guess down.

"I'm actually not; part of guarding the King and his main

advisers is tracking down threats before they occur, like in your American Secret Service."

A first trap. Israelis were always suspicious of people who maintained a career in the States while setting up residence. They wondered—some subtly, native-borns less so—where her primary allegiances lay. Not in a political or military sense, because there was no need to choose between the two.

No, it was more cultural. Israelis developed deep and caring attachments, extending themselves for friends in ways that Americans never would. Rachel remembered how one of her neighbors took in another one's five kids for six months when the woman took ill and her husband had to spend all of his free time at the hospital. As a result, though, they were careful to spend those emotional resources only on people who were in the country for the long haul.

She was pretty sure that stressing her Israeli side would be helpful in this conversation. She put on her best Hebrew, refusing to continue in English. "*Lamah hem ha-Secret Service sheli? Ani Yisraelit kamokha!*" She was protesting a bit much in claiming that she was as Israeli as he was, but using the English words for Secret Service was how Israelis would speak in conversation.

Home run; Kapdan relaxed visibly, but continued in his heavily accented although fluent English, "I am glad to hear that, because your stunt today forces you to make a choice, one you might have made already, but that you will need to make again now. I am speaking English," there was no way he could have known how much she *hated* when Israelis answered her in English after she had spoken in Hebrew, "because I want to be as sure as possible that you are clear on what I am saying. We take killing very seriously, and it doesn't matter"—he lifted a hand to cut off her protest—"that you got the wrong impression of the laws. The King and the courts have made very clear that ignorance is almost never an excuse."

"More than that, we are not talking about punishment, but about a way of helping you remove your ignorance. Ordinarily, as you may have noted, we take a fairly relaxed approach to acclimating people to the changes since the Arrival. The meetings, the rules against investigating observance, the stress on positive ad campaigns and educational initiatives—it's all a part of trying to make the transition as smooth as possible, leaving the maximum room for people to feel their free input into their lives. But once something like this happens, well...."

He let the last word sit between them for longer than she liked, but she decided not to give him the satisfaction of succumbing to the pressure to ask. "You have choices, but not limitless ones. You can decide to plead guilty and go to jail; you can claim you didn't do it, have a regular court trial, but then if you're found guilty, which I would think you would be, the punishment would be either a severe jail sentence or, maybe because you're also an American citizen, the court might give you the option of leaving the country within 24 hours of the verdict. If you go that route and get expelled, though, you could never return here."

He stopped, but she knew he wasn't finished. Again, she knew he wanted to make her ask. She wanted to wait him out, but she also wanted to get to the end of this conversation, so she said, "Are those all the options?"

"No," he replied slowly, "I was specifically sent here to present one more, but I don't know if there's any point." With that, he pulled out a fairly thick folder.

"Now you must understand that the file I am reading to you has been composed in the time since you pulled the gun on Harvey. Once someone commits a crime, we get a search warrant and instruct the computer to pull up all the records we have of you, including video recorded by the cameras that found you after Yedidya Gross alerted us to what you were planning. This is not a complete dossier yet, because even our search programs take a little time identifying you in all the situations tagged and stored by the computer."

"But here's what we've got so far. Rachel Tucker, age 34, well-known journalist and anchorwoman for ABC News, has lived in Israel part-time for about five years. Married to Elijah Zeale, known as Lije," Kapdan had said it wrong, as so many did when reading it off a paper; Rachel automatically corrected him. "That's Lije, with a long "i", as in Elijah."

Kapdan smiled in apology and continued. "known as Lije, whereabouts unknown for the last six and a half months. Not particularly observant, although no flagrant violations. Appears to attend synagogue only on Rosh Hashanah and Yom Kippur, has not been involved with any study groups, and has been seen eating milk products within an hour of a meat meal. Not terrible, but enough to suggest that religion isn't what drew you to Israel. Is that about right?"

As the words left her mouth, she knew they weren't productive, but she had no interest in holding back. "Well, at least I won that argument with Lije—cameras mean police state. Tracking my observance? How dare you!? What business is that of yours? And, on the topic of none of your business, what does my husband's disappearance have to do with our discussion here at all?"

Kapdan was surprised at her outburst, started to respond, stopped himself, inhaled and blew out, muttering, "I told them I wasn't tactful enough for this, *aval mah efshar la'asot*, what are you going to do?" He turned to her, "Ms. Tucker, I'm sorry I insulted you, I only mentioned that to give us some background for what I'm about to suggest. We don't track people in general, although we want to have the capability to do so if necessary. The cameras are there to help solve crimes and/or prevent them. We do not examine them without a warrant, as I tried to stress a moment ago; in your case, it let us avoid what could have been a much worse outcome, both for you and for Mr....Keiter."

"Truth is, we would have been interested in you even if this hadn't happened, because it's not every day that a well-known TV personality ups and moves to Israel, especially if religion wasn't the motivating factor. Given enough time, we probably would have approached you anyway, because we'd love to have you as an active citizen. But that's yesterday's news. Now that you've forced our hand, what I'm about to mention is the only positive option, although you might not think of it that way. You can..." Exhale, anticipating a storm, she guessed, "commit to more significant and careful engagement with the religion."

This didn't sound good. Rachel was put off enough by their having investigated her life; now they were going to try to dictate it, too!? Luckily for her, interviewing required listening to all sorts of insanities without visibly reacting or judging, a skill essential to navigating this conversation. Kapdan didn't notice and kept speaking.

"You know why those meetings are called Democrats' Anonymous? Because the people who have the most problems acclimating to our new society are the ones who believe in democracy, individual rights, to the exclusion of legally defined and significant responsibilities to the community. In our public community, those who want to be full members need to swear publicly to observe the laws of Judaism, and accept that the community will sometimes make demands that seem intrusive, such as making decisions for them about some parts of how they act religiously."

"So your other choice is to begin studying to do that, to become a full member of the community, which we call a *haverah*. I don't want to minimize the lifestyle changes that will involve—synagogue attendance, continuing education, giving charity, keeping Shabbat and all the holidays, and so on. The question is whether you'd rather just admit guilt and leave, or go through what you should know is a difficult change of life."

Part of Rachel's surprise was how far Kapdan's words were from anything she had anticipated, even though she had thought carefully about this meeting from the time she entered the police car until Kapdan's appearance. Thinking ahead was how she avoided shocking surprises, but this time had failed miserably. The government's PR had lulled her into thinking that they were avoiding what the secular Left referred to as *kefiyah datit*, religious coercion. She had assumed—hell, she'd been as much as told—that if she wasn't too "out there" in her lifestyle, no one would bother her, and, until now, that had pretty much been true.

Of course, there had been that one idiot who wouldn't let her take the baby home from the hospital until he checked with the *mohel* that she had, indeed, hired him to perform the circumcision the following week. And then showed up at the ceremony, as if he was just joining the celebration! But he had been the exception.

Now this. Sure, she had made a big mistake, but an obvious and explainable one, and she had to choose to become…religious in a way she didn't want or to leave the country! Calm, Rachel, calm. Gather and record the information you need, think later.

"If I decide to do this, to become a Friend" saying it that way sounded like a Quaker thing, a most unappealing image, so she switched to the Hebrew "a *haverah*, what do I do?"

"There's not a strict set of guidelines, but you would have to commit to observing all that you already know, and to study—fairly intensively—what you don't yet know. It would be sort of like studying for citizenship in another country, but with more rules and ideas. And, you would have to enlist a sponsor, a male or female Levi or Kohen who would undertake supervising your studies and overseeing your progress."

A sponsor—if only Liat were alive. Although, truth be told, it was only Liat's death that had put her in this situation. "What if I don't know anyone?"

Kapdan seemed surprised by the question. "We could assign you someone—you'd fill out a questionnaire, and we'd try to connect you with an appropriate person. But I would have thought someone like yourself would have come across many of the high-powered Kohanim and Leviim?"

The question was more concerned and curious than prying, so she decided to answer. "When Lije was around," she paused, as she always needed to when she heard herself using the past tense for him; some secret part of her still hoped he was a jerk who would show up, "we did a lot of social stuff, made many acquaintances, but it was just social. Also, Lije was more actively religious than I have been, so that there seemed little need for me to look into it—I joined Lije when he had something religious he wanted to do, and that was plenty for me."

"Even then, he made the contacts—he fit in better to Israeli society, and I was traveling to the States most weeks, coming to see him on weekends, and then when he...." She found it easier to let the thought trail off, rather than say the word, "Well, I lost touch with most people. Anyway, that was then, and I have to face now. How soon would I have to become a *haverah*? Is it a two-week course, and then I have to know everything, do everything, and get punished when I don't?"

She had meant to be sarcastic, and was happy when Kapdan winced. "Ms. Tucker, I recognize this is rough, but you should try to see this from our perspective as well. We're not trying to punish you, we're trying to respond appropriately to a criminal act and at the same time to encourage you to adhere to what we consider to be the Truth, perhaps a little more strongly than usual. I know you don't yet share that view, but try to keep in mind that that's how we see what we are doing."

"To answer your question, you'd need to make the *commitment* right away," he saw the look of panic on her face and added, "by which I mean after you've had some time to weigh the options I've given you. And then, should you decide to go this route, and name a sponsor, you would attend a commitment ceremony, and would be required to file biannual reports certifying your continued good progress. As long as that progress continued, the government would have no more reason to pursue your case."

"So let me get this straight. I can leave the country..."

"No, you can *plead guilty* and leave the country, never to return. If you leave without choosing an option, we would take that as a guilty plea as well."

"Or I can commit to working towards being a *haverah* and take on a sponsor who will oversee my continued growth throughout my life?"

"Well, at *some* point, we would expect your sponsor to certify that you were indistinguishable from other adult Jews in belief and observance, and that he or she had no further need to oversee you, that you could develop your relationship with God in the same privacy the rest of us have. Usually, though, the student/teacher relationship continues throughout one's life, although at more and more sporadic intervals. Or, of course, you could decide to fight this, by claiming that it wasn't you who was about to kill Harvey, or that you didn't intend to kill him. That's a long shot, considering the camera evidence, but you can always try it."

Kapdan's patience was clearly running out, so Rachel said "OK, last question, how long do I have to make a decision?"

"We have no interest in applying great pressure, but we can't let you walk out of here scot-free, either. What I can do is take your passport, so that you can't leave the country without registering a guilty plea, and then, when you make your decision, we'd either return your passport and bid you farewell, or put you in the care of whatever sponsor you choose."

"What if I start with a sponsor and don't like him?" She knew this was her nerves showing, but, as so disconcertingly often in this interview and in Israel in general, she couldn't help herself.

"You can always switch to a new one." Kapdan was clearly trying to end the meeting and still be sympathetic; he leaned forward and said, in what Rachel assumed was his gentlest tone, "I know this is a lot to absorb, and it's certainly not where we would have wanted to be. We had no need to mess with your life, but what you did today was a direct challenge to the society we are in the process of building."

"If you want to join us, great, and we'll do everything we can to make the process as smooth as possible—you don't click with one sponsor, find a new one; some piece of observance is a problem, we'll try to work it out or at least delay your need to adopt it until the end of your study process. And, you can choose to leave."

"So take a week, and if you need more, we can discuss it. Actually, now that I think of it, call me for any reason, here's my card, with a 24 hour number. Truth is, any Levi or Kohen, male or female, or *haver* or *haverah* should be willing to answer whatever questions you have."

He stood, done with her for now, so she did as well, her

instincts to politeness blessedly taking over. "Well, thank you, Captain. I need to digest this, but I certainly appreciate the effort you and the government have put into how you've handled this."

Kapdan smiled, a mix of pleasure at her gratitude and world-weary cynicism. "Don't get too caught up in our altruism; getting you to join us as a fully involved part of our society would also be a huge public relations coup, and I'm pretty sure that was taken into account. Anyway, good luck, and I'll await your decision."

CHAPTER NINE

Rachel stumbled out onto the street, glancing at her watch for the first time since Kapdan entered the room. 3:30. She *must* have been getting special treatment, because the whole thing had gone remarkably quickly. With the right cab, she could pick up dinner (not a cooking night tonight) and be early for the babysitter. Since she was sure she'd be obsessing about Kapdan's words all night, she might as well at least get credit with the babysitter rather than waste her time trying to do anything else productive.

A cab came right away, which Lije would've said was Divine Providence. She sat back in her seat, thinking about what to buy for dinner. Her dieting instincts said salad, but most of the vegetables she ate gave Atid gas, or at least the doctor claimed that was what was doing it. She wasn't in the mood for meat, so she settled on bagels, telling the cab to pull over at one of the many bagel stores dotting the city.

Leaving the store with a dozen bagels a few minutes later, three everything, three salt, three cinnamon raisin, and three chocolate chip, she pondered the continuing mystery of the chocolate chip bagel. How could a chocolate chip bagel *not* be an excellent idea; and yet each one she ate fell far below her minimum standards, let alone the high hopes she had held for it. She had spent several years now repeatedly convincing herself that it was that particular bagel that was no good. Soon enough, she'd have to accept the truth that there was no such thing, but for now she'd continue her pursuit of a well-made chocolate chip bagel.

She got back in the cab, which had miraculously waited for

her. Plenty of times they promised to wait, even took an advance on the fare, and then decided they had a better fare waiting somewhere else and drove off.

The moment she walked in the apartment and thanked the babysitter, any thoughts of Kapdan were pushed aside by the chaos that was the end of Atid's day. She had walked in on feeding time and, as the babysitter reminder her, he didn't like the bottles of mother's milk she constantly prepared (evenings, early mornings, and sometimes in the nearest bathroom) nearly as much as the real thing.

Not only that, he had skipped a feeding, perhaps in the hopes that he'd get what he wanted in the form of his mother. As he was screaming, she remembered, and her stomach confirmed, that all she had eaten since leaving that morning was the Diet Coke she had at the police station. Racing around the kitchen with Atid in one arm, she threw leftover egg salad, lettuce, and tomato onto a plate, to eat with her bagel.

Once he latched on and stopped screaming, the twenty minutes feeding him (she couldn't admit to herself that it was more like thirty, because one of her motherhood books had been very stern about mothers who didn't force the child to stick to a ten minute limit on each side) was actually fairly pleasant. She ate slowly and carefully, wondering whether it was true that food made you feel fuller if you took your time with it. She had thought to review the day's events, but her mind decided to float, and she didn't have the energy to force it to focus.

After the two of them were done eating and Atid took a too-quick post-meal nap, it was 5:45, which meant an hour and a half until bath and bedtime. Once the bath and bed routines had started, she knew she would be okay, but it was the hours until then that she dreaded. Despite his youth, her son seemed to have already managed to link his longest consecutive waking periods to the times when his mother was around, but she had still not worked out any routine of games that entertained him for any sustained period of time—not peek-a-boo, not the mirror, not funny faces.

As so often, she decided that a walk was in order. Getting him ready was always good for a few minutes busyness, and he liked being spoken to as she gathered his paraphernalia. She often had an inner chuckle (or a nightmare, she wasn't sure which) at her news crew's reaction to seeing Rachel Tucker tell a newborn, "And now we need some extra diapers; remember when you made doody in the middle of the mall and I didn't have any diapers?"

All packed up, she put him in the stroller and set out on their way. She never left the house confidently anymore, though, because Atid had often proven his unerring ability to need the lone item she had forgotten at home. Down the block, she remembered that she had left behind the emergency milk, which actually calmed her somewhat, since she could now convince herself that she had remembered the one item she had forgotten. What were the odds she'd forget *two* important items?

The walk was primarily for Atid, since he liked the rush of people, trees, cars, and life passing by. It also gave her time to think, she hoped with a more organized mind. She had some food in her stomach, she'd be able to buy a drink along the way, and, if the baby kept to his pattern, he would doze happily for much of the next hour or two.

She didn't want to leave Israel. First off, as Lije had always predicted, the country's quirks, even the most annoying ones, had gotten under her skin; she didn't want to contemplate a future in which service providers provided service, drivers were careful and forgiving to others on the road, and people who wanted you to wait said so in words rather than sticking a cupped hand in your face.

Leaving would also mean the search for Lije would end, make his fate a complete mystery. She knew that the police didn't have the time or interest to pursue the matter very far, even with her constantly on their backs. Liat's death wasn't even yet a mystery to anyone but her.

Leaving now would be a victory for Harvey Keiter, who she couldn't believe was as innocent as he had claimed. And what about

Pinhas, who, in Reuven's telling, also needed to be stopped? Her stubborn side refused to give in or up so easily. That she would be leaving under duress only made it that much more distasteful.

But…to act more religious because some government said so? The thought of it made her almost physically recoil in horror. Maybe she could deepen her observance because *she* wanted to? But she didn't. What if she decided that God wanted her to? Ugh, she hated sentences or people that assumed they knew what God wanted.

Then her cell phone rang, and it was Ed Appleby, her director. Ostensibly, he was calling to be friendly but, since it was past midnight in the States, she knew he was also trying to find out how soon he could get her back on the evening news. The station had been wonderful about her pregnancy, Lije's absence, and her maternity leave, but they wanted her back, and presentable, soon.

As she talked to him, Rachel stopped walking to check herself in a store window. The hair, thick and blonde, framing her face flatteringly, was always an asset. She had some bags under her eyes, but she hoped they'd go away as soon as she broke down and got a nighttime sitter, so she could start getting six uninterrupted hours a night. Even if not, makeup could easily take care of that.

The body was still good, but she'd better start getting serious about diet and exercise. She was proud of her journalistic accomplishments, but appearance was part of the job. And, as everyone knows, the camera adds at least ten pounds. All right, she said to herself for the thousandth time, no more junk food, and back to my exercise routine.

She chatted with Ed, told him she'd be back at work the minute Atid was three months old, and was about to hang up, when it struck her. It wasn't perfect, but as she laid out the idea for Ed, it got better and better.

"Hey, Ed, if you're interested in having me work sooner, I have an idea for a series that I could tape now, but that you couldn't use for about six months or so."

He was immediately interested, used to her spontaneous ideas and the ratings they brought. "Yeah, what is it?"

She quickly told him the story of her attempted murder, taking some guilty pleasure in knowing that the word would get around the network not to mess with Rachel Tucker. Ed made all the appropriate noises of shock that the civilized woman he knew had actually intended to kill a total stranger.

"A blood avenger, Rachel Tucker? We need to have a loooooong cup of coffee when you come back to the States. But I don't get it, what's the story?"

"It's a series actually. You see, I was caught in the act, so they had a lot of ways they could punish me. Instead, they suggested I agree to become a *haverah*, which is a kind of religious status; it says that you've accepted the view of Judaism that they—the government, this Messiah fellow—claim to be true, and that you have studied and will continue to study to better understand your responsibilities in the religion."

"But that's crazy! Didn't religious coercion go out of style in modern countries in, like, the Middle Ages?"

"You know, I was freaked out, too; I think part of me still is. But I think I can turn it into a bang-up news story. What if I tell them that I agree to become a *haverah,* but videotape myself as I go through the process? I could tell them it's for my own memories, but we could use it as a series, showing American audiences what's happening in their closest ally in the Middle East."

Rachel hated the phone, because she couldn't see the other person's reaction, and she had always been viscerally visual. Worried that the silence on the other end was skepticism, she plunged on, as if she were thinking out loud. "Truth is, this could turn into a great documentary; or a PBS series. You know what, Ed, I'm sorry to have troubled you, I think I want to shop this around a bit. I need to call my agent…"

Ed laughed. "Now, Rachel, give me a minute to digest. You have an idea, you blurt it out, and expect me to react within five seconds! It sounds good, but I'm trying to think through some of the logistics. When would we be able to air this? Would it be a one-week series of five two-minute segments? Two weeks? The nightly news can't use a story that spreads out over weeks and weeks, people don't have the staying power to watch that kind of thing night in and night out."

"Maybe we should plan it as a thirteen week series, a half hour a week. You tape yourself all along the way—at major events and a nightly wrap-up, would be my guess—and then we can edit it into a coherent whole. I have to run it by some of the higher-ups, but it sounds like a good start. Only, I'm not sure that it can focus solely on you. Are there going to be other people involved in this process? And, how do we explain having a cameraman follow you around all the time?"

As she was about to answer, Rachel had a sudden image of Yedidya answering a series of questions in the order they were asked. Weird that she should think of that. "You could air it as soon as I have completed my training, which I expect to be within six months. There's not that much news from the Middle East now that people have stopped blowing each other up all the time, so I don't think we'll get scooped by anyone on this in the next six months. Also, I'll return to my regular slot in six weeks; after the first intensive period, I assume I can arrange my training schedule for my return trips to Israel," she was making it up now, since she had no idea of when she'd be coming back to Israel, or how often. Would Atid join her? Would she spend weekends away from him? Later, Rachel, later, "so it's not like I'll be dead weight for the network."

"I think I could probably tape both kinds of segments, a short one for the nightly news the week the series starts, maybe two or three two minute teasers to create interest, and then other short pieces as commercials."

"There aren't other people in *my* process, but I have to have a sponsor, so I'll be interacting with him or her, and then the sponsor's going to send me to various classes and events, to give me a full taste of the kind of life they're pushing, where I assume I'll meet other people like me. On the cameraman issue, I actually thought that maybe I would tape myself; what we would lose in camera quality we would gain in realism."

"I tell you Rachel, it sounds great; good to know that motherhood and the Middle East haven't dulled your edge. Let me set up a few meetings, pitch it to the relevant people and see what happens. Meanwhile, start taping yourself; do you have a digital video camera? Carry it with you, you never know when you'll have a shot. I'll let you know when I have a meeting set up, and maybe you can e-mail me some of it, unedited, so I can show people what you mean."

"Ok, Ed, thanks. I'll be in touch."

When she hung up the phone, Rachel reflexively looked at the minutes on her cell phone, even though the station paid the bill. 12 minutes 35 seconds. Not bad for successfully pitching a reality series.

Now she just had to figure out how to use a digital video. And find a sponsor. What about Yedidya Gross? He seemed nice and knowledgeable, and had the respect of the public. She fished in her handbag for the card, and dialed the number. When he answered, she identified herself, sparking another set of apologies for the day's mishap. Rachel interrupted, told him not to worry about it, but then added that it had put her in something of a bind, which she summarized, closing by asking whether he would sponsor her training. Of course, she added, she would pay for his time, adding to herself, or at least the network would.

"It's not the money, Ms. Tucker; in fact, we're not allowed to accept payment, only gifts that people choose to give. But, sadly, my slate is simply too full right now. After I finish this week in the Temple, I'm spending three months as a judge near Machtesh Ramon, a city that needs a lot of cleaning up, and after that, I need to get my home life in order. Not only that, but after the abject failure of our first meeting, I'm afraid I'd always be overly cautious, and burden you with too many details on any question you'd ask me. Can I recommend someone else? I know a man who's had tremendous success with Americans. He's warm, friendly, and I think you'd like him."

"You know what, before you tell me—and I don't mean to be

rude—as we're talking, I'm thinking I might prefer a woman. Until you mentioned being too busy, I think I hadn't paid attention to how much time the process will involve and a woman feels more...I don't know, appropriate."

Silence on the other end of the line.

"I'm sorry, Yedidya, are you still there?"

"Yes, I'm just embarrassed I didn't think of it myself. But I don't know any women who are available. The man I was about to tell you about, though, is also connected with all the best teachers, he may be able to find someone for you."

The instant before Yedidya said the name, Rachel realized what was coming; it all fit together, a coffee shop to pick up strays from the Temple, his concern with giving others a positive feeling about that Temple, she almost said the words with Yedidya.

"Reuven HaOzer; he runs the Temple Grounds, and, since you told me you've been there often, I assume you know him at least casually?"

Do I ever, Rachel thought. Well, at least she once again had a plan and, oddly enough, it once again involved getting to the Temple Grounds early the next morning. Time to get Atid, and herself, to bed.

That night she dreamt that Lije and Liat were talking to each other, arguing about whether she should have a male or female sponsor. Lije pointed out that he was the only one who had ever convinced her to act at all religiously, so she should at least give a man a chance. Liat argued that it was immodest to get so close to a man, which struck Rachel as odd even while she was having the dream, since Liat, with her wild clothing tastes, had never struck her as particularly concerned with modesty. She woke up with a bad taste in her mouth. She was used to seeing Liat in her dreams, but since when did Lije get there, too?

CHAPTER TEN

Pinhas wasn't there when Harvey arrived at the office; he was dealing with some problem on the Mount. The trainee serving as appointments' secretary—a prestigious and competitive position, even though it lengthened the training by a year or two—told Harvey that some guy, who came often and always bought his sacrificial animals at the Temple stores, was upset because he had bought a bull that turned out to be blemished. Kohen Moshel would be back soon if Mr. Keiter was willing to wait.

Harvey had nothing better to do these days, and he'd probably spend the next few minutes reveling in someone thinking he was important enough to call him Mister. In his world, his former world he should say, everyone went by first names, or nicknames, which he'd hated. Not for the first time, he thanked God for that final conviction, where they'd threatened permanent solitary confinement, and a diet of groats and stale water.

Harvey wasn't sure why *that* threat had made such an impression, when all his time in prison had left so little of one, but there it was. And, once he'd taken the first step to change, good things had started happening. Getting Pinhas as sponsor felt like a double coup, since, aside from the contacts he had for giving Harvey a new life, the priest knew enough about his prior activities to know what Harvey was referring to without him having to spell it all out.

Frequently in their conversations, Harvey would start to say something, and Pinhas would close his eyes, wince, and say, "Yes, yes, no need to belabor that, I know about that, let's move on." Some of his friends had told him about how hard it was to actually verbalize their various crimes, but Pinhas didn't seem too interested in his doing that. He'd mention something, say he was sorry, and that was the end of it, a relief for Harvey, who wasn't much for introspection.

And he never could have appreciated Rinah while he was still caught up in the life. He'd always preferred the women who dressed in a way that made it clear that getting them in bed wouldn't be too much of a challenge. Relationships for him had generally meant women he slept with consistently for a few months, before going on to the next one. He couldn't remember even wanting more than that; he'd been too busy with work to think of women as anything but an outlet for his sexual tension.

Had he met Rinah back then, he'd have left her for some wimpy guy who cared about sharing feelings. With all Pinhas' minimalist approach, Harvey had still thought about himself a lot more these past months than ever before; when he met Rinah, he found deeper pleasures than he had known existed. It didn't hurt that, for all her modesty of dress and demeanor, she had a wild side that was exactly what he needed.

Harvey's reverie was interrupted by Pinhas entering in a foul mood, as was usual for him anytime he had to deal with actual people. Harvey had long ago realized that Pinhas only liked the technicalities of the service, the slaughtering, cleaning, and burning of the animals, the apportioning of the parts to the various priests, informing the owners that their sin was absolved, but human relations was just an annoyance.

Harvey knew and believed the rumors that it was Pinhas' poorly hidden contempt for others that had cost him the High Priesthood. Everyone recognized his brilliance and his skill at making the Temple run smoothly, but the High Priest had to be beloved of the other priests and the people, and, at least in a closed ballot, his brother priests didn't trust Pinhas to take on that role.

"Harvey." It was an acknowledgement of his presence, not a greeting.

He had hoped it wouldn't happen, but as soon as he started talking about Rachel and the day's events, he switched back to a person he thought he had left behind. "Did you hear what that crazy bitch almost did to me? I tell you, when I take care of…"

Pinhas raised a hand, imperious in his reproof. "Please, Harvey, this is ground we have already covered; it pains me to see you regressing in this way. First, watch your language in a holy place. I would discourage you from speaking that way anywhere, but your awe of this place should even more so prevent it in here. As for Ms. Tucker, you know that we need her services until we have recovered the item. And, let me add for the record, we do not condone the kind of *taking care of* I assume you meant, and your suggesting it makes me wonder if you are as far along as I had been assuming."

Harvey had to tolerate Pinhas' self-righteous side because he needed good progress reports to keep him out of solitary, but he hated it, and right now wasn't in the mood. "Oh, sure, when some… woman points a gun at me, you're all ready to tell me to ignore her. But I guess we didn't ignore Liat's threats, did we?"

Pinhas grimaced at his words. "That is a most unfortunate analogy to draw. As you well know, I warned and pleaded with Liat to be sensible. I tried to make her see that what I was doing was for her own good. And when she continued to refuse, well, it was out of my hands."

Harvey wasn't ready to stop, although he could hear Rinah begging him to hold his tongue. "Out of my hands, out of my hands! Isn't that a convenient excuse for when your reputation is in danger? But when my freaking life is at stake, well, then, that's when we have full control of ourselves, huh?"

Pinhas' eyes shone brightly. "Self-control, Harvey, is the essence of the *haver*. I'm afraid this little outburst tells me that your progress isn't quite up to snuff. Too bad, too, because your string of "satisfactory" to "excellents" was quite remarkable. Ah, well, I'm sure the judge will be relatively lenient; I'll add that I think it was a momentary lapse and that with a minimal punishment you should be back to yourself. Two beats of the lash and two days in solitary should do it this time. But please remember; the discipline and awe that mark a relationship with God is constant and unremitting.

To address your teacher so disrespectfully suggests that you have not sufficiently incorporated that lesson. This is for your good, not mine."

Harvey was so used to punishment that the words only bothered him because of Rinah. She'd complain about his being away, about the recovery time after getting out of solitary, and about the delay in his finishing his course, which would also delay their marriage. He'd have to make it up to her, and that was sure to cost him. Glum but resigned, Harvey left the office and went back to the crapshoot that was his life.

CHAPTER ELEVEN

I t took her a full hour to put herself together that morning, mostly because she had gotten used to cutting corners on self-grooming, having not been in front of a camera in a long time. All prepared, feeling virtuous for sticking to a small bowl of cereal and milk for breakfast, she sat down in front of the camera and tripod she had set up the previous evening.

"This is Rachel Tucker, bringing you the first in a series of in-depth ABC News reports on the changes in Israel ten years after the arrival of the man the country has hailed as the Messiah. That Arrival has deeply affected the country politically, economically, socially, and, of course, religiously."

"In setting up a mixed monarchy/theocracy in what used to be the foremost democracy in the Middle East, the Messiah set off alarm bells in Washington, although few incidents have caused concern thus far. Still, Washington's attitude, in the words of one State Department official who spoke on the condition of anonymity, is watchful caution." Rachel had gotten that quote months ago, but the guy was not one to change his mind; she'd check with him later today.

"To help our viewers understand the New Israel, ABC News is going to take you inside the core of the country. As a dual citizen, American and Israeli, I am enrolling in a certification course to become a *haverah*, a status that signifies, to this government, that the person involved has adopted the Jewish lifestyle, with all of its rules, as fully as possible. Were I to complete the course, viewers will be interested to hear, I would attain privileges other Israelis do not have—seats on town councils, for example, are limited to graduates of such a course, whose testimony is also considered more reliable in court. We will be investigating what makes this inner circle tick, their goals and aspirations, their failings, their hidden secrets."

"Today, my mission is to find a personal religion trainer, who will sponsor my studies. Most of the process is self-study, but the sponsor guides the student on what books to read, religious practices to undertake, ceremonies to attend to learn about Judaism in practice, and certifies eventual readiness for final exams."

"My first lead is the coffee shop of a man named Reuven HaOzer; this popular gathering spot, called the Temple Grounds, is located close to the rebuilt Temple. Its owner, a man who attracts and helps all sorts of psychologically and economically needy people, has amassed a well-established record as a sponsor to candidates for *haverut,* but also as a successful parole officer, and as a guide for non-Jews who wish to become citizens of the State of Israel. In previous encounters with HaOzer, I have learned that each meeting is completely different than the one before. Wondering what that meeting will bring, this is Rachel Tucker, ABC News."

Not perfect, but that's what editors were for. She was too busy being proud of how much background info she had managed to pull off the Internet. Like finding out that Reuven was a constant fixture in the Israeli press; the Jerusalem Post had over 50 articles about him since the shop opened seven and a half years ago.

She was also proud of the arm holster she had rigged for her camera. After getting off the phone with Ed, she decided she'd rather film without people knowing about it; it would produce more spontaneous and, she hoped, more interesting footage. A lot of this process was going to be heavy religion talk, which didn't broadcast well; the more human interest she could put in the footage, the better. The arm-holster, with the remote conveniently tucked in her purse would let her record surreptitiously, increasing the odds of catching something good on tape.

Atid had been an angel today, entertaining himself the whole time she got ready, wrote out a little script, filmed, and packed a water bottle and fruit for the day. When the babysitter arrived, instead of her normal excitement at moving on to the productive part of her day, she actually felt a pang at leaving him home. For the first time in the weeks since he was born, she was tempted to take him with her.

Resisting at least that temptation, she kissed him good-bye with more fervor than usual, and made her way to the Temple Grounds. She decided to take a different route, part of her continuing attempt to learn all the multiple pathways of Jerusalem. She walked around the Old City to Zion Gate, but as she came through the Gate, she forgot to take the left that would have gotten her to the Old City and instead headed down towards the Mount, where the old Wailing Wall had been left intact, a reminder of the thousands of years Jews had longed for a rebuilt Temple.

She had almost gotten to the bottom of the steep hill before realizing her mistake; walking back up worked up quite a thirst. Entering the shop, she decided she didn't need coffee yet, and got water and an iced tea instead. She nursed the two drinks, knowing that Reuven, whom she did not yet see, would find his way over there.

He did not disappoint, smiling his way to her table within five minutes of her arrival. "Well, if you're drinking water, I guess it's not the coffee that keeps dragging you back. Are you here just to show off your good looks or is there some other purpose to your visit?"

Rachel was surprised at how flattered she was at the lightly tossed compliment. Before Atid had been born, she had often been noticed for her looks, had known that anytime she attended an affair, pictures of her in full dress would be posted on the Internet, and had sometimes even consulted with a stylist so she could make a "Most Beautiful" or "Best Dressed" list. A part of her missed the attention that had come with that radar, gone with her pregnancy and absence from the States.

It hadn't helped that no one on the streets of Jerusalem, even the construction workers, had seemed to notice her appearance, although she was still in her camera-ready clothing and makeup. Old insecurities, kept at bay since high school by a steady stream of admirers, were never too far below the surface—had one child destroyed her looks?

Rachel tried to adopt the same light tone as he had, but her underlying irritation at the situation made her words sounds more bitter than sardonic. "Well, I'm here to join the ranks of those who can't manage their own lives, who have to come to you for solace and sustenance."

The smile left his face as soon as she said it, because of course, she mentally flogged herself, *he* took his work very seriously. To try to take back the insult, she hurried on, telling him of her conversation with Yedidya and her decision and failed attempt to kill Harvey. Not waiting to see his reaction, she moved on to her meeting with Kapdan, her tentative decision to train to be a *haverah*, leaving out the TV angle, her asking Yedidya for help, and his suggesting that Reuven might know a good sponsor.

Reuven listened in his perfectly receptive way, and, when she finished, waited, both to be sure that she was done and to think. "I knew about Harvey; I have a police radio so I can help out at various kinds of crime scenes—*you'll* probably think it's a big joke, but I am a certified grief counselor as well, for all those "needy" people looking for solace after a tragedy. But I didn't know what they had decided to do with you; when I saw you walk in, I thought maybe they had let you off with a warning. How long did Kapdan give you to give him an answer?"

"A week…"

"Well, then, my plan would be to spend Sunday together, for two reasons. First, I want to take you to a city of refuge, to show you how it actually works, so we can be sure you won't jump to rash conclusions in the future. Second, those places are usually filled with sponsors, since the residents are required to meet with sponsors regularly as part of living there. Third…"

"I thought you said two reasons."

He smiled. "So sue me. Third, I think we'd have fun."

She was relieved that he had so quickly put aside his pique, but tensed at this latest leading comment, which hinted at a more than professional interest, an interest she had no clue how to handle. She hadn't even let herself think about her feelings towards him, because, well, whatever she thought about Lije's fate, *officially* she was a married woman; especially since yesterday, how would the government take her going on a daylong trip with another man?

When in doubt, equivocate. "Is that such a good idea? You know I'm a new mother, right?"

"I think it'll be a great idea. You'll get out of Jerusalem, it's supposed to be a beautiful day, we can bring a picnic lunch—there are lots of wide open fields right outside the city where people go to hang out, tan, sleep, you know. And, you'll be taking a step in your education towards being a *haverah*! You can leave the baby with a sitter, right?"

She'd have to address it head-on. "And it's not a problem for a married woman to be…" She couldn't find the right word, so she went with the wrong one, "consorting?"

Reuven laughed. "I don't intend to *consort* with you at all. Look, I found out about your…situation…with your husband, so I know that this is in no way a date. And the government, well, they haven't been clear yet about how we distinguish between consorting, as you so nicely put it, and friends getting together. Certainly any physical displays of affection would be a problem, but I'll keep my hands to myself if you will."

"We can tell whoever asks that we're looking into a sponsor for you, or whatever. The government trusts me, you know, because I don't break the rules, and certainly not in public, where we'll be *all the time*. And, to be clear, I'm not planning or hoping to break any rules with you, either; you're married as far as I'm concerned, until we find out what happened to your husband. But that doesn't mean you can't ever enjoy yourself, does it? Anyway, it's up to you; you have to feel comfortable going, or you won't enjoy it, and that'll miss the whole point. Would you prefer a chaperone? Male or female?"

Rachel knew he was teasing, and it made her feel like she was acting kind of prudish, a word that had never before applied to her. "No, it's all right. I was only worried because I'm so unused to this whole social thing, and especially with the new rules, and my warning yesterday," and then, to her mortification, she began to cry.

When she cried in front of men—and she tried hard not to; she hated thinking she had gotten her way by acting the damsel in distress—she never wanted physical comfort, even with Lije. As she was sobbing, she felt the stares of other men, which only made it worse (the women had turned, sure, but they had the good sense to turn back when they saw a woman crying); some of them even started to get up to ask her what was wrong.

Reuven handled it perfectly. He motioned the other people away, wordlessly, got her a box of tissues from somewhere, and waited her out. She wasn't a big crier, but this time felt long. As it went on, she felt fifteen points of angst combining to keep the tears coming. Would she ever find out what happened to Lije? It would be bad enough to lose him in the middle of the work-in-progress that had been their relationship, but being stranded forever would be worse. She had never let herself focus on that, but Reuven's saying it straight out made it hard to avoid.

And what did that mean for the baby? Rachel knew that her guilt feelings at having brought him into the world without being able to know his father were part of the reason she hadn't found a way to respond emotionally to him, but the thought that he might not even ever know what *happened* to his father made it worse.

And soon, she knew, she wouldn't be able to hide from how to handle these issues. She'd have to start answering awkward questions, from the network and other members of her New York social circles. She'd have to tell the awful story, again and again and again, to whoever asked, pretty much. Oh, God, she might even have to do one of those awful interviews laying bare her tragedy and her "courage" in facing it!

The crying helped. By the time she ran down maybe ten minutes later, she felt better and had made some decisions about how she was going to handle these kinds of situations. As she wound down, Reuven asked her if she wanted to freshen up, and pointed her in the direction of the bathroom.

When she came back, he was pensive. Uncomfortable at having acted so intimately in front of a stranger, she put on a joking face, and asked "Come here often?" Which, in the context of their previous conversation, was exactly the wrong thing to say.

"Rachel," Reuven said, "I don't want to complicate your life, and I know the last couple of days have been stressful. I like you, but you have to believe me that, as long as you don't know the story with Lije, I am not looking to develop a relationship that is anything other than friendly and professional. I slipped by making clear how much I'd enjoy a day in your company, but I do think you should visit Hevron, if only to see the changes since the Arrival. I have a feeling that you will gain more than either one of us know, and I *know* it's a good first step to finding a sponsor."

Hearing him speak so carefully, measuring each word to be sure that it not carry the wrong connotation, she regretted that circumstances forced them to turn what might have been a nicely developing friendship into a stilted, deliberate negotiation of terms. In fact, she had not seen Hevron since the Arrival, she did wonder what the government had done with the squalid Arab city, and she would enjoy a day trip with him. Maybe, having made their positions clear, they could step back to some spontaneity.

"Look, I'm sorry I've been difficult about this; let's start over. Let me introduce myself—my name is Rachel Tucker, but you can call me Rachel. I am an *agunah*, an abandoned woman," it was in fact harder to say it in English than in Hebrew; the Hebrew sounded clinical, so she could ignore the emotions that were unavoidable when she said it in English, "and am also having a hard time with the recent death of a close friend. I am looking into becoming a *haverah* and need advice on how to do that. If you think going to Hevron on Sunday would be a good idea, it would be my pleasure to join you. Shall we meet somewhere, or would you like to pick me...I mean get me at my apartment?"

He smiled at her approach, and responded in kind. "It's a

pleasure to make your acquaintance, Rachel. I was thinking we'd take the bus; there's a whole inspection thing when you get to the city, so it's easier to get it out of the way in Jerusalem. It lets us bypass some of the traffic outside the city. They have fairly regular service, if that works for you."

"Sure. My babysitter comes at 8:30, I can be at the Central Bus Station at….nine-fifteen." She hated giving times because she knew that something would happen to make her late; it always did.

"Great, I'll see you then."

CHAPTER TWELVE

Rachel left the Temple Grounds walking considerably more lightly than when she had gone in, feeling as if she was finally making progress in at least one area of her life. She went to a health club near her house that had early and later hours—proximity, accessibility, and ease—and signed up for a membership, even though the doctor wouldn't clear her for serious exercise for a few weeks yet. Taking action in that direction made her feel efficient, and the more efficient she felt, the more she got accomplished. She spent the rest of the day strolling through Jerusalem.

Of course, she couldn't allow herself to call it strolling, she thought of it as investigating her surroundings. She found parks for Atid, categorizing them by how old he would have to be to enjoy each one, bookstores for when her current supply ran out, locations to film, and still got home at 6:30, feeling thoroughly refreshed and renewed.

Which was probably why Atid chose to be in an awful mood. She held him, rubbed his back, put him over her lap, sang to him, bathed him, each of which worked for five minutes at a time. By the fourth cycle through the routine, it was 9:30, when he usually took a long sleep beginning at 8:00. She placed him over her shoulder and began patting his back, trying to relieve what she thought might be gas. At each pat, he calmed a little, as if she was on the right track, but soon started screaming again.

When frustration got the better of her, she gave him what she thought was a fairly hard whack, immediately sorry and resigned to the screams to come. Instead, he burped loudly, sighed happily, and went to sleep on her shoulder. A harder pat? Rachel was almost ready to cry in relief. This squalling bundle who had ruined so many of her nights with his crying was looking for a firmer hand to help the gas come out. She knew he would go down nicely now, but she held him for a few minutes, reveling in the tenderness she felt. She wasn't a harridan, she told herself, just a woman whose bonding had gotten off to a slow start for many good reasons. Kissing him gently on the forehead, she put him down on his back and went to bed herself.

It was only once she was comfortable in bed that she realized she hadn't filmed a commentary, although she and Ed had agreed she'd do a morning and an evening. Truth was, she hadn't filmed that much; she didn't often remember that she had the camera with her. Should she get out of bed, do her makeup all over again, just to film two minutes of commentary? Nah, she'd do twice as much next time. She turned over and slept soundly.

Friday and the Sabbath passed quicker than usual, as Rachel repeatedly wondered what a city of refuge would look like. Since she only had a half day of babysitting on Friday and none on Saturday, those were always hard days, filled with Atid time. In between the diapers, feedings, walks, and crying, Rachel stayed home, rested her overworked body, slept a lot, and did some reading. She even took out a Bible to read the original passages about cities of refuge.

By the time she went to sleep Saturday night, embarrassingly early for the bon vivant she had once been, she felt ready to at least do an introductory voice over in the morning. Her alarm woke her at 6:00. Atid's last waking had been at 5:00, and, if he stuck to his pattern, he'd be good til 7:30. She quickly showered, blow-dried her hair, put on her makeup, and sat down to record. Her research of the night before helped the words flow easily.

"The city of refuge. Even the name makes it sound like a relic from a primitive time of blood feuds, of relatives serving the role of police in securing the safety of the members of their clan. And yet, the new leader of the State of Israel re-established them as one of his first acts. Aside from the population transfer involved—buying residents out of their apartments, installing Levites as owners/operators—the system also shifted the direction of much of Israeli criminal justice."

"Murderers now often handed themselves in, showing up at these cities of refuge for protection from an overzealous blood avenger. While authorities readily admit that many murderers are not yet brought to justice, they nonetheless point to their smaller than average cold case file. Knowing that a family relative will kill you as soon as he can convince the authorities to certify him as a *go'el hadam* does wonders to encourage proactive surrenders. Today, we will be visiting one such city, the ancient city of Hebron, to see how the system works."

Rachel tucked the camera in her arm-holster, ready for the day. Before then, though, there was a baby to feed and a bus to catch. She hated herself for it, but she was actually looking forward to a day with an attractive man who felt the same about her. It had been too long, with too much intervening mess, since the last time.

Closing her eyes, she remembered. She and Lije had decided to take a spring picnic up North. Lije loved it there, and she had to admit that over the years she had enjoyed the many beautiful hikes, waterfalls, and pools he had found. This time, he had surprised her by bringing along a tent and a change of clothing for her, and taken them on a two-day excursion to the Banias. They had had a wonderful day; the weather had been unseasonably warm, although the water was still extremely cold from the winter. They had played silly games in the waterfalls, taken walks as well as hikes, and enjoyed warming the steaks he had brought from her favorite Jerusalem steakhouse. That night, as far as she could tell, was the first of Atid's life.

Since he seemed to know how to punish her for feeling good, Atid interrupted her memories by cheesing in her hair and all over her outfit and the babysitter showed up late. She re-showered, put on new clothes, and got out of the house already behind schedule. Then, the bus she took didn't go to the Central Bus Station (she thought all buses went there; isn't that why it was called the Central Bus Station?), and her cab got stuck in traffic. It was only 9:30—fifteen minutes late wasn't bad by Lije's standards, for example—when she finally showed up, but she felt as if she had already lived two full days. A nagging voice in her head claimed this was a sign she should not be going to Hevron with Reuven. As per usual, the nagging voice was more of a nuisance than an obstacle; it didn't change what she was going to do, it only made her feel guilty doing it.

When she did get there, she realized that they hadn't set a specific location, so she found out when and where the next bus to Hevron would be leaving, which was where he found her.

"Hey."

She turned to see him standing there smiling. He was wearing what Israelis thought of as dress-up clothing—dark slacks ordinarily reserved for Sabbath, holidays, and weddings. Had he worn a white shirt, she would have been sure that he thought of this as a date. Even so, she felt underdressed in her jeans and button-down Polo shirt.

"I'm sorry, I thought this was a casual kind of thing."

"For you it is, but the likelihood is that I'm going to meet mentors and bosses, who track my progress. We get rated on how well we're spreading the Word, you know" he managed to be both serious and self-deprecating at the same time "so I need to look like I'm on the job, not spending a pleasant day with a beautiful woman."

If she'd *felt* married, she'd have bristled at the repeated compliments; in the States, she would have known it was an attempt to test the waters in the hopes of initiating some kind of affair. But she knew that they both knew that they both assumed that it was only a matter of time before they found out that Lije was...well, she'd deal with that when it happened. Besides, he looked pretty good, too. When dressed up, his bulk was more clearly muscle than it might seem in his ordinary clothes. This was a man she could feel good walking down the street with or, she dared say, bringing to a black-tie dinner.

The bus should have been an ordeal. The ride was only forty minutes, but before they pulled away from the station, each passenger was individually questioned and searched for weapons or other contraband (any notably heavy items were held back, since they could be used as a "blunt object," like coroners always named as the cause of death).

As annoying and inefficient as the authorities handling the questioning were, she was enjoying the time with Reuven so much that she barely noticed her surroundings. He told her about growing up in LA, a city he despised at the time, but had come to appreciate more on his return visits to his parents, of his moving (he referred to it by the more romantic Hebrew term, "making *aliyah*," going up) to Israel at eighteen, joining the Army (priests were not yet exempted from service), his failed first marriage, his loss of his toe leading to a downward spiral of alcoholism, recovery, and, finally, setting up the store that had come to fill almost (he carefully stressed the word) all the voids in his life.

Rachel was touched and yet uncomfortable at how freely he was opening up to her. She sensed that he did not do so easily, that his listening to others masked a personal guardedness, and that this was the kind of openness he would give on first dates, back in the day. For once, though, she shoved her concerns to the back of her mind and enjoyed the moments as they passed. How Zen of me, she thought, surprised, amused, and delighted.

CHAPTER THIRTEEN

A s they approached Hevron, each side of the road was populated by openly armed people. At first she didn't pay attention; Israel, from its founding, was a country whose private citizens were part-time soldiers, owning guns, and tending to wear them as they saw fit. But she couldn't help notice that they turned their guns towards each vehicle that passed, lowering them only after a long look.

"Who were those people?"

Reuven smiled. "Avengers; they stand at the last point before the city limits. Lots of people who need to get to a city of refuge come in a car or bus, figuring it's fastest. Most cars have bullet-proof windows, left over from the old days, but occasionally one of them will be stupid enough to leave a window open. Every year, one or two people get killed on the road into town."

She didn't like seeing life and death treated like a game, and also felt a little nervous at the possibility that they were going to be shot at, but she didn't want to ruin the mood by getting into a religious argument. Her marriage to Lije had taught here that even calm men got worked up about religious stuff, at least in Israel. She steered the conversation in a different direction.

Once the bus pulled into town, people began lowering their windows, although a few didn't, probably refuge-seekers still not confident they were safe. As the bus eased its way through town to the courthouse, she was surprised at how calm the place was. No soldiers patrolled the streets; people walked casually around town, without any of the tension she'd assumed would pervade the air of a city populated by convicted criminals.

"These people are all murderers?"

"No, no, most of them are the Levites who are asked to live here to set a tone for the place; they are trained from birth for this job—they spend their entire day, pretty much, in study, thought, meditation, you know."

"Like Shaolin monks on *Kung Fu*?"

Reuven laughed. "Actually, yeah. When I was recovering from…my bad time, my sponsor had me try a lot of that martial arts stuff. The calmness of mind that Buddhists cultivate bears a lot of relationship to what they strive for. You gotta remember, these are people whose job is to relate to *anybody* lovingly and respectfully."

"But even the convicts are usually perfectly normal citizens. They didn't plan whatever happened, and they aren't sure they're responsible. They get here, pretty much all they know is that *out there*" he waved vaguely towards the boundaries of the city "is somebody who wants to kill them for something they don't think was their fault. From their perspective, they're good people who got stuck a bad hand."

Something had changed about him once they got into town; it was as if he had put his sponsor-persona back on, and the open, friendly seatmate of the ride had receded behind a veil of…she couldn't put her finger on it. Something here bugged him, although he was the one who had said they should come.

A greeter welcomed people as they got off the bus, checklist in hand. Each person said something, and she directed them either inside the courthouse or to other sites around the square. Rachel was going to ask Reuven what that was about, but he was already up and headed off the bus. She followed, and as she got to the front, she heard what the people were saying to the woman at the bottom of the stairs.

"Visitor."

"Refuge."

When Reuven got there, he identified himself, showed an ID card, and took her with him.

"You've got pull, I see. I better stick with you or I might get in trouble," she teased. He smiled, still tense.

"What do you want to do, eat, see some of the traditional

tourist sites—the Cave of Machpelah, where the Patriarchs and Matriarchs are buried—or go into court?"

"Yes, yes, and yes." She loved wandering around new places, picking up information as she went along. She almost wanted to run down one street after another, going anywhere and nowhere, until her feet were too tired to go any further. And then she wanted to sit at a café, with a soda or a latte, until she was ready to go out and see the city, inch by inch. What was it Lije had always said when dragging her on tours, even walking in the Land fulfills a commandment? She was ready for that one, here and now.

At the thought, she remembered Lije teasing her that she was most Jewish when it served her own purposes. Truth is, touring had been one of her continuing fights with him—when they went to a new place, he had always wanted to go to specific spots, on a specific schedule. She liked to soak it up, seeing how real people lived, hearing them talk, and fight, and flirt. She wondered what life was like in a city like this, where murder was always the backdrop.

Reuven picked up on her enthusiasm and seemed to relax as he enjoyed it. "Ok, but what first?" The day passed in a whirlwind of walking, eating, talking, laughing, and learning. As she reflected on the day on her way home, her feet complaining at bearing the burden of her good time, she took a moment to worry about not having come at all close to finding a sponsor.

All the ones she had met that day seemed to be the social misfits of the Levi class. She had particularly liked the men who had refused to look her in the face, but thought they could handle her training. The women were somewhat better, but she hadn't clicked with any of them. She felt a little nervous, like there was something wrong with her.

Reuven tried to be reassuring. "There could be lots of reasons you haven't found anyone yet. Look, we like to assume that all the Levites are in control of their own issues, but maybe all those women were jealous of you. I mean, you're Rachel Tucker, and you're all dressed up, maybe they were intimidated. Or, maybe they saw you with me, a well-known priest and sponsor" he puffed himself up exaggeratedly, but she was too tired to do more than smile, "and assumed they weren't in your league. Anyway, don't worry about it; worse comes to worst, I'll speak to Kapdan and explain the situation. Meanwhile, you've got plenty of time til he needs an answer. What are you doing tomorrow?"

She didn't know how to take the question; but was nervous that he might be going somewhere she didn't feel comfortable. "I don't know yet, I wanted to go through my mail at home, get in touch with my boss in NY, see how the baby is, why, what did you have in mind?" He'd been excellent company, and she didn't want anything to ruin it.

"Nothing. I have to be at the store tomorrow, I thought we should keep in touch with your progress, suggest ideas as they come along. Tell you what, why don't you come up with a plan, and if any of it is relevant to studying, call me, and I'll give you my thoughts. If you want."

"Ok, great. Um, is it appropriate to thank you for a wonderful day—I could not imagine that visiting a city of murderers would have been so enjoyable."

Reuven almost blushed. "Please don't thank me, the pleasure was mine. And anyway, it's part of my job, you know. So, here's my card, call me. Bye." He walked off hurriedly, as if to avoid a drawn-out good-bye.

She got home at 7:00, which tonight was a big deal for the babysitter. It was a measure of how much she had enjoyed her day that the woman's tantrum washed right off of her. Her feet hurt, she hadn't eaten too much, she had learned a lot, and *she had gotten it on tape.*

Maybe because of her attitude, the time with Atid flew. He was in a good mood for longer than usual, and when he started fussing, her new forcefulness got a burp out of him easily, she gave him a bath, a bottle, and then he went down for his long sleep. She checked her watch, 8:15, figured she'd watch film for two hours, send the best of it to Ed, and then get to bed.

As she sat in front of the TV, fast forwarding through the

three hours of crap she had chosen to record for posterity that day, she gained a new respect for cameramen. In that whole time, she had gotten maybe ten minutes that she wasn't embarrassed to send along, and most of that was from a discussion she had had with a guy at a café, who had approached her. She could only take credit for having turned on the camera.

CHAPTER FOURTEEN

Hi, Reuven. Got a new recruit here?" He stuck out his hand to Rachel, rough- hewn, heavy and strong. The tattoo on his left triceps, a heart with an arrow and the word Marcia written on the shaft of the arrow inside the heart (Marcia? For a tattoo?) was unusual in a country whose laws now forbade Jews from defacing their bodies with permanent markings. "I'm Zeke Long, pretty much the senior man around here. How'd yours happen?"

His questions flustered her. She hadn't thought of the possibility that people would assume she was there for refuge; wouldn't it be great if the Enquirer or some other rag picked up *that* story? But also, there was something threatening about this man, not out in the open, but right under the surface, violence and anger aching to be released.

"Oh, no, actually, I was stopped before I managed to do anything. But the police ordered me to do some retraining, or whatever." Inanely, she was reminded of Alice's Restaurant, where Arlo Guthrie sang about all the other convicts moving away from a guy arrested for littering, only moving back when he added "and disturbing the peace."

"And they gave you Reuven? Wow, you must really be a tough case, they only give him the lost causes—I was one of his, too. Took me maybe a year to even resign myself to being here, I'll tell you that. When I first got here, man, was I pissed, sorry, I mean peeved. I mean, I had just gotten married, and I'm on a job, you know, in construction, and I'm coming down the ladder from the roof, and as I'm going down, my foot slips, and I fall, and that idiot Slim is at the bottom of the ladder, and I land on him and he up and dies on me. Next thing I know, his family's taking potshots! I only just got here before they killed me."

"And then, when we have the trial, I don't get a lawyer, I just get to tell my story to the judges, all 23 of them, which is pretty nerve-racking itself, and then *they* do all the examining, so I can't even get in a word on how I think they should ask the questions! I gotta admit, though, they did a good job o' it, I'll give 'em that, but *then*, get this, they say that I have to stay here, and I say "how long" cuz you know I'm figuring with parole and time off for good behavior, maybe it's just a few months, like back in Rikers or wherever" thank you, Zeke! That familiar feel she'd been trying to place since he started talking, it was the mannerisms of the felons she'd met when reporting on prison reform (or, more accurately, on prison not-reform), "And they tell me, it depends on when the High Priest dies; well I nearly sh.. I mean had a fit."

His monologue needed explanatory voice-over, to give the background to what he was saying, but other than that, boy, was it great. She watched, relieved that she'd captured him on camera.

"Anyway...I'm sorry, am I bothering you? My advisor—Reuven was just a short-term whatdotheycallit? Yeah, intervention to get me started—anyway, my advisor tells me I'm a little too, what's his word? forward with people. So, if I'm being too forward, I can just go..."

She'd assured him that he was doing fine, but was happy to get in a word, so whoever saw the film would know that it was a Rachel Tucker news story. She didn't want the network thinking this could film itself.

"No, please go ahead, you were saying that it was difficult for you to reconcile yourself to your sentence."

Zeke savored her word. "Yeah, that's it, it was difficult to reconcile. At first, I did my "reconciling" by vandalizing the town at night, but Reuven took me aside and pointed out that while they couldn't kick me out, they always had options for disciplining, and he mentioned a few unpleasant ones, like rationing my food, forcing me to take a tiny apartment, whatever. He made it clear they weren't going to put up with…well, they meant me, but they used some fancy word with a "d" for it."

"A disruption?" She guessed out of politeness.

"Nah, something else, but that's good enough. They weren't going to tolerate my disrupting their town. So I thought about it, and realized that this was definitely a lot better than prison, and what the hay, I might as well make a go of it. I'll tell you this, though, cost me my wife, this whole thing did, she decided she couldn't be bothered to move here, and I knew that that was the beginning of the end…I didn't get the letter, though, til last month, which is why I'm walking around kinda glum, you know, not interested in talking really?"

Ok, never meet up with Zeke when he was in the mood to talk. A glum Zeke, however, was exactly what she needed. "Maybe you could answer a few of my questions, and that would take your mind off your troubles?"

He brightened up. "Sure, I'd love to; my sponsor's always happy whenever I play well with others, as he puts it. So fire away. Although I gotta tell ya, I'm not sure you can understand this place until you've lived here. I mean, it's a little crazy. Like, for instance, my sponsor thought I wasn't showing enough regret—all right, I probably wasn't, I mean how much can you regret falling off a ladder? None of this was my fault, that's what I kept telling myself—so he decided to make me listen to a victim impact statement. They made me sit in a room while relatives of the dead guy could come by to let me know what I did to them by killing their father, husband, son, brother, you know."

"And I'm sitting there, and they come in one by one, some of them the same ones waiting to plug me if I ever leave town, but when they were done, man, it was powerful."

"What was?"

"Well, after hearing those stories, I wasn't convinced that it was my fault Slim bought it, but I knew I didn't ever want to do anything that could lead to people feeling that kind of pain again. Which was funny, a little, cuz the other time I killed somebody, I didn't feel that way at all."

"What happened that time?" She had barely been able to maintain the neutrality of tone that was so essential to keeping him talking. He had told her of killing a girl, mid-20's, light brown hair, a hiker's backpack, one rainy night when he was drunk, somewhere north of Jerusalem was all he could remember.

Along with his other remarkable qualities, it turned out that Zeke enjoyed having a few drinks and then taking nighttime target practice, trying to knock branches off trees. This night, he'd been standing inside the woods, and hadn't paid attention to the woman hitchhiking at the side of the road. One of his shots, instead of hitting the tree he had aimed at, went a little left and killed her.

He'd run down to the side of the road, instantly sober, looking desperately for a passing car. Or so he told Rachel and audiences in America. She'd been standing at a spot where many people picked up rides, but nighttime was very light on traffic, both of those seeking rides and those providing them. She died within minutes, never regaining consciousness.

Afraid of the consequences, he'd buried her a little further into the forest, cleaned up any blood he could find, and gotten out of there. Memories of Lije washing over her, Rachel could think only of the poor family wandering the country, maybe the world, looking for their daughter, sister, wife, mother, or friend. The tears she had kept inside when Zeke told her the story the first time came pouring out now, as she was again shocked by how oblivious he was to the suffering he'd caused, regardless of the impression Slim's family had made on him.

And yet he seemed to think he had taken her death seriously. He had said, somberly, as if it was a big deal to him, "From that day to this, I haven't touched a gun, and I used to be a pretty good shot." As if that made a difference to the family. "When nobody found her, I figured I was safe, and then this happened. So I guess what goes around comes around, you know? No use crying over yesterday's news, and all that, right? Anyway, I gotta go, I got a meeting with some people about possibilities for when I get out of here. Nice meetin ya, though, see ya around."

As she watched the tape of him leaving, she again felt a fervent hope that the High Priest would live for the rest of Zeke's lifetime; she felt safer knowing that a guy like Zeke Long was not in general circulation. Then she chuckled to herself as she remembered Reuven coming over after Zeke had left and, unprompted, saying he prayed for the High Priest's welfare every time he thought about him. Great minds and all that.

The interview with Zeke had buoyed her spirits. It was footage she could send to Ed; it was strange enough to American audiences that it could be a whole report, with some expert giving the background about cities of refuge, accidental murder, and how all of that worked. More important, it gave her a job where she could provide a real service to people in distress.

She rummaged around in her apartment, found the notebook that used to be her never-fail companion, and jotted down the information about the young woman. He'd said it had been about ten years ago; she could go through missing persons' files, track down the victim's name, contact the family. If she couldn't find Lije or nail Harvey, she could at least do this. Excited about the prospect of actual investigative reporting, she went to bed without reviewing the rest of the footage, a mistake she never would have made had she been at the top of her game.

CHAPTER FIFTEEN

Police headquarters Monday morning provided a completely unwanted reminder of the old Israel, where manners was a dirty word. The desk sergeant had time for everyone but her; Rachel watched her file and polish her nails while talking on the phone to her boyfriend, shushing her anytime she tried to ask a question. After hanging up on the boyfriend, she announced that it was time for her break and went to get coffee. On her way back, she had a lengthy and apparently heartfelt discussion with another female officer, ending with tears and a hug, joked with friends, joined a round of Happy Birthday, and finally came back, almost annoyed that Rachel was still standing there. Only then did she bother to tell her that they no longer kept Missing Persons' files.

Rachel was pretty sure this was a lie, but didn't press it, because a moment before the woman had come back, she'd realized that she could find what she wanted in newspaper archives—when Lije had gone missing, the papers had focused on it for a long time. Even factoring out the extra coverage for her celebrity, there should have been at least a few articles on this woman as well. She took her name and badge number, since she'd be talking to Kapdan later that week, but left it at that, going instead to the library to troll the Internet archives of the local papers.

It took a little while because her Hebrew reading wasn't what it should be, but good old-fashioned research yielded three possibles. Shlomit Hami, a dark-skinned Yemenite girl, 21, had disappeared while hiking the country North to South. She was Rachel's favorite possibility, but she couldn't completely rule out two others who disappeared within six months of Shlomit. Which complicated matters, since she couldn't go to any of the families. She also couldn't show Zeke pictures, since he would clam up. How would a court treat drunk target practice, anyway?

Reuven, he'd know what to do. She was about to get in a cab, but remembered that she had his card and could just call him. It was an odd conversation, and she had the impression that the stakes were higher than she realized.

"Hello, the Temple Grounds, how may I serve you?"

"Reuven, please; you can tell him it's Rachel Tucker on the phone."

Surprisingly, maybe because Reuven had specially trained them, the person actually put her on hold, instead of just yelling. After a pause, he came on. "Rachel, how are you? What are you doing today?"

When she told him, there was a silence so long that she checked that they hadn't been cut off. "Reuven?"

"Yeah, yeah, sorry. Listen, Rachel, I have to make a few phone calls, and then I can get back to you. What number are you at?"

She resisted the temptation to point out that she had given him a business card with a cell phone number; he didn't seem in the mood for teasing. When they hung up, she was once again without a plan. In her lexicon that signaled a meal, and, more out of luck than anything else, it was 12:45, so she could go for lunch.

She sat at an outdoor café, eating a bowl of French onion soup, served in a hollowed out loaf of bread. As she savored the meal, she set an agenda for at least the next few days. She couldn't go on looking into the missing girl unless she wanted to ignore Reuven's request, and she didn't want to do that to him. She couldn't film any more news reports, because she had no sponsor and was not going to be going on with her training. And she couldn't send footage to Ed, because she hadn't gone through all the material.

That, at least, she could change. She walked home, working off lunch a little, and resumed editing the footage to send to Ed. While going through it, annoyed with herself for being such a poor camerawoman, she almost missed it.

They had been watching a court case, because Reuven had wanted her to see how the court decided who stayed in the city of refuge. Some were required to; some begged to, worried that the avenger wouldn't believe the court's finding that they had no liability; and some stayed because they were bound over for trial for murder.

Mostly she had been dozing, because the proceedings were painfully exacting. For defendants, that reduced the chances of a false conviction to almost nil, but it produced a spectacle that was deadly dull and several synonyms thereof. She didn't even remember this one scene, but there it was on tape.

The accused was trying to prove he couldn't have killed the victim. Rachel couldn't follow it all, because there was some technical issue about rabbinic rules and open fields, but it seemed like the victim had been killed in a place where priests couldn't go. The accused was a priest, and argued that that proved he hadn't been involved in the crime. In response, the victim's family brought evidence that the killing had actually taken place elsewhere, and the body was dumped there (Rachel thought of Harvey, and wondered how big a clientele he had; would he be willing to cover evidence by moving a body from one place to the other?).

As she watched the tape, she was struck by how everyone in the courtroom could easily accept that a murderer would refuse to enter a field because he was a priest and the Rabbis had legislated a requirement to act as if there were ritual impurity in certain places. She could only assume that their assumptions reflected reality, but she found it shocking that anyone could insist on observing a ritual rule when having transgressed one of the most fundamental human ones.

She spent the next forty-five minutes struggling to write a voice over that would convey this paradox to an American audience. The best she came up with was: "Perhaps more than any other, one scene in court captures the dichotomies that the religious side of Israel brings to the fore. Arguing about whether Joel Shearith, a priest, could have committed murder, both sides of the debate assumed that Joel would never have entered an abandoned sandlot, because it is off limits to priests."

"It was possible, everyone agreed, that Joel had killed someone and was currently lying about it; but they could not conceive of his having violated this rabbinic rule about ritual purity. That strange mix of ordinary humanity and deep commitment to an extensive theological regimen lies at the heart of the New Israel, and will be one of the factors we will be looking to explain further in these reports. For now, this is Rachel Tucker, ABC News."

It wasn't her best work, but her mind kept wandering to Liat's diary. In those last few weeks, Liat would almost obsessively steer the conversation to it. Each time, she would say, in a way that sounded important to Rachel even back then, "Well, at least Pinhas can't get to it."

She had dismissed it as an idiosyncrasy, and in the rush of events around her death and the baby's birth, hadn't thought about it since. But now, as she watched the footage, images of Liat came flooding back, and she could almost physically hear her say, "Well, at least Pinhas can't get to it." What could have been there that mattered to her so much? Did it still exist and if so, where?

She'd have to start in Liat's apartment, although she couldn't imagine why that was particularly safe from Pinhas or his minions. She'd start there because she didn't know any other places Liat might have hid a diary, she had a key to the apartment, the family hadn't sold it yet, and she had no other way to feel useful.

The apartment was just a few blocks away, but as she made her way over there, her phone rang. "Hi, it's me." She had, in fact, recognized the voice, but wasn't sure how she felt about his confidence that she would.

"What's up?"

"I had a friend of mine talk to Zeke, steering the conversation towards the incident. Before he realized it, he had spilled the beans, and knew that he was looking at a long spell in jail—there are serious penalties for covering up a murder, for shooting guns in unsafe places, for owning certain kinds of guns—unless he cooperated as fully as possible. He couldn't help us with who the girl was, but he was more exact with the location; it's on a small side road off of the main Tel Aviv-Jerusalem highway. I've told the authorities about the tip, and they've started a search, which you're welcome to join. If you'd like."

Rachel was a little upset (which is how she always described when she was hopping mad), especially at how proud he seemed to be at what he had done. "Reuven, who asked you to do that? I was investigating this, and I asked for your help in confidence. I would have found the answers I needed soon enough, and now you've burned my source! I know you don't believe this, but I can look into things just as well as you. I've been doing it professionally a lot longer than you have, I might add."

She knew she sounded snippy, and there was a perfectly good reason; she was feeling snippy. She hadn't known him long, but she had become fairly confident that Reuven consistently walked the line between concern and nosiness. This time, he had gone over. Way over. And she wanted him to know it, and to know that, at least with her, he wasn't going to get away with it.

Infuriatingly, he refused to take the bait, answering calmly. "Rachel, give me a little credit. Zeke thinks he was too talkative with that Levi and that that's how it got out; he's done that before, so he's not going to connect it to you. And I told the government people only about Zeke's role. So don't get so upset!"

She hated how he always had a reasonable-sounding explanation for everything he'd done. Explanation or no, she knew she felt like he was intruding on something that was hers. Now she felt childish for being so territorial; after all, the point was to find the girl, right? To ease the pain of the family, right? She didn't want to think about how much her pride had been wounded by his getting so much more information with a few phone calls, so she just focused on the original question he had asked her.

"Are you going? Do you want to pick me up?"

He didn't answer, and as the silence stretched, she knew she had said something wrong. Without seeing him, though, she had no idea of what. Finally, he burst out, "Rachel, I'm a priest, remember? I can't help search for a dead body!"

She was about to say, but your toe means you're not a priest anymore, when she realized that he knew she had been thinking that, which is what had led to his impatience and now his pained silence. Well, one part of her thought grimly, that makes us even. The rest of her resolved to talk less and listen more. This purity thing had nothing to do with being able to serve in the Temple. Check. She wouldn't forget that again. Time to backtrack.

"I'm sorry, I misunderstood, I thought this was a general search of the area. You know what, though, I think I'm not going to go. I'd end up just saying something wrong or uneducated, and you wouldn't be there to correct me, so how much fun would that be?" She hadn't meant to sound quite so sarcastic, but didn't mind that much, since it gave her a chance to vent a little more of her own feelings about his having intruded on her finding out about the missing girl.

"All right, Rachel, I'm sorry. I'm a little sensitive about the toe; I told you that in confidence, and sort of felt like you were using it against me, trying to give me a little dig about all the ways in which I can't serve anymore. But you know what, that's my issue, so let's leave it."

Rachel didn't want that, either. She wasn't used to having so much trouble getting clear of personal issues in a relationship. She thought of herself as a good communicator, who worked hard to keep her personal neuroses to herself. But with him, one of them always seemed to be stepping on the other's toes. A cell phone was not the venue in which to work it out, though, so she switched topics.

"All right, let's forget it. The truth is, I'm not interested in going. But do me this favor—make sure that if they find anything, they tell everyone, especially the media, that they were acting on a tip from Rachel Tucker; if I can get my name on a scoop, ABC's happiness will be worth losing Zeke as a possible future source. Also, if they're ever going to go to the family, maybe suggest that I can help. I've seen it done many times, and, well, you know, I might be able to...help."

He seemed relieved at the change of topic as well. "Ok, great. Listen, I had one other thing for you. I was thinking about your situation, and I know I'm not your sponsor or anything, but if I were, I think I'd start by trying to help you understand the connection that *haverim* feel to God, which I think is the fundamental first step. So I thought you might want to try to get a handle on that, for which I thought I'd suggest a prayer group that I think you'll like..."

Rachel didn't mean to groan out loud, but it escaped before she could stop it. "A prayer group? You mean, like a synagogue, where I have to sit behind a curtain and watch? Don't you think I've been to synagogue? Can't this wait? Couldn't I do that last, when I'm finishing the program?" She'd never been big on prayer, communal or otherwise, and didn't envision any great changes now.

"Trust me, this is not your average prayer group; I firmly believe that you'll enjoy it, but I *know* that it's an important step on your road. It's 9 o'clock every morning, third floor of Shaare Tsedek hospital. Ask the receptionist. OK?"

An offer, she sensed, that she couldn't refuse. "Ok."

He tried to cheer her up, saying "And afterwards you can call and yell at me about sending you to such a boring place. Or thank me for changing your life." Rachel smiled politely, which of course he couldn't see, thanked him for his interest, and hung up as she got to Liat's building.

CHAPTER SIXTEEN

Pinhas surprised Harvey by opening their meeting with what seemed like sincere interest in his progress. He commented almost praisingly on Harvey's having accepted his punishment well, and actually opened his file to note that he was attending communal prayer regularly, had joined a study group, completed several correspondence courses in Judaic Studies, and was occasionally volunteering. Looking up from his file, Pinhas said, "Of course, that is all technical performance; the *haver* has an internal experience to match those acts. What's going on with you inside?" tapping his heart for emphasis.

Surprised by the changed demeanor—their meetings usually were about errands he had run for Pinhas, with a purely pro forma check on other progress—Harvey made the mistake of speaking unguardedly and, worse, happily. "It's really wonderful. I've come to enjoy reading the Torah in public. It takes a lot of preparation, but when I'm done, and I walk off that stage, you know, it's like, wow, those people would not have heard those words without me, and it's just....great. And my time with Rinah is great; I mean, she is just such a wonderful person that I can't imagine how I got on all these years without her. I don't think I'll find the professional thrills my old work gave me, but Rinah and I are hoping to buy a farm, put my energy into producing instead of destroying."

He had been about to go on, relieved to have an opportunity to share the concerns he couldn't burden Rinah with, but too late realized that Pinhas hadn't actually been *that* interested. The priest cut him off, tone indicating that this was the end of one segment of their conversation, "Good, good. Definite progress, I'd say; keep it up and I may need to scramble for excuses to keep you much longer."

A smile, with little warmth; Pinhas hated admitting that he needed Harvey, even to himself. The comment about making up excuses had been meant as a joke, Harvey knew, but was uncomfortably close to the truth. To hide his discomfort, Pinhas shifted to their usual agenda. "But let's discuss slightly more pressing matters, shall we?"

Harvey knew what he meant, and with a sigh took out his notes. "We checked all the usual possibilities. Not in the apartment, not at work, not in the safe deposit box—yeah, I'm pretty proud of that one. I figured since I didn't steal anything, no real crime was committed, right? Anyway, it's not in any of those places, that much we know."

Pinhas smiled, a chilling show of teeth that might easily have also been a grimace or a snarl. "That's too bad, because I had been thinking that finishing this one errand should be enough to bring our relationship to a close." Harvey had spent a lifetime hearing such promises from a series of men who held the key to the various prisons he'd been in. He knew that, like Pinhas, the person mentioning the possibility of freedom always found a way to back out. Still, against his will, his heart quickened. Finished? Rinah had told him that once he was certified, she could introduce him to her family, which was only one step away from the Golan, growing grapes and figs in peace.

Caught up in his reverie, Harvey had tuned out, a dangerous mistake to make with Pinhas. He zoned back in time to hear him say, ".... for her to do it for us."

Had he managed to force himself to think for a minute, he'd never have said, "I'm sorry, what did you say?"

Sometimes Pinhas yelled in situations like these; today, he limited himself to making a mark in Harvey's file, smiled in a satisfied way (what, he's got me for another month now?), and said, "I said that since we have sparked Ms. Tucker's interest, perhaps she will do our work for us, losing dear Harvey Keiter his shot at having completed his training. Ah, ah, ah...hurting me would be a biiiiig mistake, as I am sure you well know. Why don't you go along on your way, and see if you can beat her to the punch?"

Harvey left fuming. As soon as he was out of the room, Pinhas' shoulders slumped, and he buried his face in his hands. He had known he wouldn't be any good at sponsoring another person's training; he was about rituals, slaughtering animals, waving fats and bloods. Why had they insisted he do this? And now, forcing him to string along a man who he wanted to hug and say, good job, my man, and send him off to live with Rinah happily ever after?

When would it end?

CHAPTER SEVENTEEN

A s soon as she opened the door to Liat's apartment, Rachel knew she was on the right track. She hadn't been back since the night of the murder, but remembered that it had been perfectly neat. She had also called Liat's mother before going over, to be sure she didn't intrude on anything. She had said that no, she had been there a few days ago cleaning up, and was forcing herself to go only once a week, to keep from wallowing.

So when Rachel entered an apartment that had been dumped, she had no doubt about what had happened. Liat's clothing, every stitch of what she owned, was strewn around the place, the pictures were off the walls, the furniture moved aside. Someone had been looking for something. The diary? But why? And why now? As she asked herself the question, she knew the answer: enough time had passed that whoever was looking for it was no longer worried about surveillance.

Rachel looked around the apartment for a bit, but knew she wouldn't find anything; whoever had been here before her had done a very thorough job. She went home to Atid, frustrated that she hadn't found the missing girl, hadn't found the diary, and had to go to prayers in the morning.

The baby sensed that his mother needed an easy night, and cooperated. No gas, lots of smiles, good sleep. She woke refreshed, but nervous. Dear God, she found herself saying, make this as quick and as painless as possible. There, the group had stimulated her to better prayer already.

She got to Shaare Tsedek at 8:45, wanting to be sure not to walk in late. The security guard at the front desk told her to go to the third floor and make a left off the elevator. She took the stairs, having decided that it was an easy way to put some exercise in her day, but when she got out at three, realized she didn't know which way to turn. She stopped a vivacious young woman, maybe 23, with luxurious black hair cut to about two inches below her shoulders, sparkling green eyes and a welcoming smile.

Dressed casually in a jeans skirt and oxford shirt, Rachel admired the way her clothing showed her to be well-attired while in no way emphasizing the qualities of the body underneath. She certainly was neither significantly overweight nor appallingly thin, but she wore the outfit in a way that signaled that further information about her body shape was a private matter between herself and whomsoever she chose to share it with.

Hesitantly, Rachel asked if she knew where there was "some kind of a prayer group" on the floor. Flashing beautiful white teeth, the woman introduced herself as Esther Kevuda, and said she was going there, too.

"This is your first time?"

"How did you know?"

"I haven't seen you around here before, for one thing, but you could be used to going to a different service and be a guest for today. Mostly, it was because people tend to call these groups New Tefillah. You seemed not to know that, so I figured."

As she was talking, Rachel realized that American audiences would love to hear and see Esther Kevuda, and managed to work her camera into a comfortable filming position. She was about to ask a question, but Esther beat her to it.

"You know, we have a few minutes, why don't I give you a run-through of what's going to happen?"

"That would be great, I'd appreciate it."

"Ok. Pardon this question, but it's so I can know how much background to give. What's your experience with organized religion?"

"Well, I grew up in a somewhat observant home, and became more so when I met my husband. But synagogue, well, that was always a High Holidays, Passover, sometimes Shabbat kind of thing. Why?"

"Well, we do things a lot differently, but if you don't have so much experience with regular synagogue, I don't need to explain how we've changed. First, we're not a synagogue, we're preparatory for synagogue. After spending a half hour here, some of the people go to the more traditional service at the hospital's synagogue. We're about using the group experience to help each of us open a conversation with God, to get in touch with His presence. Is that clear?"

"The words, sure, but I don't know what they mean."

"Ok, well, it's like this. Prayer's supposed to be about talking to God, asking Him for help with your needs. Too often, we found..."

"Esther, I'm sorry for interrupting, but who's we?"

She blushed, a rosy color that only made her skin all that much more beautiful. "Well, actually, I was one of the founders. Me and a couple of friends were schmoozing, and realized that we didn't enjoy traditional synagogues—they were rushed, they had too many words, and too little opportunity for self-expression. So we wanted something that would have more flexibility, more of the flavor of actual communication, without insulting traditionalists." She glanced at her watch. "Oops, I'm sorry, I didn't realize the time; I need to get ready for the group. Would you mind if we spoke afterwards?" When Rachel nodded, Esther smiled her gratitude, turned, and went into the room.

Rachel didn't think anyone was going to get her to feel connected to God—it had been way too long since she had stood arm in arm at candlelight vigils singing about love and peace to think she'd recapture that sense of connection to a greater whole—but the effort seemed worth witnessing and filming. How bad could a half hour be?

The room she walked into hosted thirty men and women preparing in different ways. Some had pads, laptops, or other note-taking implements in front of them and were busily scribbling, typing, or whatever; others were stretching various parts of their bodies; others were deep-breathing with eyes closed—but many were chatting in the relaxed way of people who feel comfortable with themselves and their surroundings.

When Rachel entered, several pairs of eyes turned towards her, a set of them belonging to Yedidya Gross. He left what he was doing, a kind of hamstring stretch, and came over to her with a smile.

"How nice to see you again, Ms. Tucker. Can I once again apologize for having gotten you into this mess?' Yedidya had been sending notes, and occasionally books or articles on forgiveness, for the past week, even though, truthfully, Rachel blamed no one but herself for her situation.

She smiled her best smile in return, which was pretty good. "Yedidya, please. First, call me Rachel. And, second, stop agonizing over this. You caught me before I did anything crazy, no one was hurt, and I'm learning a lot. Maybe it was all part of God's plan; don't *haverim* always say, it's for the best?"

Yedidya smiled back. "That's very understanding of you. May the Lord repay your forgiving nature by leading you and all of us on the path to greater fear and love of Him and His ways."

It took her a minute to realize that he was blessing her, and blushed when she did. Although it sounded perfectly natural to him, as if he blessed others often, she couldn't remember the last time she'd received such a personal and direct expression of good wishes. She tried to reciprocate.

"Well, thank you, Yedidya, and…may all your blessings of others come true for them and for you." Dissatisfied, she hurried on. "Um, but I'm also looking for help with what's about to happen here. Are you a regular?"

"Depends on what you mean by regular. I tend to float through various styles of services, but I try to make it here at least once a week. And you, what brings you here?"

It was harder in a big room with many people around, but Rachel started filming again. Esther and Yedidya spoke with the kind of practiced confidence and genuine warmth that easily translated onto film. They could probably have been successful actors, Rachel thought, and Ed could edit out whatever parts he didn't like later.

"Reuven urged me to come, thought it would be a good step on my road, but I don't know what I'm getting into. Can you give me a quick rundown?"

Yedidya glanced at his watch. "No, I don't think so; we tend to start pretty promptly, and it's time. Why don't you see how it goes, and we can review afterwards, ok?"

Understanding his response, but no calmer about what she was about to undergo, Rachel took a seat and prepared for the worst. They started off with a breathing exercise Rachel had done in various classes, yoga or whatever, sitting quietly and focusing only on the breath. When they opened their eyes, Esther had them recite a short Psalm about the beauty of brothers living together in peace, a sentiment Israelis had shared for a long time before achieving it.

The first time they said it was fine, the second time better, and by the third time—in a row!—Rachel felt as if she knew it well enough to put her own meanings into it. She wasn't quoting anymore, she was talking, with the Psalm as the pretext. Too soon, Esther asked who wanted to speak, and a list was formed.

People spoke much more briefly than at Democrats' Anonymous, maybe a minute each. They told of current challenges, past failures, and hopes for future successes. Thinking back, Rachel noticed that her reaction to these talks was so much different. People here weren't talking out of self-centeredness, they were sharing a thought they hoped others would find meaningful. As if to confirm their skill, she found her thoughts turning to her own life, to Lije, to Atid, to Reuven (to Reuven? Rachel was so embarrassed she almost blushed, which would have been even more embarrassing), to getting her career back up and running, to all the topics she could imagine including in a true talk with God.

And then they sang a song, but the person who picked and taught it was completing his recovery from brain surgery. He claimed—Rachel got it on video, because she knew it sounded hokey unless you saw and heard him saying it—he claimed, and he put you into his shoes so well that you actually felt as if you were about to go under the knife for a procedure that could easily leave you blind or worse, that he had heard the song, over and over again, the whole time he was under. Moved by the story, Rachel still also wondered whether the surgeon had been playing it in the operating room.

Despite her cynicism, she was disappointed when it ended. Shocked at how much it had moved her, she wanted to thank Esther, who had run the half hour gently but purposefully, without allowing anything to get too long, clinical, or sentimental. She was apparently not the only one, as a long line of people was waiting to talk to the young woman. Yedidya came over to ask if she minded if he went to the synagogue downstairs, and she decided to go along, to see if she could maintain the mood. As she turned to walk out, Esther called to her.

"Rachel, wait up a moment!"

She turned, a little self-conscious at Esther's excusing herself from all those people to come talk to her.

"How'd we do?"

"Surprisingly well—I was actually thinking of going to the synagogue for prayers. In any case, Yedidya had said that he could explain some stuff to me afterwards as well."

"Oh, great. As soon as I finish with these people, I'm going, too. Maybe we'll get brunch after?" Rachel nodded and left. She entered the synagogue expecting a similarly exciting experience, but didn't get it. They used the traditional prayer book, familiar enough but written in Hebrew too opaque for her. Distanced by the language, she felt herself slipping back into her usual prayer mode, bored resentment and impatient anticipation of when it would be over. Then, she caught sight of Esther, eyes closed, as intent in here as upstairs.

Well, if she can do it, so can I, Rachel thought, a little too grimly for what was supposed to be a spiritual moment. She took a deep breath, and another, and another. Finally, she closed her eyes, and shut out the world around her. She tried to put herself back into the room upstairs, to turn time back to the moment that Esther had said, "All right, that will be all for today; remember there is a synagogue service downstairs for those who want, and that we meet here every day at 9:00."

And then she just started talking. To God. Later, she could only remember that there had been more of it than she would have expected. She remembered tears and hopes, and a sense of Presence. Most of all, she remembered that her thoughts kept circling back to Liat and Lije, to being able to put them both to rest, being able to feel like she had avenged the one and found out what had happened to the other. She talked until she ran down, which must have been a long time, because when she opened her eyes again, the room had emptied, and Esther was waiting, a smile on her face.

"Wow, we really got to you, didn't we?"

Rachel smiled sheepishly. "I have a lot on my mind, I guess."

"I know, Reuven actually called me about you last night. Before I forget, though, Yedidya Gross left you his card; he had an appointment he had forgotten about, but wants you to be sure to call him with any questions you have. Reuven was nervous about you hating it, and wanted to make sure I provided an extra-special service today. Which did wonders for my nerves, since he mentioned your name, and, not to make you feel old, but I grew up watching you on TV!"

Which, of course, did make her feel old. Brunch would have to be a salad and nothing more. And she'd head straight from there to the gym; the time had come. And then a facial, and a manicure/pedicure, and...but Esther was still talking.

"My family only moved here a few years ago, so I got the best of both, an upbringing in America, and a life in the Holy Land. Now if only I could find a husband with the same qualifications..."

Away from her official capacities, Esther exuded a lilting youthful quality. As they walked to a café, ordered brunch, and talked, she spoke with the unguarded enthusiasm of those who have not yet experienced real disappointment, or who could still assume that any such tough times were a temporary break in the path to a wholly positive future. A future, she assumed, that would mean marriage, homemaking, and lots of kids.

Rachel desperately wanted to question those choices. This was a woman who could easily succeed in any number of careers, not least of which would be the rabbinate, or whatever it was called when a woman brought people to a closer connection to God. Knowing now wasn't the time to bring it up, she determined to keep in touch with this clearly talented young woman, to do her part in making sure that she didn't confine herself to the role of mother and housewife. The country and world needed her too much.

It was probably youthful exuberance that led Esther to ask why Reuven had felt that she would need to come to a service like that one. Rachel ordinarily would have answered minimally, letting her journalists' instincts edit what she would and would not say. But she liked Esther, and it had been so long since she had had a nice girl-to-girl chat, that she found herself telling her the whole story, of Liat, her death, Harvey, her meeting Reuven, and her failed attempt at being a blood avenger.

She did edit herself somewhat, mindful of Reuven's warnings about the law's distaste for tale bearing. She didn't mention Harvey by name, or her suspicions about Moshel. Afterwards, there was a silence that extended for so long, Rachel was worried that she had offended Esther in some other way.

"Esther? Are you ok?"

The young woman startled when Rachel called her name, as if she had forgotten where she was. When she looked up, her eyes glistened with moisture. "I'm sorry, but your story of sudden respiratory distress reminded me of Liat Moshel, a dear woman who I miss terribly."

CHAPTER EIGHTEEN

Rachel's intake of breath was painfully sharp. "You knew Liat? That's the friend I've been talking about!"

Esther nodded sadly. "I suspected. What a terrible, terrible loss. I had been sad enough when I thought she just died, but now that you've told me this...I'm stunned."

Rachel, too; there went her care about talebearing. "But, how did you know Liat?" Did Reuven know? Was he manipulating her into finding information about Liat? Why wouldn't he tell her directly?

"She used to come to our group, with her husband, Pinhas. When we moved here—we used to meet at the old Yeshurun synagogue, on the other side of town—she came by herself a few more times—he couldn't come here, of course; I gave them the names and times of a few more services like this one, but he wasn't interested—and she eventually stopped coming. I saw her one last time a few weeks before she died."

Rachel's head was spinning so fast, she almost couldn't keep up with the story. Why hadn't Liat told her about these groups? What did Reuven know, and when did he know it? A distinct effort dragged her back to Esther, who was still telling her story.

"It was one day, she just showed up again. I was happy, of course, but, as usual, I walked into the room two minutes before we had to begin, so I had to wait until after to talk to her. She told me she'd gotten divorced, and spent the last two months moping. She had just had some minor surgery done, and since she was in the hospital anyway, figured she'd drop by and say hello, and thank me for all I had done for her."

"She was being very final, like she was closing a chapter of some sort, so I pushed her more than I normally would, asking her straight out to start attending regularly again. She said no, she didn't think anything could help her now, but at least her story was safe, and she was at peace."

Rachel remembered that surgery. Liat had found a mole, and her grandmother had died of skin cancer, so she'd rushed to take care of it. It was only one night in the hospital and she had forbidden Rachel to visit her there; in Liat's superstitious mind, pregnant women did not visit the sick, for fear of casting an evil eye on the unborn baby. But now that Esther had made the connection, she realized that that was also when she had first mentioned that her diary was safe. Safe? Why safe? Why after the surgery?

"Esther, when Liat died, didn't you tell anyone about the conversation?"

She looked embarrassed and uncomfortable. "You know, I thought about it, but it seemed so insubstantial. I mean, what would I have told them? I think you should know that this woman who stopped breathing one day, by natural causes as far as anyone knows, came to me 10 weeks ago and told me she was at peace and her story was safe?"

Said like that, she was obviously right. But if the police couldn't do anything with that information, she was pretty sure she could. "Esther, did Liat give any indication *why* she felt she was safe?"

She shook her head. "No. But she didn't say she was safe, she said her *story* was. I remember noticing, because I didn't know how you made a story safe."

Rachel didn't either. As they chatted over coffee, though, with Esther regaling her with some of her funniest blind date stories—apparently she went out a lot, something Rachel would never have done at that age—she suddenly realized that she didn't understand the earlier story about Liat and Pinhas. Unthinkingly, she interrupted.

"Esther, why did you say Pinhas and Liat stopped coming to the group?" As soon as the words left her mouth and she saw the look of chagrin on the other woman's face, she realized she had committed a cardinal sin, letting someone else know how little their stories mattered. Rachel knew, from experience and from the look on Esther's face, that she took this interruption to mean that Rachel thought of her friendly and funny stories as so much fluff compared to the real issues she, Rachel, was pondering. Which was a) not true, and b) would hurt her chances of mining the treasures that Rachel felt sure resided in this impressive young woman.

She tried to make up for it, even as she knew it wouldn't work. "Oh, I'm so sorry for interrupting; it's not that I wasn't enjoying your stories, I'm just a little obsessed whenever there's more information about Liat. Please forgive me?"

There was no way she could refuse, but her tone of voice, body language, and entire presentation changed markedly. Having been twenty-three herself, Rachel knew that she had made her feel like a child, focusing on dating stories. She remembered the anchorwoman who had treated her that way when she was first breaking in to the business, remembered her mental decision to take that woman's job from her within five years, and her delight at doing it in four.

She knew she had to find a way to repair this relationship, both to take away the hurt and because she liked Esther more than most people she met. Right now, though, she had to follow this train of thought. "So, I'm sorry, why couldn't they come anymore?"

"Because we moved to Shaare Tsedek and Pinhas was—is—a priest, he couldn't risk being in the same rooms or hallways as a corpse."

"And how long had they been coming before they stopped?"

Esther thought, looking up at the ceiling for inspiration. "Maybe three, four months. I remember when I heard that they broke up, I thought that maybe they had come to me as a kind of last gasp to save their marriage; lots of couples, after exhausting ordinary therapies figure they might as well try God, a last resort before divorce."

Something about all of this was niggling at Rachel's mind, but she couldn't get to it. She had to talk to Reuven, because if he was trying to hint her into figuring out something he already knew, she wasn't playing. But first, she had to mollify Esther, and the pride in her voice as she mentioned people coming to her to save their marriages told her how she could do it.

"Esther, I don't know how much Reuven told you about my situation, but I was wondering, do you sponsor *haverah* candidates?"

Score! The smile on her face—so talented, but so young and sensitive, mixing determination to perfect the world with the first hints of a realization that she might not be up to the task alone—told her that she had wiped away the insult she had caused.

"Well, I do, sometimes, but I thought Reuven was doing that for you. Actually, I thought the two of you were..."

Rachel mentally inhaled, unused to sharing confidences with people nine or ten years younger than her. But what the hell. "I know. But you know what? And I don't want to say that anyone has behaved improperly or anything, but I think that between the two of us, there's a little too much chemistry for it to be quite...healthy."

"Oh." She thought for a few seconds. "You mean, like you'd like to go out?"

"I don't know whether I'd like to, or whether he'd like to, but it's not so comfortable because I'm pretty sure one or both of us would like to." And then it hit her; Esther had assumed she was unmarried, despite her new motherhood. "But what makes you think I'm not married?"

She blushed. "Reuven told me you weren't, I don't remember in what context." Which was a polite way of saying he had mentioned some kind of interest in her. "Why don't you just ask him out? I bet he'd say yes; anyway, that's what I did."

Oh, great, she thought to herself, tell someone you barely know that you're interested in the guy she's maybe still interested in. Tread carefully, lest you put your foot down your throat again. "And what happened?"

Luckily, Esther's girlish devil may care attitude had returned. "Oh, we went out a few times and it was nice and all, I mean look at him, and talk to him, and you know that you'd have to be crazy not to love him, but you know, he's at least *thirty-six*—not that there's anything wrong with that—and we just weren't interested in the same things. He was focused on building a family and a home *now*—I mean, he doesn't want to be marrying his kids off as a doddering old man—and, well, I want all of that, but I'm still looking for a little adventure before I get tied down. But somebody like you might be perfect. I could suggest it if you want, so he wouldn't know it was coming from you."

All right, enough was enough; it was 11 am, she had errands to run, a death to investigate, she wasn't starting on her sob story about why she couldn't date. She needed to check in with Reuven, and wanted to wander around Shaare Tsedek—maybe Liat's ghost would tell her where to go next. So she sidestepped the question, saying she wasn't dating right now, innocuous enough not to arouse suspicions, and brought the meal to a graceful close.

When they said good-bye, Rachel reached into her handbag for her cell phone, which, of course, wasn't there. Thinking back, she realized that it was gracing her kitchen counter, recharging. She went to the Medical Records office, where she'd seen a pay phone. Picking up the receiver, she dialed the Temple Grounds, a number firmly engraved in her memory by now.

"Hi, it's me!" she said when he picked up the phone.

"Hi, you. So, do you hate me? Do I owe you a big dinner to make up for sending you to the most boring prayer service ever?"

"Actually, no. I had a very nice time and learned a lot—"

"Too bad, I was hoping I'd have to buy you a nice dinner."

When he'd said it, she, too, had thought that dinner with Reuven would be, well, pleasant was as far as she'd let herself go, but that wasn't for now, so she went on as if she hadn't heard, "...and I especially liked Esther. I asked her if she would sponsor me."

"There you go! I was hoping you would hit it off; it's the main reason I sent you there."

"Are you sure? Cuz I have to tell you, I was feeling a little manipulated when Esther told me that Pinhas and Liat used to come to Esther's group."

"They did? You have to believe I didn't know that! Wait, how could they have, it's in a hospital?"

"It only switched there a few months ago, which is when they stopped coming. You weren't steering me here, like it would help me pick up the trail?"

"No, not at all, what made you think that?"

"I don't know, it all felt a little too neat, you send me to a prayer group and it turns out Liat went there, stopping only a few months before she died."

"You're right, it is freaky, but I give you my word it wasn't me." There was a silence, but with Reuven it felt comfortable, a pause in what would soon turn back into a pleasant conversation; until then, she was happy to wait on the phone. As her money ran down, though, she was saying goodbye, when Reuven suddenly said, "Oh, I almost forgot to tell you…" and the line went dead as she frantically tried to find another phone card.

She didn't have one, or the time to get one, because she had remembered why Liat and Shaare Tsedek were linked in her mind: it was here that she had first met her! Lije had disappeared three weeks before, and Rachel had been going out of her mind sitting in the apartment waiting for news. She had taken a leave from the network, and was about to tear her hair out with the combination of worry and boredom that came from a tense life in which nothing happened from one day to the next.

Anxious for something to do, she remembered her father telling her that if you want to feel better, help the less fortunate. You'll have done a good deed, and will appreciate the good in your life all that much more.

So she had found and joined a society for visiting the sick, and Liat had been one of her first visits. When Rachel walked in the room, she instantly recognized the attractive brunette who lived nearby; in the days before this one, they had bumped into each other several times on the street, with Liat always initiating a friendly, if superficial, conversation that had never gotten as far as introducing themselves. Perhaps because of that connection, her nervousness about visiting people she didn't know, and the stress of Lije's disappearance, Rachel ended up telling Liat her whole story, being pregnant, Lije, not knowing what she should be doing now.

Liat had listened, but she'd sensed that her story had deeply moved the Israeli woman. When she left, Liat made Rachel swear several times that they'd see each other again, although not in the hospital, since she was nervous about Rachel's baby and the evil eye.

And that's how it had begun, she supposed. She hadn't thought to look back to the beginning of their friendship, even after her death, because by the end it had become so much more than a kindness. Liat was the only person who seemed to imagine herself in Rachel's position, whose questions and ideas for how to spend time consistently matched what she herself was thinking.

She sat in one of the chairs outside the Medical Records office, thinking about Liat. She was in Shaare Tsedek six and a half months ago—for what? Rachel didn't remember. She was in Shaare Tsedek again two months ago to remove a mole but also for a last try at Esther's prayer service. Why did she feel like there was something else here? C'mon, Liat, what is it about this place?

She would never say, *ever*, that her friend had answered her. But she did, at that moment, have a flashback to Liat's ramblings about the story being safe. Safe, safe, safe. As she ran the word over in her mind, Rachel was trying to understand why her thought processes had decided to connect Liat's obsession with safety and the first time she had ever met her. Safety from what?

Or whom. And then Rachel had it, or thought she did. But where would Liat put it? Not in her room, those got cleaned thoroughly after each patient left. In a common room—the library maybe?—but how would she guarantee that someone wouldn't walk off with it? Was there a safe for patients who didn't want to leave stuff in their rooms? Or maybe a drop-off of some sort?

Running now, she found the visitors' coat check, and asked whether they also took items for long term storage. Not generally, they told her, only for people who have to come back repeatedly for follow-up checkups or treatments; they could leave items in the back room, and pick them up whenever they came in, with the hospital taking no responsibility. But, of course, they couldn't let Rachel in there, because she wasn't a returning patient.

She thanked them and walked away, her mind already formulating plans for how to get into the room. She watched from a discreet distance for about fifteen minutes, and already had a Plan A and B. Plan A depended on diverting the attention of both of the people who worked there, and it wasn't long in coming. One went to the bathroom, the other saw a friend down the hall, and got into a loud and excited conversation.

Rachel waited until her back was turned, and slipped in. Through the racks of hangers, there was a door to the back, which led into a small room lined with shelves and personal possessions. And there, on one of the shelves, was a little red book, which could be a diary. Rachel opened it, recognizing the handwriting. She also was happy to see that there was another door, so she wouldn't have to face the coat check women on the way out. Slipping the diary in her handbag, she walked confidently, knowing if she looked like she was allowed to do what she was doing, no one would stop her.

CHAPTER NINETEEN

She wanted to sit and read the diary right then, but her guilt about leaving Reuven hanging finally got the better of her. She'd go to the shop, get a biscotti and coffee, and read the diary. Her day was taking shape already, with four hours till she had to be home for the baby.

They already knew her at the shop; as soon as she walked in, the girl behind the counter said, "Oh, hi, I'll go get Reuven," before she even got a chance to order. He came out, looking worried.

"Are you ok? We got cut off, and then when you didn't call back, I wasn't sure what was going on."

"That's sweet, and I'm sorry I didn't call back, but I had no change, and I was working on an idea...and then I wanted to share my news with you in person, so here I am." Rachel knew that most people didn't get as wrapped up in what they were doing as she did, but she had long ago given up on changing herself. She wished she had called to say that she'd be over in a bit, but it was a quirk she had no expectation of changing. People who would be her friends had to learn to live with it.

He didn't disappoint. "No, as long as you're ok, it's fine, I was just excited about some news I wanted to share."

"Me, too! But you go first."

"What kind of gentleman would I be if I went first? More important, what kind of coffeeshop owner would I be if I didn't ask what you were having?"

They took her coffee and biscotti to a table, although he insisted on bringing over mini- chocolate chip muffins as well, which were, unfortunately, heavenly; she considered it a real triumph that she ate only two. Dinner would have to be low-carb, low-cal, low everything. She told him about the diary, which excited him almost as much as her, but also sent a shadow across his face.

"What's the matter?"

"I wonder why Pinhas didn't get to it."

"What do you mean, it was in a hospital, like I told you!"

"Have you forgotten Harvey? And you think there aren't others like him, happy to do what Moshel wants?"

Surprised, she realized she *had* forgotten Harvey. Now, it did seem weird that the diary was still there. "Maybe Liat never mentioned it to Pinhas?"

"Then why was she so obsessed with keeping it safe?"

"Maybe she didn't believe that he'd look for the diary, and that even if he did, he couldn't send Harvey to check the whole building, and since he didn't know about the coat check, he couldn't direct Harvey there? Whatever, I've got the diary and Pinhas doesn't, so let's drop it."

She had said the last louder than she anticipated, and the shadow of worry on his face turned into anxiety, almost fear. "Shhhh! Don't talk about him so loud—you never know who's listening!"

It was disturbing, how every so often he would do something completely at odds with her picture of him. The Reuven she thought she knew—and she made a very good living based to a large extent on her ability to sense people's characters and turn them into compelling news stories—was fundamentally fearless. Yet Pinhas Moshel worried him greatly. Why?

He had moved on, however, and while she had been pondering his worries about Pinhas, he'd been telling her a story, but she only caught the end.

"...and that's how they found her!"

"I'm sorry, Reuven, my mind wandered. Who did they find?"

"The body Zeke told you about. It was Shlomit Hami, the Yemenite girl. Her family's so excited!"

Her face must have registered her surprise at his choice of

words; what family would be excited to find out that their missing daughter was in fact dead? He tried again.

"Sorry, maybe relieved is a better word, or, or, well…what's the word for having something you have dreaded for years actually turn out to be true, which is terrible, but at least means that you won't have to dread it anymore? I guess I should have said that they have the comfort of knowing, which means they can grieve. And, they can have a funeral, which is always an important stage of mourning. Which reminds me, Esther asked me to have you call her if I spoke to you."

"Esther? Why?"

"She didn't tell me, but it was connected to the funeral, that's what reminded me."

She wanted to borrow his cell phone, but he was worried about ritual purity, and asked her to use the one behind the counter.

"Hello?"

"Esther? It's Rachel Tucker. I'm with Reuven, and he said you wanted me to call?"

"Oh, yes, he told me about Shlomit Hami; what a terrible tragedy. I wanted to suggest that you think about attending the funeral; I might be going anyway and would certainly come along if you wanted company."

Puzzled, Rachel asked, "Why should I go? I've been to funerals before—I was at Liat's just a couple of weeks ago."

Esther was stepping carefully, she could tell. "I suspect this would be the first time you would be paying close attention to the rituals, and I think it would be good experience, both as a prospective *haverah*, but also, well, Reuven and I were talking more about you, and he explained your situation a little more fully, and, well, this would be good preparation in case you were ever to be mourning someone close to you."

Like if they find Lije. Pretty perceptive and proactive, actually, Rachel thought, impressed, I have to remember to fit that into the tape—sponsors give information but also make judgments about how and when to convey it. Meanwhile, Esther was still talking. "I'm sorry, what?"

"Would you like me to go with you?"

Rachel repeated the question out loud, a favorite stalling mechanism. Reuven waved his hand to get her attention. She excused herself, put her hand over the transmitter, and looked at him expectantly.

"I'm going anyway. Do the two of you want to come?"

"Why are you going?"

"Well, when the search was going on, I made a connection through a friend of a friend's friend, went over there a few times, and now they want me there."

"You went over there a few times and now they want you to be at the funeral?"

"Well, yeah. Is there something strange about that?"

The first rule of journalism, she felt like saying, report the story, don't become it. He clearly didn't buy it. "How did it happen that in visiting a few times, you became so close to them that they are asking you to be at the funeral?"

He grinned, pleased that she had noticed his talent for serving people in crisis in ways they appreciated. "It's a gift. Look, when people are hurting, they want the presence of others. Sometimes they want to talk, sometimes they don't, but they want people around who are there to give them whatever they think they need. I went there, introduced myself—people assume that priests are trustworthy—and spent an hour or two with them on a few different occasions. It's actually always pretty interesting, to see how different family members react in different ways.... But don't you think you should get back to Esther?"

Horrified, she realized she'd been so interested in his story, and obvious enthusiasm for that part of his job, that she'd completely forgotten the phone in her hand.

"Esther? I am soooooo sorry! Reuven was talking and we got off on a tangent" She didn't go on because there was loud laughter from the other end of the phone.

"Oh, don't worry about me. The two of you go on with your tête-à-tête; I don't want to get in the way. No, good old Esther can sit around all afternoon, waiting for Rachel Tucker—should I say the *famous* Rachel Tucker—to get back to her. Please, don't let me interrupt you two."

She knew she was teasing, but was uneasy enough with her dynamic with Reuven that she couldn't laugh about it. She tried to tease back, but her heart wasn't in it.

"Ok, miss smartypants, so did you hear the conversation as well? He's going to the funeral and wants to know if the three of us should go together."

"Oh, I'd hate to intrude on such a wonderful twosome." Esther was enjoying this.

Getting exasperated, she spoke slowly, emphasizing each word, "You won't be intruding. Yes or no?"

"I'll be there. When should we meet?"

Rachel turned to Reuven. "When should we meet?"

"Nine o'clock Sunday morning."

Back to the phone. "Nine o'clock Sunday morning. Is that ok?"

Esther hesitated. "Sunday? I assumed it was tomorrow. Why are they waiting so long?"

Back to Reuven. "She wants to know why they're waiting so long?"

He understood the question, although she didn't. "In the years since she disappeared, her crowd has dispersed, kind of, and they want a chance to find as many attendees as possible. Also, they want to have the neck-breaking"

"Neck-breaking?"

"I'll tell you later. Tell Esther they want to have the neck-breaking the same day, so that everyone's still around. Anyway, they got permission to wait til Sunday."

She relayed the answer to Esther, who said, "Well, Sunday's usually one of my days to lead the group, but I guess I can find someone to cover. I'll see you at the shop, Sunday, 9:00."

When she hung up, one of the staff called for Reuven, and he excused himself, too abruptly for her taste. Angry at what felt like rudeness, she decided to leave, too, without waiting for his explanations or finishing her coffee.

The second was definitely a mistake, since she could have used caffeine to help her cope with the baby. It was one of those nights where she had to hold him and/or walk him just about the entire time until bed (not to mention the bath he needed after an explosive diarrhea got him everywhere, and a little bit on her). Once she got him squared away, changed her clothes and washed herself, especially her hands (a dozen times; manure on the hands freaked her out), she collapsed on the couch for twenty minutes.

She desperately wanted to go straight to sleep, but felt an overpowering urge to read Liat's diary *tonight*, or else something dreadful would happen. The last time she had ignored a feeling like that, she had had nightmares the whole night anyway, so it wasn't as if she could even count on a good night's rest if she ignored that feeling.

Before she could read, though, she had to tape a segment for Ed. Not in the mood, but feeling guilty about neglecting the project—she'd definitely do a real segment in the morning—she rushed through, knowing she'd be furious when she reviewed it.

Turning to the diary, which she had thought would be riveting, she instead found it dreary and sad. Their marriage had never been good, and some of the stuff should have been pretty shocking. Rachel hadn't absorbed the awe of the priesthood she saw on the streets (where people instinctively drew back, so as not to accidentally touch a priest), but she was surprised at how cruel Pinhas could be when under stress. That he could speak insultingly didn't surprise her, but for him to then air commercials offering marital counseling (for a fee, of course) as part of his services...

Rachel took it in stride, a remnant of her days on the celebrity-watch circuit, whose pure and consistent strangeness meant that nothing would ever truly shock her, certainly not Liat's diary. After dozing off five times while trying to read it cover to cover, she flipped to the end and started scanning backwards.

She was skimming when she saw her name. Checking the date, she saw it was March 7, a week after Lije disappeared. They had met in a fruit store, according to Liat's diary, which also claimed—Rachel didn't recall this—that they had discussed the difficulty of finding avocadoes of the right consistency to satisfy their spouses.

Rachel smiled, always surprised at how impressed some people are by meeting a celebrity. As she continued from there, though, seeing Liat's comments about how well the friendship was working out, she had the distinct feeling that there was a more specific goal in mind than just getting to know an American celebrity who lived nearby.

Flipping back to before the fruitstore encounter, Rachel saw her name on each of the preceding seven days' entries as well. She selected a passage at random to read more carefully, but a slight sound caught her attention. She couldn't say what it was exactly, but her mind flashed to a movie, she couldn't remember the name. She remembered hating it, but a crucial scene had stuck with her, where the victim inside the house hears one little noise and ignores it, the minimal sound the murderer had to make to get into the house.

She didn't want to be melodramatic, but she also didn't want to die because she was too stupid to check out a noise. She looked at her clock, a little shamefacedly, to be able to tell the police the exact time she heard the noise. 11:30.

But what to do? In the movies, you pick up a heavy something, which she'd never understood. Was she going to overpower whoever had broken into her apartment (if anybody had)? Then she thought to go to the baby's room, but who would want to kidnap the kid? Calling out also wasn't an option, because that just told the guy she had heard him (or her; no need to be sexist about the phantom intruder).

With no other options, she did all three. She put the diary under her bed, picked up her bedside lamp with the marble base, called out loudly, and ran down the hall to the baby's room. She knew how remote a possibility it was that he was here for Atid, but she couldn't help herself, she had to know he was safe.

As she ran out of her room, he was waiting on the other side of the hallway, stepped behind her, put his arm around her neck, and pressed a long knife into her jugular. At least she assumed it was her jugular, he was a professional wasn't he? Although, come to think of it, a slice through any part of her neck would be pretty bad.

Cliché or not, she couldn't think of anything else to say. "What do you want?" (At least she avoided saying please don't hurt my baby, the single thought running through her head).

"I'm here to give you a message. If you stay calm and quiet, we can do this quickly and nobody has to suffer." The voice, speaking quietly through a handkerchief, was familiar, but she couldn't place it. "The rightful owner of the book you've got wants it back. He's very pleased that you figured out where it was, and would be happy to compensate you for returning it to him."

Pinhas! She might have known. But why wasn't this guy asking for the diary itself? She instinctively tried to turn towards him, but his grip tightened and the knife moved a fraction of an inch deeper into her neck.

"Uh, uh, uh. Calm, lady, I *really* don't want this to end in blood."

"It's all right, I wasn't trying to fight you, I'm just not used to talking to someone I can't see."

"I could let you see me, but then I'd have to kill you, and I've sworn off that."

"So how do I get this book back to its owner? Do I give it to you?"

"Nope, I'm not a lost and found, or a delivery boy. Truth is, I'm not even a messenger anymore; this is just a last quick favor for an old friend. You take the book tomorrow and you put it back where you found it; then you bring a receipt to the David's Citadel and leave it at the front desk under your name. My friend'll pick it up when convenient. And, lady, please don't mess around with this; nobody wants to see anybody else get hurt, you get what I'm saying?"

Anybody else? How many had there been? Whatever it was, Rachel wasn't going to fight Pinhas Moshel directly, or this man in her apartment. But how to get him out? "Ok, I'll do it. Just don't hurt me or my baby." Desperate mother wasn't her best role, but she didn't think he was going to be critiquing her acting.

When she woke up, the bump on the back of her head brought the incident immediately to mind, and also told her how he had gotten away without worrying about her identifying him. Awareness washed over her slowly, with Reuven's face one of her first sights, as he wiped her face with a wet washcloth. She was in her bed. Elsewhere in the room, she could sense conversations and people, but turning towards them felt like it would hurt. A lot.

"Reuven? What are you doing here?"

"I heard the call on the radio, recognized your address, and came over."

"Well, I'm glad I woke up to see you…I mean, a friendly face."

"Me, too. But Rachel, what happened?"

Hearing their conversation, a police officer and doctor came over, whom Reuven introduced. "Rachel, this is Officer Regel; he was the first to respond to the call, and he got the doctor over here to look after you." She nodded her head to them, then winced at her mistake.

"Ms. Tucker, I'm relieved to say that he didn't hit you that hard. You'll have a bruise, and you should take it easy for the next few days, but I don't think there's any serious injury. If your headache is still there in 48 hours, call me, but other than that, I think you'll be fine."

She took his card, then remembered her mother's stories about concussions turning into comas. "Can I sleep tonight? Or do I have to wake up every hour or something?"

"It's sort of a judgment call. I think you're fine, and I've seen lots of concussions. But certainly the safest thing would be to have someone wake you."

The police officer interrupted. "Actually, my superiors have told me that we're posting someone here for the rest of the night anyway, purely as a precaution, in case the guy comes back. He doesn't seem to have gotten anything, so we think that he was interrupted in the middle. Those are the ones most likely to come back. I could have the woman we leave here knock on the door every hour."

That wasn't her idea of a good time. Luckily, Reuven popped in. "Well, if there's going to be someone else here anyway, I could stay, too; I'll bet I'll wake you up more gently than that."

She smiled her thanks, and was about to go to sleep, but the officer wasn't done. "I'm sorry, Ms. Tucker, I know you're tired, but the sooner I get any information you have, the better the odds of catching your intruder and restoring your peace of mind."

Rachel told him the story, leaving out the diary and the message, having realized, as she was talking, that if she told him about it, he'd take it in for evidence or something, and she wasn't willing to risk her baby's life to help the police catch Pinhas Moshel.

When the two had left the room, Reuven said, as he moved the washcloth slowly and gently around her face, "What did you leave out?"

"What? What do you mean?"

"I mean, you edited the story. What did you leave out?"

"He spoke to me, the guy. He wanted the diary."

"Really? Did you give it to him?"

So she told him the full story, pleased he knew her well enough to catch her omission, relieved to share the story, and hopeful he would have some advice about what to do next. The thing that puzzled her most was the intruder's refusal to take the diary with him. She once again heard his voice in her head, and had that tantalizing feeling she knew it from somewhere. The more she focused on it, though, the more it slipped away. Sighing, she let it go, hoping it would come back when it was ready.

Reuven was upset and worried. "What was in there that would make Moshel take such a chance?"

"What chance did he take? He sent some lackey, and we don't even know who." But as the words left her mouth, she thought of Harvey. Was it his voice? She couldn't remember.

Reuven was adamant. "There has to be something vital—no, damaging—for him to be willing to be so blatant. When did he say you had to put it back?"

"Tomorrow, why?"

"I'm thinking of options. We could stake out the check room at the hospital; we could photocopy the diary, so that we have it even after we give it back; or we could read it all tonight." He was pacing back and forth as he was thinking, which left her without the washcloth on her face. She tried to pick it up herself, but moving worsened the ache in her head from a dull throb to a pounding, so she groaned and lowered her arms.

He came back to her side, immediately apologetic. "I'm sorry, here." And he patted the cloth around her face, too energetically.

"No, no, smooth gentle strokes, not patting all around." She didn't want to complain, but he was making it worse, not better. "And I don't care what you do, but I'm not reading a whole diary tonight. And I'll bet he'll have us, or me, followed, so I don't think we're going to get a chance to photocopy it. And he wouldn't have told me to put the diary back in the coat room unless he was sure he had some way to get it undetected."

He thought about what she had said, ending up shaking his head as if in disagreement. "You're right, but we have to do something. Here's what I think. I'll read it tonight. In the morning, if I've noticed anything, I'll run it by you and you can tell me I'm right. If I don't notice anything, we'll try copying it, and go from there."

She wasn't going to copy it. If he was willing to send someone to invade her apartment, whatever was in that diary was much more important to him than Atid's life, and she wasn't going to risk that.

Reuven could read all he wanted, she was tired and wanted to go to sleep.

"Wait, what about Atid? I can't get up with him tonight."

He thought. "How many times is he going to be up?"

"What time is it?"

"12:30."

"You mean it's only been an hour?"

"Yeah, you were lucky. When he bopped you on the head, he let you drop on the floor. Your downstairs neighbor heard the bang and was furious with you for making such a racket when he was trying to fall asleep, so he called the police. When they came to the door, they heard Atid crying, saw the jimmied door, and came in."

"Wait, so who put Atid back to bed?"

"He did it himself. The cops weren't going to deal with a baby, and by the time I got here, he had fallen back to sleep. I got everyone to stay quiet, but he behaved beautifully."

She had nursed at 8, and he usually only went 5 or 6 hours; but if he had been forced to fall back asleep on his own, who knew? "I think he'll need to feed in about two hours, and then again three hours after that."

"No problem. Do you have formula?"

"No, but I have breast milk in the freezer. Take out two bottles and start defrosting them. When he wakes up, you can heat them up the rest of the way, but be careful it's not too hot." She barely waited to hear him agree before falling into the fog of sleep that had been becoming ever more insistent as she talked.

CHAPTER TWENTY

Bright sunlight streaming through the window and the sound of the baby crying woke her. Opening her eyes, she saw Reuven asleep at the night table with the diary under his face. Focusing on the baby, she instinctively sat up to go feed him, a huge mistake. As she fell back on the pillow, the ache in her head brought her back up to date on the previous night's events. Still, she felt already too indebted to ask Reuven to get him another time.

Moving more slowly, she sat up, put her feet on the floor and inched her way to a standing position. The damn housekeeper insisted on putting her slippers so far under the bed that she had to get on all fours to find them, which she wasn't going to do now; she'd have to go barefoot. There, that wasn't so bad. Now put one foot in front of the other, and go feed your baby.

He was frantic by the time she got there. It took her at least a minute to calm him down, which involved bouncing him lightly in her arms, a move her head complained about loudly. Somehow, she managed to down two of the pain relievers the doctor had left, calm the baby, and get him to nurse so she could sit without moving her head while he ate. This being his morning feeding, he didn't go back to sleep when he was done, but nestled in her arms, ready for a little face to face contact time.

Rachel made a few googly faces, but didn't have the energy. Feeling guilty and wanting to take her mind off of it, she stood up and walked back to her room, carrying him as motionlessly as possible, both because it would keep him calm and help her not move her head.

When she got back to her room, she arranged her pillows so

she could sort of lean back, which Atid would tolerate, without fully lying down, which he would not. As she slowly tried to position her body so that he still felt her presence but she didn't have to be sitting up, Reuven heard one of his whimpers and woke up. Rubbing his eyes and nose, he looked at her, bleary-eyed and disoriented.

She started to say good morning, but he held up a hand, walked out of the room and into the bathroom down the hall. She heard the toilet, the sink, the shower, and five minutes after that he was back in her room, more awake, although still in his clothing from the previous day.

She smiled. "Good morning."

He smiled back, but his heart wasn't in it. "Um, Rachel, I read the diary, and I know exactly what's in it that's the problem. And it has to do with you."

"Me? What about me?"

"You have to read it yourself, but let's wait a few minutes. I'm here for you, but I also called Esther to come over, in case you need, you know, a shoulder to cry on, and she should be here soon."

She looked at her watch, and saw that it was only 7:30; he had called Esther over at this time of the morning? Now she was getting nervous, but he refused to tell her anymore, or to give her the diary until Esther got there.

Which she did, five minutes later. He gave her the diary with a block of three pages marked off, and said that he had to go to prayers, but would be back in about forty five minutes. Esther sat down next to the bed, asking how she was feeling. She wasn't in the mood for small talk and realized, with a twinge, that these two people, whom she had known for less than a month, were her closest friends in this country. She longed to be back in New York, with her mother, her work friends, people she'd grown up with.

Before she read the diary, she had to call someone from home. Who stayed up late? Ed for sure; he was usually editing tape til 2, 3 in the morning. The others? She wasn't sure. It would have to be Ed. She explained herself to Esther, who pretended to understand completely, excused herself, and told her to call when she was ready.

"Ed Appleby." Hearing him say his name, connecting back to a life without diaries, mystery men, priests, and Temple ceremonies, brought tears to Rachel's eyes. She had been so busy trying to find out what happened to Liat, avoiding worrying about Lije or her future, and taking care of Atid, she had way overdrawn her emotional bank. Ed certainly wasn't her best friend, but he'd have to do.

"Oh, Ed, it's so good to hear your voice."

"Rachel, is that you? What time is it?"

"7:42 my time, Ed. I just woke up, but I think I'm onto something here, because someone broke into my apartment last night, warned me to return that diary that I showed in the footage I sent you, and then knocked me out."

Ed was shocked. "Are you ok? Should I come over there? What could be so important about a diary?"

But Rachel had already stopped listening, because she had thought of a way keep the diary while returning it—she could film each page, and then read it off the film! She felt like shouting hallelujah, but didn't want to wake the baby. She quickly hung up on Ed; in the end, it was good she hadn't been able to call a close friend, since Ed was used to reporters hanging up on him in mid-conversation. She called Esther.

"I've got it! I've got it!"

"Got what?"

"We can film each page of the diary, and then read it later."

Esther wasn't as impressed with the idea as she was. "I don't know. Reuven seemed to think that you should read the part he marked off as soon as possible."

Rachel was not to be deterred. It took her a few minutes to set up, but then she flipped slowly through the diary, panning her camera up close over each page. She was a genius! Reuven came home when she was halfway through; she excitedly told him her idea, but he, too, was underimpressed. "Did you read the part I said to?"

She shrugged. "I figured I could get to it later, since we'd have the whole thing."

He came over to where she was filming, took the camera from her gently but firmly, and said, "I think you should read it now. It starts here"—he pointed—"Liat's in the middle of telling about a drive she forced Pinhas to take her on, to try to save the marriage." Not pleased with his bossiness, but unwilling to flagrantly ignore his certainty that she should read it now, she began to, resentfully.

We drove up north, where we used to go when we were dating. I thought remembering other trips might put us in more of a mood to talk out our feelings. Really, I should say, put *him* in more of a mood to talk out his feelings, since I was always ready to. Of course I was wrong; he was busy insisting that everything was fine, that his position in the Mikdash just meant he had to be away from home a lot. And that when he got home he was just tired, and didn't have the energy for any looong conversations (his words and inflection, the bastard!).

I was fuming, because all I was trying to do was make sure we didn't grow apart (obviously, I'm already too late), and here he was pretending that there was nothing wrong in his working 10-12 hour days, in addition to all sorts of errands after the Mikdash closes for the night, and then having no energy for me when he gets home. I asked him when he thought we'd start a family, which you'd think an important priest would care about, and he had no answer! He's focused on himself and his position; to his friends and peers, he can always imply we don't have kids because of some fertility issue on my part. I'll bet that's what he does.

But that's not the worst part—the marriage is over, I can see that now, so it's no use agonizing over it anymore, it's time to start moving on. But while we were busy arguing, we had stopped watching the road.

We were on a pretty deserted highway, just after the sign that says Katsrin, 25 KM. There's a new turnoff there, that takes you on a much shorter path straight to the Kinneret, but few people know about it, so it's generally deserted—it can be an hour between cars. There was nobody around, so we could really focus on our fight, on pressing just the right button to infuriate the other person.

Well, certainly, *I* wasn't paying any attention to the road. As we were yelling, I remember something catching the edge of my vision, and I turned to look out the front window just in time to see us hit a man head on! It happened so fast we not only hit him, we ran right over him and went another 30 meters before we stopped.

Of course we jumped out of the car and ran back to see if we could help him. When we got there, though, it was clear he was dying; there was blood everywhere, several bones were obviously broken, and I think there were internal injuries, too.

I was so upset, I said the first thing that popped into my head: "What are you crazy, stepping out in the road like that?"

Every breath an effort, the poor man said: "Car broke down, got tired of waiting for someone to stop for me. Mistake." And then he sort of laughed. "Always wondered how it would end. Not what I would have asked for, but I hope it is a *kapparah* for all my sins." And then his lips started to move, and I knew that he was reciting his confession, preparing for the absolution of death. I didn't know what else to do, so I just held his hand and waited for him to finish. Pinhas, of course, had moved far enough away not to have to worry about impurity from contact with a corpse.

Every minute or so, he'd fight for air, cough up some blood to clear his airways. Suddenly, he interrupted himself and turned to me. "Listen, my wife, she needs to know what happened to me. My name is Elijah Zeale, and her name is Rachel Tucker; we live at 24 haPalmach in Jerusalem, phone number 555-9234. Tell me you'll get her the message, please!"

So I promised, never realizing what a hell that would put me in. The whole thing took maybe four minutes, and then he was gone. I had never seen a man die, and never want to again, but I tried to record every detail in my memory. The harsh rasp of his breath, the way his eyes looked out, as if they could suddenly see hidden aspects of the world, and, of course, the desperation when he worried about his wife.

When I got back to the car, Pinhas asked whether he was dead, as if he was hoping for some miracle. I said yes, and he pulled a shovel, a bag, and a body parts recovery kit—like from after a terrorist attack, but why did he have them?—out of the trunk, and said, "Ok, you go clean up the scene while I dig the hole." He had apparently come up with a plan in case he didn't get his miracle.

At first, I didn't even understand what he meant. "What are you talking about, the police will handle all that stuff." And then he flipped out. I knew he had to restrain himself from grabbing me, because I had just held a dead man, so I would make him *tamei*, and keeping him out of his beloved Temple for a day.

So he just walked up to me real close—touching him would have provided a momentary victory, but he would have taken it out on me in so many ways that it wasn't worth it—and said, "Listen carefully, Liat,

I've always shielded you from parts of my business that you had no need to know about. But you need to know this—messing with me is a very bad idea. There are many people, not people you want to meet, who would be verrry upset if I got caught up in a scandal around this man's death. We are not reporting this to the police, and we are not letting the world know that Pinhas Moshel had anything to do with a fatal accident! We have to bury him right here and right now, and quickly too!"

I tried to protest that I had promised to contact the widow, but he wouldn't hear of it. He was in a frenzy of—what?—self-preservation, but something else, too, that I have never been able to figure out. So then I suggested leaving the body there in the middle of the road, so that at least it would be found and his wife could know what had happened, but he was too paranoid that the police would find evidence connecting it to us.

Disobeying would be a mistake, I knew. So I put a bag over the body and picked up as much of the blood and other stuff as I could. By the time I was done, you couldn't tell that a corpse had been there unless you were really looking for it, and who would be looking for it?

I buried him there, in the hole Pinhas dug. When he wasn't looking, I found six large and odd looking stones, red, blue, and orange, arranged them in a circle over the grave, hoping that someone would notice it and wonder.

Rachel couldn't read anymore, because her tears were making it impossible to see. Poor Lije, with his dreams of great ideas, great deeds, and changing the world, ending up dead in a car accident, buried without mourners or eulogies. Unbidden, the thought welled up in her head, an oath to her dead husband: don't worry, Lije, that won't be the end of it, you will do greater deeds in your death than you were given time for in your life. You and me, buddy, we'll bring down Moshel together.

She looked up at Reuven, who had sat down next to her and buried his head in his hands. The first of too many questions burst from her. "How could she? She pretended to be my friend! How could she not have told me, or found a way to let me know?"

He sighed. "I don't know; maybe when we read the rest of the diary more carefully, we'll figure it out. But if I had to guess, I'd say she was afraid of Moshel. I know that I'm afraid of him, and I haven't done anything to bother him since...since, well, you know when. I'm glad you haven't felt that kind of fear, but it's more powerful than you imagine; you get paranoid, you get to thinking that he knows everything, that he knows where you eat, where you sleep, who you talk to, what you say. It's not an excuse, but it can be paralyzing if you let it."

"I'll bet she befriended you as part of her rebellion against him, and was trying to build up the courage to tell you, or maybe only drop a hint. It wasn't enough, I know, but I'd go easy on her; after all, she did pay for it with her life."

"Not enough? It's not even close to enough! She should have...I can't begin listing the things she should have done! At least the diary gives me a new reason for wanting to get Moshel. Can I kill him myself now?"

He thought about it. "I don't know; the diary's clear that Moshel was there, but it doesn't say who was driving. We should bring it to the police, and let them sort it out. They can get an opinion from a court about whether you qualify. But let's make a copy first—I never know where he has spies and thieves. Also, then we can go find the body, and give it a proper burial. Get dressed, and we can get going."

Rachel was relieved that he didn't mention that finding Elijah's body would change her from being a married woman to a widow; it would have been weird for him to be the one to point out that she would be free to remarry as soon as the body was found and id'd. Mixed with that relief, though, was nervousness about how they'd handle it. Luckily, she didn't need to think about that yet. One task at a time, she told herself, as she headed to the shower.

Fifteen minutes later, she was ready, but felt hollow, listless. Ordinarily, setting a bunch of tasks and moving to get them done provided a deep sense of satisfaction, of using her time wisely and well. Now, more intensely than any time since right after he disappeared, she kept seeing Lije's footprints, in the bedroom they had shared, in the shower he had always made a mess of, in the toilet seat he had always left up, in the breakfast nook where he ate his sugar cereals. Let the mourning begin, she thought.

CHAPTER TWENTY-ONE

T hat's it; debt paid in full. I'm out. Sign my paper and let me go."

Pinhas Moshel had known that he would pay dearly for what he was about to do, but Harvey Keiter, he had said to himself, had suffered enough. It was time to let the man start his new life with...what the hell was her name? He *had* to start listening more. With a deep sigh, he'd signed the paper, given it to Harvey, shaken his hand, and watched him run off in joy and shock that it had actually worked.

Which had led directly to his current meeting. The tall man with no body fat sitting opposite him exuded strength, inner and outer, making Pinhas squirm with the kind of discomfort he had not felt since the old days in Brooklyn. Reminding himself that he was Pinhas Moshel, master of the Temple finances and accounts, he said, careful to keep his tone as commanding as it ordinarily would be, "With Harvey gone, you'll have to retrieve the diary. It is going to be returned to the long-term coat check at Shaare Tsedek hospital," a rather clever hiding place, if you think about it, good for you, Liat, Pinhas thought, impressed but also chagrined that he hadn't considered the possibility she had prepared so far ahead of time, "by 10 this morning. You can pick it up there."

When the man shook his head, rejecting that idea, Pinhas would have liked to vent, but controlled himself enough to say, "I'm telling you, the property will be returned to its proper place this morning! I know my business, I know how to insure what needs to be insured, and you'll just have to trust me."

"Actually, no, I won't. I was hired for a certain task, and I will perform that to the best of my abilities in the way I deem fit. If I don't deliver the diary, safe and unreplicated, my own reputation will suffer, which concerns me more than any other issues you may have. If you ask me, this operation has been bungled from the beginning. I won't add a failure to my résumé simply because you are unwilling to do what needs to be done to make this work."

As the man left the room, Pinhas noted he didn't only hate feeling out of control, he also hated actually having lost control. He'd set a ball rolling; for now, there was nothing he could do.

CHAPTER TWENTY-TWO

Reuven and Rachel left the house and headed to his car to drive to the nearest Kinko's; it turned out that filming the diary produced an image that was only rarely legible, and would have taken much longer than the morning deadline. Within a few feet of the house, they picked up a tail.

Reuven noticed him before she did and started walking faster, urging her to do the same. Unfortunately, the tail wasn't trying to hide what he was doing; when they picked up their pace, so did he. Reuven started to run.

She tried to keep up with him, but she had never been a big runner, and neither the months of pregnancy and recovery nor the previous night's attack had done anything to improve her stamina. Too soon, she found herself gasping for air, head throbbing, and knew she just couldn't run much longer. Irrationally, she found herself annoyed at the various action movies Lije had forced her to see; none of *their* heroes or heroines ever ran out of breath in the middle of life-threatening chases. Now what would she do?

"I...can't...keep...here, take the diary!"

He hesitated, but said, "All right, if I have the diary, he'll go after me, and you should be ok." He took the diary openly, so their tail would see, put it in his backpack, and took off. The man at first started to run faster after him, but as he reached her, he changed his mind and stopped. He put his arm around her waist, in a way the casual observer would think was cozy, but instantly let her know that a wrong move would end very badly.

"Hey!" His voice and face were unfamiliar, but there was no mistaking his type. He had done this or something like it many times before, and Reuven wasn't going to outthink him. Reuven heard him, understood his blunder, and turned around. "It's a simple thing; you have what I want and I have what you want. Come over here and we'll handle this quietly."

This was one scene she had never figured out. How was Reuven going to trust him? How was he going to be sure the guy would let her go when he gave the diary back? How could the guy know Reuven didn't have a second notebook in his backpack and would slip him the wrong one? And besides, they were on the street. It might have been a quiet street, but it was a street, there were enough people that the guy couldn't do anything he wanted.

She needn't have worried; he was a professional, he knew what to do. As Reuven got within fifteen steps, the guy said, in a tone that would have sounded friendly to any eavesdroppers, "No need to come closer, I don't want to bother you. Why don't you throw me the book, and when I see that it's what I want, I'll go home."

Reuven didn't trust him, but couldn't make a scene without risking her safety. He answered, keeping his voice casual as well. "Do you have to go? Maybe we should go to a café and have a drink, and we can make the trade there, where we can both be sure we have what we want."

Waist-holder wasn't going to be deterred, and his voice slipped a shade towards threatening. "I'm kind of busy today, and can't spend a lot of time on this. There's not a lot of room for bargaining here, so why don't we do this and get me on my way?"

Reuven hesitated, but then pulled out the diary and tossed it to him. Thinking he would be distracted by catching the book, she poised to run, but he one-handed it without letting go of her, flipped through the pages, satisfied himself that he had what he wanted. Without another word, he pushed her towards Reuven so hard that she staggered, but managed to keep from falling. Reuven ran towards her, and helped her steady herself.

Her near-fall had attracted some attention on the street, and a few people came over to ask if she was ok. By the time she had gotten rid of them and looked up to see where their assailant was, he'd disappeared. She started to go after him, thinking maybe they could catch a glimpse of him, give his description to the police. Once again, Reuven had a different idea. He grabbed her hand, and pulled her in the other direction.

"Come on!"

She pulled back, as shocked by his initiating physical contact— with anyone, since that meant he couldn't go to the Temple that day, but especially with her, officially still a married woman even though they both now knew otherwise—as anything else. "What are you doing? Let's go to the police and tell them what happened!"

She had spoken a little too loudly, and some people turned once again in her direction. He let go of her hand, and moved closer, dropping his voice so that no one else would hear what they were saying, and shifting his body language to make it look like it was a romantic moment. Sure enough, most of the people smiled and turned away. For the benefit of the few remaining, he leaned in and whispered in her ear.

"The police aren't going to believe some crazy story about a diary and a robbery. Even if they do, they have no evidence or clues to follow up, and they are not going to bother an important, and apparently pious, man like Pinhas Moshel, just because you and I claim we read a diary that made some outrageous accusations against him. So going to the police isn't going to help us much; but if we get to my car, pretending that we are out for a drive together, we can go to where your husband was buried, and dig him up."

"Once we do that, we'll have a lot better chance of finding evidence that connects Moshel to the killing. As soon as Moshel gets the diary, and realizes what we know, you can bet he's going to send someone to move the body, and then we'll have nothing, so why don't we go? Oh, and by the way, you might want to act like you like me, so that these nice people don't lynch me while I'm trying to help you!"

Sure enough, one of the remaining onlookers, several inches taller than Reuven and massive, came over and asked Rachel if she was ok, if he could help her. Still reeling from the events of the past five minutes, she managed to nod, thank him, and say that yes, she was fine, this was her boyfriend, they had had a bit of an argument, but everything was ok. He didn't seem convinced, but there was little he could do about it. As they walked off, he followed at a distance, until they got to Reuven's car. Reuven got in first, she walked around to the passenger's seat, and they drove off.

Her willingness to help him avoid a beating did not translate into her being happy with him, though. After a few blocks, she said "All right, you can let me off."

"What?"

"Let me off. Nobody who was there this morning will see, so you're safe. You want to go up North, fine. Me, I a) don't remember where the diary said, and b) think we should be going to the police. So you let me off, I'll go to the police, tell them my story, and you can look for the body."

Surprised, Reuven looked over at her to see if she was serious. When he saw the set of her mouth, he said, "Look, Rachel, you've got to believe me..."

She wasn't interested. "Please pull over right now, or I'm going to open my window and start screaming my head off."

"All right, all right, don't do anything crazy. Look, I'm going to pull over, but you have to promise me you'll give me a minute to try to convince you I'm right."

"I don't have to do anything, and no promises. But I'll listen for as long as you're convincing."

He pulled over, but didn't turn off the engine. "I know that this is hard to accept, but Pinhas Moshel is not the ordinary run of the mill bad ex-husband. Think of the diary; he was awful to her when they were married, he cared more about his career than letting Lije have a proper burial or your suffering, and that's the stuff you know personally. Think about this, he sent one guy last night to tell you to put the diary back and a different one to take it today. How many people do you know who have minions like that?"

"None."

"Right. Now think. Is a guy like that without influence with the police? You think he's come this far without protection of some sort? Going to the police will let him know that you've decided to pursue this, whereas driving off outside the city limits could be for a hundred different things. Our safest course of action, our likeliest road to getting this guy, is to go find Lije's body, use it to find corroborating evidence for our otherwise cockamamie story about a diary, and then bury him properly."

He breathed deeply. "Or at least that's what I think. My instincts, I gotta tell you, are to start driving so fast that you can't get out, but I'm not going to do that. If you insist on my letting you out, I will, but you'd be putting yourself in danger and probably me, too. But look, you're an adult, so you get to make your own choices. I'm going up North either way, because I think that's our best hope for getting out of this without getting hurt. You with me or you want out?"

Slowly, she nodded her head.

"Is that yes you're with me, or yes, you're out of here?"

She wasn't sure and hated not being sure. Reporting had given her a profound respect for police, who, in the vast majority of cases, were efficient and concerned public servants. She'd like to believe that was true now as well, but Reuven made sense. What about Shomer Kapdan? If she called him, shouldn't that be ok?

She told Reuven of her compromise; he knew Kapdan, as it turned out, and was willing to have her call. She got a machine. She debated leaving a message, but with Reuven sitting there impatiently, decided to go with him and call again from the road.

"All right, let's go." Nodding with satisfaction, he put the car in drive, pulled out into the street and drove off. The first fifteen minutes passed in silence, with him weaving in and out of traffic, trying to get to the highway that would take them up North. Then it struck her that she didn't know the road Liat had referred to in the diary, did he?

"Reuven, do you know where we're going?"

"Not exactly, but I have a friend who lives up near Katsrin. I figure in a couple of hours, when we get closer, I'll call and have him tell me where the new turn-off to the Kinneret is. He'll know, and, worse comes to worst, we'll stop and ask directions."

A couple of *hours*? She was so used to thinking of it as a small country that she hadn't thought about commuting time. If it was two hours there, they'd have to leave by 4 for her to be back for the sitter (better 3:30, to be sure about traffic). It was, what, 10:15 now, would take till at least 12:15 to get there. Even if they didn't stop for lunch or anything, would three hours be enough to search for a poorly marked grave?

"Reuven?"

"Hmmm?"

"Are we for sure going to be home by 6? The earlier I tell the babysitter I want her to stay late, the better it works out for all of us."

"I don't know; what time is it now, 10:15? Figure a little over two hours there, assuming I get in touch with my friend, but then we have to search a pretty large stretch of road, and we don't know what we're looking for, and then we'd have to leave by, like, what, 3:30 to avoid traffic? Sounds kinda tight to me. Can she stay late?"

Rachel called and the answer was no. Dammit! All the times it wasn't anything all that important, she was so helpful. Now that Rachel actually needed her, all of a sudden she couldn't do it. What would she do now? She could have Reuven drop her off, but that would mean missing the search for Lije, which she desperately wanted to be part of. Was there anyone else who could fill in? The baby didn't have any stranger anxiety or anything yet, so as long as it was a responsible adult, he should be fine.

Although she mentally ran down her list of her friends and acquaintances in Israel, she knew she wasn't going to think of anyone. They were all perfectly nice, but she had never developed attachments that involved mutual imposing. Lije had, but she couldn't call those people, because she didn't know them.

In the end, with Reuven's encouragement, she called Esther, knowing she was burdening their relationship too greatly for its current level. She hoped it would grow, but she knew it wasn't yet the kind of friendship where you on the spur of the moment ask the other to take care of your infant. True to form, Esther was nicer than she would have imagined; she actually had been planning to have five or six friends (quiet friends, Esther threw in reassuringly) to her apartment to listen to some music and hang out, so if she could bring them along, it would work out great for everyone. Thrilled at having solved her problem, especially since the baby might hear some actual music instead of her own weak attempts at singing, Rachel hung up, full of gratitude for the angel named Esther Kevuda.

Promising herself she'd take Atid for a whole day of fun and attention to make up for tonight, Rachel turned her thoughts to Lije, spending the rest of the ride seeing him being hit by a car, again, and again, and again.

She must have dozed, because when they got hit, she at first thought it was part of her daydream. When the car went off the road, though, she snapped awake. At first more startled than scared, she caught a glimpse of a blue license plate on a Mercedes-Benz taxicab straightening itself back onto the road and driving off. Looking out front, she saw the edge of a cliff hurtling towards them, which meant, she instantly knew, that they had been driving on one of those twisting roads through the hills of the Shomron, where there wasn't much room between the road and the abyss. Turning back to Reuven, she saw that he wasn't reacting at all and his hands had dropped off the steering wheel.

Luckily and uncharacteristically, she didn't think. She called his name twice, got no response, and then focused on controlling the steering wheel and the brake. Shoving her left leg over Reuven and as far as it would go, she managed to reach the brake, but only just. As she reached farther and farther, she felt herself squeezing the brake slowly, as her driving instructors had always told her to do, instead of jamming it, as instinct would have had her do had she only had the reach.

At the same time, she turned the wheel back toward the road, hoping the car wouldn't spin or flip, or whatever. The brake worked too slowly to stop them going over the side, but when they went over, they were probably going only five miles an hour, which, she later thought, was what saved them. As they went over, she screamed, expecting a drop to the valley floor far below, and death.

Instead of shooting out into an abyss, though, the car slid down about fifteen feet, landing on a platform of some sort. She sat there motionless, too relieved at being alive to think clearly. After a minute, she realized that they had been driving on a hill whose sides were graduated, platforms for growing olives every few feet along the way.

Her headache was now back in full force, which reminded her of the blue-plated Mercedes Benz. If this was an attack, was he coming back for more? Getting out of the car carefully but quickly, she looked up to see whether their assailant had the professional pride to stop and insure he'd done the job right. Sure enough, she saw it a few hundred yards down the road, a stretch taxicab, light blue with a luggage rack on the top, slowly moving back to where they had gone over.

She looked over at Reuven, who was not conscious, but moaning. Relieved that he was alive, Rachel had no idea how she was going to keep him that way if this man was coming for them. She got back in the car, thinking that at least he'd have to come down the mountain before he could know whether they had survived. She closed her eyes and played dead, hoping that Reuven wouldn't move while the man was looking, and trying to come up with a plan for what she would do when he came down the hill.

She had held her breath for maybe thirty seconds, when she heard shouts and voices moving down the hill towards the car. Had he had a whole crew with him? Her heart sinking, she tried desperately to come up with a plan for survival, especially one that didn't involve abandoning Reuven.

First things first; she had to get away from this car alive. She opened her door as quietly as she could, hoping it might go unnoticed since her side faced the valley, away from the road. Looking in through the window, she desperately sought some sort of weapon, but didn't find any.

A car starting up and driving away caught her attention; it

was the blue taxicab. Shifting her view to the hillside now, she saw that several passing cars had noticed them and stopped to help. The growing crowd had been enough to to scare off whoever had attacked them. Adrenaline rush over, she sank to the ground and passed out.

An hour and a half later, Rachel was sitting at a nearby hospital, having been seen by a doctor who had prescribed great painkillers (would they let her take some home?), and was waiting for word on Reuven. With a moment to herself, her thoughts turned to the car. A blue license plate meant an Arab car, but what Arab would care about her or Reuven? If it was an Arab thing, at least, she could tell the police without worrying that she'd be spreading rumors about Moshel.

"Ms. Tucker?"

Startled, Rachel looked up to see a middle-aged woman smiling down at her. Probably in her mid-50's, a head of gray hair. Not fat, but overweight enough that you wouldn't think of her as being in good physical condition. The face itself was pleasant, although generally unremarkable in size, shape, or features.

When she pointed questioningly at the seat next to her, silently asking if she could sit down, Rachel said, "You seem to know me, but I don't know you." And then, of course, kicked herself for not saying, like in the movies, I'm sorry, but you seem to have me at a disadvantage.

The woman laughed without any warmth. "Yes, of course, I apologize; when one is a minor celebrity, one assumes that everyone knows who one is."

Rachel was not a fan of speaking of "oneself" in the third person, and was becoming less and less of a fan of this woman's evasiveness. Instead of expressing her frustration, what the pre-Atid Rachel would have done, she merely smiled and waited, a mark of the patience a colicky baby teaches. The woman continued to expect Rachel to figure out who she was, so the conversation didn't get any better.

"Well, I'm Gaavtan Yoshor."

Smile from Rachel.

"Chief of Police here in Nitzots haYeshuah; we're the town nearest to where your car crashed."

Waiting her out was perfectly fine with Rachel; before she invited her to sit down, she would have to actually explain what she wanted. Her silence apparently worked, as the policewoman shifted demeanors remarkably. Whereas before she had oozed bonhomie and camaraderie, she now reverted to bored bureaucrat.

"I need to ask you several questions about today's crash. Would you like to do it here or down at the police station?"

Rachel waved her into the chair, and composed her thoughts for the fiftieth time in the last two hours. She had told the story to the people who first arrived, to the medics who took Reuven out of the car and put them both into an ambulance, to the admitting nurse who apparently needed to know exactly how they got here before she could allow them to be treated, to the doctor who examined her, and to any number of casually interested people in the waiting room.

She didn't mind telling the story, but it was becoming a bit numbing. The trauma of the telling was gone, for now; she had only the post-traumatic effects to look forward to. "Look, I can't tell you very much, except that an Arab ran us off the road, and meant to get us, because I saw him reversing the car, as if to check that we were completely.... hurt. It was only when the other people came along that he got out of there."

"And how do you know it was an Arab, Ms. Tucker?"

"His car had one of those blue license plates."

Yoshor laughed. "Ah, Ms. Tucker, I see you were not cut out for investigations." Not a way to get on her good side, but Yoshor either didn't know or didn't care. "A blue license plate might mean an Arab did this; even if it did, though, you'd have to wonder who hired the Arab to do it. But the car might have been stolen or borrowed, with or without the owner's knowing what it was going to be used for. It might even be that someone simply stole the plate itself and put it on the car he was using, to camouflage himself. Anyway, we're having that checked out right now with the authorities."

Rachel didn't like being mocked and would have tuned the

woman out, answering only the minimum required, but the last comment got the better of her. "What do you mean, the Arab authorities?"

Yoshor nodded, as if the question fit her picture of Rachel Tucker. "I wouldn't expect most people to know about this, but Arab self-rule isn't a slogan, it's real. They have their own officials, who oversee their cities and villages. We maintain close cooperation, to be sure that crimes committed from one group to the other don't fall through the cracks. It's sort of a quid pro quo; they govern themselves and get the same unemployment benefits, health, plumbing, electricity, and so on that other Israelis get. We're not there yet, but we're almost at parity between Arab and Jewish services."

"Sounds expensive," Rachel said, wishing she had her camera with her.

"True, but thank God, the economy's been good these last several years, so we've had the money. Anyway, we called them as soon as we heard about the license plate; other witnesses got four of the six numbers, and they're going to call us back soon."

Rachel knew she should care, but was having trouble freeing any part of her mind from Reuven and his condition. She hadn't let herself feel anything for him while there was a chance that Lije was still alive, but since reading Liat's diary, feelings had started popping up that she hadn't had since those first heady days with Lije. To lose Reuven so soon after Lije's death was confirmed...she could not think about that now. She *could* think about getting rid of the annoying little woman who apparently thought she could engage Rachel in a conversation about New Israel's handling of resident aliens.

"Listen, Officer..."

"It's Captain Yoshor."

Good, insult her, Rachel, that's always the way to ingratiate yourself with people in authority. "I apologize, Captain Yoshor. You seem like a straight shooter, so let me be blunt. I'd like to help you with your investigation; in fact, I think my life might depend on it.

But right now, until I hear what happened to...my friend who was driving, I'm not going to be able to focus."

Yoshor wasn't happy, but there was little she could do without seeming completely insensitive. She restrained herself visibly and said, "Of course. You know what, I'm going to go get a cup of coffee, and maybe by the time I get back, or finish drinking it, you'll have had some good news, my colleague from the local village will have set your mind at rest about whether it was the owner of that car who attacked you, and we'll be able to talk some more. I apologize for intruding on your time of tension; it must be very difficult to have a..." Rachel realized she was trying to get a sense of their relationship, but felt no need to help her even if she had known, "...friend hurt so badly. May I bring you a cup of coffee as well?"

At the mention of coffee, the exhaustion from events of the last—Rachel looked at her watch, and realized it wasn't even 12 hours since last night's break-in—hit her all at once. She absolutely *had* to have a cup of coffee, even though she knew that the hospital probably only served mud mixed with coffee beans. Maybe her accepting a favor would put Gaavtan Yoshor in a better mood. She tried her best smile and said, "That would be terrific, thanks very much."

CHAPTER TWENTY-THREE

Pinhas Moshel was distressed; his intense dislike of the emotion worsened his already foul mood. Still, conscious of the evenhanded demeanor expected of him, he relaxed himself before calling for his intern to usher the tall thin man into his office. As he entered, Pinhas noticed that his face was smudged with dirt, his clothes were askew and his shoes were scuffed.

"I admit that my news isn't good, Kohen Moshel, but believe me that the situation is fully under control."

Relaxation exercise or not, Pinhas' frustration boiled over, leading him to speak more harshly than he ever would have allowed himself under ordinary circumstances. "Look, you whatever your name is....."

Thin Man apparently sensed that Pinhas had reached a breaking point, and responded in the calm that can only be summoned when it will clearly infuriate the other person even more. "For your purposes, as I've explained before, I don't have a name. If you insist on calling me something, call me Mr. Tall."

"That's not good enough."

"As a consultant, Kohen Moshel, I often work for opposing sides of a disagreement, although not at the same time, of course. Were my name to be known, my activities on one job might prevent me from getting others. I can't trust your security, or anybody else's, nor can I trust that people seeking revenge against me wouldn't find ways to elicit that information from you or some other of my clients. It is truly best for all concerned that I have no name."

Pinhas wasn't happy working with someone who openly admitted that he worked for whoever paid him—it should be about the Mikdash, dammit!—but waved it away with an irritated gesture.

"Look, *Mr. Tall,* when you were in here last, I told you explicitly that I didn't want to go down this road. Now, you've made things worse, not better. Instead of trying to stop them, you might have thought of *tailing* them, seeing where they were going, and then gotten in touch with me. Just for instance. Or, if you were *going* to go the route you did, you could at least have succeeded in stopping their progress completely, not delaying them temporarily."

The phone rang, interrupting his flow of words. Calming his breath, he put it to his ear, purring with his usual practiced smoothness, "Kohen Moshel here, how may I be of service?" He listened for a moment, thanked his caller with more enthusiasm than he had been able to muster in a while, and turned to the man behind the desk, who was watching him with narrowed eyes.

"Well, it seems that they were taken to a hospital fairly near a small city I know, Nitzots haYeshuah. Despite your bungling, the Lord has seen fit to help me protect my service to His Temple. I can handle this from here, thank you."

Thin Man (Pinhas decided to make up his own name for him) clearly didn't appreciate being dismissed. "You'll keep me posted as to what occurs, yes?"

Moshel blew the air out through his nostrils, willing himself to the kind of self-control that had gotten him to where he was today. "Yes, I will keep you posted. For now, that will be all." He watched Thin Man leave with no little satisfaction; with a little more help from Above, he should soon be able to rid himself of such people.

CHAPTER TWENTY-FOUR

Yoshor came back a few minutes later, gave her a cup of coffee and, to Rachel's surprise, moved a few feet away, leaving her to drink, alone with her thoughts and prayers. She didn't have any books of liturgy or Psalms, certainly what Lije or Reuven would've been saying at this kind of time. Well, she'd have to go it alone.

Closing her eyes, she tried to loosen the tension she felt, squeezing it out of some of the muscles that didn't respond to her mental command. At first, she felt a little foolish—what must it look like to stand in a hospital waiting room, moving her lips but not saying anything? At the thought, she flashed her eyes open, but realized that nobody else had noticed what she was doing, nor would they care if they had. In fact, several other people in the large room were doing the exact same thing.

She closed her eyes again, and said, "Dear God," no, that didn't sound right, He wasn't an advice columnist nor was she close enough to Him to start with that. Maybe it was just a formality, like opening every letter with Dear So-and-So, but she didn't feel like starting a plea for someone's life with a meaningless phrase. What to say?

God was too abrupt, Hey more so. What about an adjective— Good God, or Great and Holy God? No, she wasn't ready to think about how she'd describe God. What about another Name?

She started again, "Master of the Universe," Good, but not enough. Maybe one or two more of those, "Master of the Universe, God of Abraham, Isaac, and Jacob, He Who Granted the Torah to the Jews, you have taken one wonderful man from me and sent me another one..." Ok, the beginning was good, but then she had gotten caught up in herself.

Once more, with feeling. "Master of the Universe, God of Abraham, Isaac, and Jacob, Granter of the Torah, please spare the life and restore the health of Reuven HaOzer." Needs something else; why would God listen to that? Reasons, Rachel, give some reasons.

"Master of the Universe, please spare the life and restore to full health the wonderful man, Reuven HaOzer, who, despite suffering greatly when he lost the right to serve in your Temple, has built a life of service to others, helping administer murderers' reeducation in cities of refuge, overseeing *haver*-students, and providing a warm and pleasant haven at his coffee shop. In my own case, he has eased the pain of my abandonment, has helped me see begin to learn of Your ways, and has provided kindnesses small and large."

Ok, that was at least an argument, but how to close? Well, she wasn't saying the prayer over again. "Thank you for listening and caring about my prayer, as you have listened to and cared about people's prayers throughout history, and I hope You will see fit to grant this request, a request that will help smooth the path to others recognizing Your greatness." And then, feeling a little overdramatic, "Amen."

She opened her eyes, half-expecting to see Reuven walk out, fully cured. Of course that didn't happen, but she was surprised at how much better she felt, enough to notice that she hadn't eaten in many hours. She walked over to Yoshor, and said, "I need to go to the cafeteria for a sandwich; if you'd like to walk with me, I can answer some of your questions along the way."

Surprised by her change of attitude, Yoshor happily acceded. Rachel told her everything about the accident itself, which wasn't all that much. Yoshor, in turn, told her about her conversation with the Arab chief of police. It turned out—Yoshor only narrowly avoided actually saying the words I told you so, but the expression on her face was clear—that the car had been reported stolen two months previously, with a proper report filed.

Yoshor was unfazed. "Ms. Tucker, my job is to get the information I need to catch criminals and make the public safer. The possibility existed that you would tell me more when you were ignorant of the facts than if you knew what had happened. For example, let me ask you why you were driving up this way?"

She was about to tell her the whole story, but suddenly realized that Yoshor had herself raised the idea of a highly placed priest being in control of the police. Had that been a self-congratulatory reference to herself? Was she working with Moshel? Rachel couldn't figure this out now, so she decided to avoid the whole issue. "We wanted a drive, I guess."

Yoshor nodded sadly. "You see what I mean? Had I managed to get that question into our conversation ten minutes ago, I'll bet you would have answered differently. This makes it harder for me to do my job, harder to catch the perpetrators, and harder to protect you from another attack. Ah, well, such is the lot of the police."

Rachel thought she was being sincere, and would have followed her instincts, but hesitated because the decision affected Reuven, too. She was about to tell Yoshor that, but Dr. Besorot waved to her, giving her a legitimate excuse for waiting before responding further.

"I'm sorry, I've got to go see Reuven. If you wait for me, though—the doctor said I'd only have five minutes—I may have more to say when I come back."

"I'd be happy to wait."

CHAPTER TWENTY-FIVE

She walked down the hall toward Reuven's room, wondering what he would look like. She'd seen wounded people before, so she wasn't worried about that, unless it was really bad. But it probably wasn't really bad, because the doctor had said he'd be ok. But sometimes they looked really bad for a while even if at the end they were fine.

And then she turned a corner and, there he was, a huge bandage on the side of his head, his shoulder thoroughly taped, but other than that, the same old Reuven. Seeing him alive and relatively well lifted her spirits more than a little. She was about to run over and hug him but realized that wouldn't go over too well, with either Reuven or the hospital staff, although for different reasons. She couldn't resist taking one of his hands, though, and saying "Oh, Reuven, I'm so relieved you're alright."

He smiled, pale and exhausted. "Me, too." The two words seemed to take a lot out of him, because he leaned his head back on his pillow, closed his eyes, and his next words were inaudible.

She leaned forward so that her ears were right near his mouth. "What? I'm sorry, Reuven, what did you say?"

She heard him whisper, "But seeing you makes a lot of it better."

She felt herself blush, and then, embarrassed at her reaction, blushed even deeper. Feeling the ticking of the clock, she realized she had to talk to him quickly about Yoshor.

"Listen, Reuven, I know you're exhausted, but I need your permission for something. There's a police captain here, investigating the shooting, and she wants to know why we were heading north from Jerusalem. My instincts are to trust her, but she also mentioned that there are some who think that the police have been infiltrated by some kind of organized crime group, so I didn't want to do anything until I got your ok."

Reuven opened his eyes, and forced his voice to a more normal volume. "What do you know about her?"

"Well, nothing, except that she has a uniform and a badge, and the doctor seemed to know her." As she said it, she could hear how it sounded; but she had to face Yoshor when she left this room, and didn't know what to do. Reuven came to her rescue.

"Call Shomer Kapdan again, see if you can get him. If he knows Yoshor, his word's good enough for me."

It took seven minutes—she was staring straight at a clock at the nurse's station—and four people, but she finally got Kapdan on the line.

"Hello?"

"Capt. Kapdan, it's Rachel Tucker."

Kapdan was surprised to hear from her. "Yes?"

Rachel had no time to waste on pleasantries, so she tried to be as brief as possible. "Captain, Reuven HaOzer and I were in a car when an unknown assailant shot him and forced the car off the road. We're in a hospital near Karne Shomron, and the head of the investigation is a police captain named Gaavtan Yoshor, chief of police in Nitzots haYeshuah. I wondered if you know her."

"Is Reuven ok?"

"He will be, but I don't have a lot of time now. Do you know Captain Yoshor?"

Kapdan answered fairly excitedly, at least as far as Rachel knew him. "I do, we were at the academy together. What do you want to know?"

She hesitated, and was about to ask Reuven what she should tell him, but he had fallen sleep. It was up to her. "Well, we were up here looking into something fairly sensitive and she's asking questions that I would instinctively answer completely, but I am somewhat nervous about trusting strangers, particularly after having been robbed and Reuven having been shot. If you vouch for her, though, we'll go with that."

"Ms. Tucker, does this looking into something that you were doing have anything to do with the original incident that first had our paths cross with each other?"

He certainly didn't miss many tricks. "Yes, yes, it does."

"All right, I can be there in an hour. What hospital are you in exactly?"

"Wait, why are you coming? Is Yoshor a problem?"

"I can explain more fully once I get there. Meanwhile, feel free to speak fully to Yoshor, but *only* to her. She and I have several times collaborated on matters indirectly related to yours. I suspect the information you have is particularly valuable. Tell her I am on my way. In fact, can you call her to the phone?"

Rachel didn't like his taking over, but didn't have much choice. "Yes, hold on."

She stepped out into the hallway, where Yoshor was across the lobby, facing her. She was speaking to two men who, from her body language, were superiors of some sort. As soon as she saw Rachel, without pausing in whatever he was saying, she reached her right hand around one of the men as if to remove a particle from his back, and frantically waved Rachel back to her room. Startled, she stepped back in and closed the door quietly.

Picking up the phone, she told Kapdan what had happened, by way of explaining why Yoshor wouldn't be coming to the phone. Kapdan's reaction was immediate, but not reassuring.

"Well, *that* can't be good."

"What?"

"From your description, it sounds like some higher-ups have arrived and want to speak with you, which would be very bad. Yoshor's trying to fend them off, but who knows how long that will last? Stay in the room with Reuven; the doctors won't tell them where you are—patient confidentiality. Yoshor knows, so when I get there, you can let us both in."

Rachel soon found that waiting in a room with a closed door, possibly hostile people outside, and a sleeping patient is harder than it sounds. She had no book, couldn't watch television. Meditate;

focus on breath in, breath out. No use, she was too busy wondering what the two men were talking to Yoshor about, wondering when they would come into the room, and wondering what she was afraid of. Why was Kapdan so immediately alert? What did he know that she didn't?

She played with the questions again and again, in all their permutations and then some, working herself into an ever more frenzied tizzy, even though she didn't know what was so frightening. It had only been half an hour, but seemed like more, when a knock on the door interrupted her private time.

The combination of adrenaline and fear was almost painful. She looked at the door, startled, as her mind flooded with possibilities as to who stood behind it. Her palms instantly clammy, she forced herself out of the chair and walked to the door. Absurdly, she reached for a chair, some feral part of her thinking that she could fight off whoever was behind the door if necessary.

"Who…" Her voice came out as a squeak, and she stopped herself. And then she got mad. Between Reuven and Kapdan, her mind had been filled with conspiracy theories. More than almost anything, she hated living in fear. Anger was good, it cleared her head. What could be behind the door that would be so fearsome? What, would they kill her here in a hospital with a thousand witnesses? Maybe, but she wouldn't live her life letting them get to her. She cleared her throat, and tried again, just as there was another knock at the door.

"Who is it?"

Gaavtan Yoshor whispered, "Ms. Tucker, it is I, please open up, I only have a moment before my superiors return."

She opened the door a crack, saw that it was, indeed, only Yoshor standing out there, and let her in. The woman who came in the door, however, was almost completely different from the one she had met; her air of superiority had disappeared, and she was more businesslike, and seemed more competent, more trustworthy.

"Ms. Tucker, you must listen carefully. I know you do not know me, but we must leave this hospital, with Mr. HaOzer, as quickly as possible. I cannot explain right now, but the longer we stay here, the greater the danger to you both."

"But Shomer Kapdan is on his way here, and he told me not to leave this room until he got here. In fact, he told me not to let anyone into the room except you."

"Kapdan? When did you speak to him? Why is he coming?"

It took her a few minutes to explain her relationship with Kapdan; she decided to tell her the complete version of the story, Moshel and the fixer included. Yoshor listened carefully, and when she was done, said,

"Well, at least now my suspicions are confirmed. My superiors, the regional commanders, are men whose loyalties to Moshel are unbreakable. Yes, yes, I know all about Moshel; I was testing the waters by mentioning that rumor earlier. Their appearance here, to look into what I had reported as a fairly routine traffic accident, already alerted me that something was out of place. I assume you have information that has driven Moshel to some very desperate acts. I don't need to know what it is now, but you should make sure, at some point, to tell somebody else. Should something happen, whatever you know about him must not be allowed to die with you."

Yoshor wasn't making her feel any better, but she knew she was trying to be realistic. Without any answer—she wasn't going to tell her about the diary without Reuven's agreement—she had nothing to say, so she said nothing. Yoshor seemed to understand, and they sat in silence for another ten minutes.

At that point, looking at her watch, Yoshor said, "Well, they are going to be back from their coffee; I told them that you had gone to sleep and had left orders not to be disturbed. When Kapdan comes, we'll find some way to get in touch with you. Until then." She surprised Rachel by patting her briefly on the back, and slipped out the door.

CHAPTER TWENTY-SIX

Alone again, but slightly reassured that at least one other person in the building was intent on helping her, Rachel watched Reuven sleep. His chest rose smoothly up and down, except for when he moved and pain from his injuries made him catch his breath, wake partially and go back to sleep.

With nothing else to do, trying to keep her mind off what might be going on outside her door, she watched him until she could predict his breathing pattern perfectly. Every two minutes, something would catch in his chest and he'd gasp four short breaths, followed by two extraordinarily deep ones, four more short ones, on the last of which he turned on to the other side, pain, partial wakening, back to sleep, and the whole thing would start over again.

Having milked that for all the fun it was worth, she was moving on to counting the tiles in the floor when she thought of Ed and the video camera she had not been using nearly often enough. It was in the car, which meant that if anybody took it and watched the tape, her cover was blown and her plans for a series of news reports was down the tubes. She hoped, though, that the car was at some garage where they'd be too busy finding ways to overcharge Reuven on the repairs to pay attention to her camera.

Being cheated was one of her hot-button points, so much so that she could already feel her anger rising at the unknown garage mechanic. She was deep into the scene, with the mechanic claiming he had had to do some esoteric repair, her and Reuven having no choice but to pay what he said, and leaving knowing they had been taken. The best would be if the car was totaled, then they could take the insurance money and be done with it. As they drove off, her screaming epithets back at the satisfied mechanic holding their money, she heard a knock at the door, and the voice of Shomer Kapdan saying, "Ms. Tucker, I'm here with Gaavtan Yoshor. Will you let us in?"

They came in talkatively, reintroducing themselves, asking how she was feeling—which they meant as polite conversation, but made her notice the beginnings of a return of the headache—how Reuven was, all the while wandering the room, looking under the telephone, in the air vent, under the bed, searching, Rachel realized, for some kind of listening device.

Not finding one, Kapdan pulled a CD player out of his bag and was about to turn it on, but she pointed at Reuven, and said, in a normal voice, "Perhaps we should whisper; I don't want to wake Reuven." At the same time, she pulled a pad of paper out of a drawer, and three pens, and started to write a question. Kapdan quickly shook his head and pulled his PDA out of his pocket, turned it on, and gave it to her.

Whispering the version of the story that she had already told a dozen police officers, with Kapdan and Yoshor interrupting to ask questions to which they already knew the answer, they also took turns typing or writing questions and answers on the PDA. Yoshor told Rachel that she and Kapdan were members of an informal group of police officers who had realized early on that the return of the Temple had opened up new possibilities for organized crime. Kapdan told her he had managed to get assigned to her case after she tried to kill Harvey because he suspected she was getting herself in deeper than she realized, and had hoped to put her out of harm's way by occupying her with becoming a *haverah*.

Reuven, it turned out, worked with Kapdan often. From his vantage point in the coffee shop, he met all the people coming back from the Temple, and often got first wind of scams. One of the most common, they told her, was selling an animal with a carefully hidden but significant blemish. The victim would bring his animal to the Temple, get sent away to find an unblemished one, and find that the seller had disappeared.

The problem was that they caught up with a lot of the small-timers, such as the goons who threatened to maim livestock unless their owners paid protection money and so on, but they couldn't get to the higher-ups. Harvey had been an excellent lead, except that a few months before Rachel confronted him, he had been caught by some other policemen, and given the same choice as she. When he joined the *haver*–training program, he had shifted his social circle and activities, presumably on Moshel's orders, and their lead had dried up.

They were quickly running out of false conversation for the listening devices, so Kapdan interrupted to write, "Can you tell us where you were going?"

She hesitated, her mind cluttered with bits of thought, few of them rational. Reuven had said to trust Kapdan, so that should mean she should, right? But why should she? How did she know he, or Yoshor, wasn't planted by Moshel to sabotage them? How did she know that they wouldn't cut her out of the picture as soon as they found out the information she had?

She wished Reuven were awake. She trusted him unquestioningly, she knew not why, but there it was. Taking a deep breath, literally and figuratively, she typed, "We had a diary written by Liat Moshel, whose death was the reason I almost killed Harvey. In the diary, she named a location where she and her husband accidentally ran over my husband, and buried him there. We were on our way there to try to find the body."

Kapdan and Yoshor were so shocked by what she had written that they sat silent for long moments, not even remembering to keep whispering a fake conversation. Rachel picked up the slack by pretending, out loud, to tend to Reuven, who was—damn him!—still sleeping.

Finally, Yoshor typed, "Do you still have the diary?"

"No, we were assaulted in Jerusalem by a man who wanted only the diary. We were on our way to copy it when it was taken from us."

Kapdan ground his teeth in frustration when he read Rachel's message. He tried again. "Can you prove that Moshel was driving the car?"

"No. We were going to find the body, thinking, first of all, that finding my husband's body would be a good thing regardless of whether we can tie it to Moshel," good, they were properly chagrined at not paying attention to her personal interest in the matter, "and, second, that having a body would help gather more evidence about it."

Kapdan stood up and said in a normal voice, "Ms. Tucker, thank you for your time. Capt. Yoshor and I need to speak privately for a few moments about how best to pursue this investigation; would you mind waiting for us here? We'll be back in a few moments."

Left alone, Rachel digested what she had learned. She knew she had just been handed tremendous scoops—corruption in the Temple, extortion, racketeering, unbelievable!—but she needed people who would speak on the record. Kapdan and Yoshor obviously wouldn't, since it would compromise their investigation. Same for Reuven.

By the time Kapdan and Yoshor returned, Rachel had a plan, but she had to first find Lije, and then get back to Jerusalem. Which reminded her, she'd better call Esther soon and explain why she was going to be even later than she had thought.

Kapdan said, in his normal voice, "Well, Ms. Tucker, you've been very helpful, but I think that's all we're going to need to ask you for the moment. Are you heading back to Jerusalem? I can give you a lift." Meanwhile, he typed on the PDA, "Can you take me to the location named in the diary?"

She hesitated; in her normal voice, she said, "Actually, I had thought about staying with Reuven, to make sure everything's ok; I had already arranged extra care for my baby anyway, so I'm in no particular rush to get back." On the PDA, though, she wrote, "I'll take you there, but I want a guarantee that I get an exclusive on this story when it comes out."

The two police officers exchanged looks, and Yoshor, smiling, took out a five-shekel bill, gave it to Kapdan, and said, "Ms. Tucker, while you're welcome to stay, I am placing two of my top men here to make sure Mr. HaOzer rests comfortably and safely." And then typed, "Shomer knows you well; he bet you'd be with it enough to realize that this will make a great story. Yes, we agree that whenever the story can come out, you get it first, as long as you cooperate fully with us from here on."

Having agreed, they quickly closed their conversations, oral and typed, and headed out of the room. Outside the door, as Yoshor had promised, were two police officers who certainly looked tough, although Rachel wondered how Yoshor could be sure they were not working for Moshel. She'd have to ask Kapdan in the car.

At the door, she stopped and turned back to Reuven's bed. Leaning over his sleeping body, she whispered, "Rest well, Reuven, and get out of here quickly. Stuff's moving, and I think we're on the road to getting Moshel. It...well, it won't be the same unless you're there with me when we finally get him." She leaned forward, about to give him a quick peck on the cheek; not knowing what he would think about it, she stopped herself and went with Kapdan to his car.

CHAPTER TWENTY-SEVEN

As they headed toward Katsrin, Rachel called the babysitter to remind her that Esther Kevuda—she described her so that the sitter wouldn't be nervous—would be watching Atid for the first few hours of the night. She felt blessed that all this was happening when the baby was still young and couldn't feel neglected by her involvement with this investigation. There'd be enough time for him to resent her career in the future; at least this wouldn't be on the list of complaints he brought to his therapist.

On the drive, after Kapdan assured her that he had personally vetted the two officers outside Reuven's door, they argued goodnaturedly about theocracies. Rachel thought Moshel and company proved that they were bad ideas, however benign they intended to be. Kapdan disagreed.

"I think, Ms. Tucker, that you are making the common error, made by many of us as well, that the Arrival would be the end, but it's actually only the beginning. Sure, we have a Temple, we have real sovereignty, less worry about world pressure, and are on the road to building a religious country, but we don't think we're there yet. We're just on the road."

"And Moshel?"

"Ms. Tucker..."

It only now struck her how incongruous it was that they were still addressing each other so formally, when he was the one keeping her safe from Moshel's men, or Moshel himself. She had been so angry at him for representing the government that was forcing her to study religion that she had forgotten ordinary manners. "Please, call me Rachel."

Kapdan smiled his appreciation. "Rachel, free will means that some percentage of people will make bad choices; we can reduce that number, and we have, but murder, theft, extortion—these are part of human nature. It will be years and decades before even the Messiah could wipe those out."

She wasn't convinced, and lapsed into a moody silence. Growing up in a not-so-religious family, she hadn't thought a lot about the Messiah, but whatever she *had* thought, this wasn't it. Wryly, she realized that the Messiah she hadn't believed in was one who would perform miracles. Now that he'd come, she was surprised that it had happened at all, but also disappointed in how ordinary it seemed.

Come to think of it, her marriage hadn't been what she'd dreamed of, either. She had loved Lije, sure, but they saw the world so differently that the good times were all too often mixed with tension, or anger, or resentment. She had spent five years resenting this country because Lije had dragged her over here, which had made her commute, which had made her more nervous about her career, which in turn had led her to delay having kids, which meant she hadn't started a family until she was older than she had wanted, and put a cap on the number of kids they'd ever have.

Then he disappeared, and she spent months hating him for abandoning her, hating the system that couldn't rule him dead without solid evidence, hating (and loving) the fetus and then baby he'd left fatherless; now, she was struggling to absorb the reality that all that pain came from one man caring more for his status as a priest than her and her family's suffering.

Her headache was fully back. She only had two of the painkillers left; the rest were in Reuven's room, which was ok, since it gave her an excuse to go back to visit him tomorrow. Meanwhile, she popped them, told Kapdan she needed to close her eyes until they took effect, and leaned her head back for a moment.

Lije was telling her something, something important, but she couldn't quite catch it. "What?" she said. He opened his mouth to say it again, when she heard someone say "Rachel? Rachel?" As he reached for her, she felt herself sucked backwards in a vortex, and woke up.

It was getting dark already. She looked at her watch; 5:00, they'd been driving for two hours, and she had slept for one and a half of them.

"We're at the new turnoff the diary mentioned. Where do I go from here?"

It came back to her as she thought about it. "She said after the sign for Katsrin, 25 km," Rachel looked back at it, "there was a new turnoff, built since the Arrival."

Kapdan was driving slowly so he could follow her directions. "Yes, I turned there."

"Well, that's it, then. Soon after that, they hit him, and she buried him somewhere near where he died, putting six strange colored stones near each other. I guess we get out and look around."

Kapdan called Yoshor, and gave their exact location; she said she'd have one of her colleagues in Katsrin send a car out to assist them. He hung up, parked as far over to the side as he could, turned his flashers and brights on, took several roadside flares, the kind she was used to seeing at accident scenes, and lit them behind his car. He smiled sardonically at Rachel, "If my car gets hit, I want it to be clear that it was on purpose."

She had never looked for a grave before, so she started wandering up and down the road, looking for stones. He called her back. First, he pulled out two large flashlights, which gave almost as much light as a streetlamp, from his car.

"Here, let me explain how we do this."

She laughed. "There's a way to do this? How often do you look for unmarked graves?"

"Pretty often, actually. Priests are notoriously careful about that kind of thing, so we get requests to check out certain areas. We first block off a piece of road and side road—say, five meters at a time—and check that. Then we'll move on to the next piece. For each piece, I'll walk back and forth lengthwise and you do the same widthwise; try not to bump into me too much."

By the time they got to their fifth piece of land an hour later, she was getting frustrated. Only the thought of finding Lije kept her going. She looked over at Kapdan, who seemed completely unperturbed by their failure to find anything. He felt her look at him, and smiled. "Welcome to my world. I've been doing this for so long, I can do it for hours without noticing the tedium. But we'll take a break in a minute; you can clear your head before we keep going."

She had continued walking while he spoke, and almost walked right by it. As she looked down, reassured by his words, she saw a bright blue stone which stood out from all the other ones around it. Excited, she called him over and showed it to him. "I don't understand, though; the diary said there were six oddly colored stones!"

"Rachel, it's been several months; stones don't stay in one place!?"

"They don't?" She thought that was the essence of being a stone.

"Well, *some* do. But a stone like this, any of a number of things could have happened. Maybe some kids came for a walk, or a young couple went for a picnic, or who knows what, but the stone got moved. At least it lets us know we're on the right track. The question is whether this was the original place and the others got moved, or this one did. Hmmm."

He thought for a while, at least a minute, and then said, "Perhaps we ought to search separately rather than together. I'd like to try checking the road itself; I'll bet Liat didn't get all the blood from the accident, it's notoriously persistent, especially on asphalt."

So they started again, she on the side looking for stones, he for blood. Every once in a while, a car would pass, stop to find out if they were all right, and then continue on. The police officers from Katsrin arrived, and joined the search. One of them found a startlingly red stone almost right away, but it too was alone.

Kapdan was perhaps ten meters further on when he let out a shout and called them over. When they got to him, he was pointing to a patch of black asphalt, "There! See it?"

Rachel looked where he was pointing, but couldn't see

anything. She bent closer, and, as she bent, caught a glimpse of red on the roadway. "Now I do. So what now?"

Kapdan looked around. "I'd bet anything that it's here. What's on the side of the road?"

Fifteen minutes later, they found three colored stones near each other. The two officers from Katsrin started to dig, and, ten minutes later, uncovered a decomposed body. She looked down into the hole, expecting to be horrified, but all she saw was a skeleton in clothes, like in the movies. That it had once been Lije was still only an intellectual fact; it hadn't penetrated her emotional consciousness yet, and she wondered when it would.

Kapdan was suddenly all business. "Well, Rachel, we have a body; the task now is identification. The pockets are empty. We'll have to take a plaster cast of the teeth and send it to dental records. I'll get the process rolling."

Dental records? Plaster cast? Couldn't they leave him alone? The man was hit by a car and buried without eulogy or mourning, did they have to defile him further? Now, she felt herself reacting the way she had expected to when she looked down the hole. Think, Rachel, think! Could she get them to stop touching him, to let him be? As they hoisted the body out of the grave, one of them climbed out, took the body from the other, placed it on the ground, then the other climbed out, she turned away, thinking.

She tried to remember Lije as she had last seen him; the jeans and short-sleeved shirt on the skeleton was one she knew well, but that wouldn't be identification enough. What about the watch she'd given him for Hanukkah? She called over to Kapdan, who was leaning over the body, examining it, "Is Lije...I mean, the body, wearing a watch?"

He looked. "No."

It wasn't Lije. The tears came unbidden, and she heard herself crying, only at that point realizing the extent to which she had been hoping that it would be him, so that he could find peace and she a new start. It couldn't have been more than two minutes that she was crying, but when she turned around, having regained her composure, she saw Kapdan, a black eye beginning to form under his right eye along with a nice sized welt on the side of his head, pointing his gun at the two police officers from Katsrin, who were standing with their arms in the air.

"What….what's going on?" Rachel had the awful thought that Kapdan had betrayed them, that he was actually one of Moshel's men, and was going to remove the body to a safer locale.

"Officer Boged here jumped me; he apparently was interested in recovering the body and hiding it again, so that Moshel would be safe."

Right idea, wrong person, Rachel thought to herself. Which was unfortunate, because the two police officers apparently sensed her ambivalence and began calling out to her, "Hey, lady! Be careful! This guy's crazy! *He's* working for that guy in the Temple, not us! We were just here to do a job!"

She actually didn't know who to believe, but since Kapdan had a gun and she didn't, she'd hope Reuven's judgment was correct. "But I don't understand; why didn't they jump us when they got here?"

"They didn't know where the body was; only you did. Once we had the body, they could go back to their superiors and tell them they had accomplished their assigned task. Apparently, the police in Katsrin aren't as Moshel-free as Gaavtan Yoshor assumed." As he was talking, Kapdan had also been dialing his phone; when he got an answer at the other end, he spoke briefly and then hung up.

Before he spoke to Rachel again, he had the two policemen undo their belts, drop them to the ground and kick them over to him. Keeping his gun trained on them, he reached down and pulled a set of handcuffs off each of their belts. Taking another set off of his own and three more from his car, he handcuffed their arms behind them and to each other, then had them kneel, buttocks on ankles, handcuffed their ankles together and to each other, and then the two joining pairs of handcuffs to each other. It would be a while before they went anywhere, and even once they did, it would be at a slow pace.

And it was all handled with ease, as if controlling two trained police officers posed no challenge. After which, he told Rachel, "All right, I spoke to an associate I know personally from the area. She's going to bring a handpicked squad of people to come watch the scene for us until Jerusalem's Body Recovery Unit can get here. I assume you'll want burial near Jerusalem?"

She hadn't thought about it. "I...I...I...don't know. But how do you know I get to make that decision? I mean, he has no identifying marks, no watch..." The tears were dangerously close to flowing again.

Kapdan seemed confused by her concerns. "Rachel? What's the matter?"

"Lije was wearing a watch; he always wore a watch, he was fanatic about knowing the time. If there's no watch, it's not Lije. And I'm back to where I started." She managed to limit herself to one sob.

Kapdan shook his head firmly. "You mean, you think it was a coincidence that we found five odd colored stones, three of them together, and a body buried underneath? No, I'm pretty sure it's Lije; somebody took the watch and the contents of his pockets either for their value, or, more likely, to make him harder to identify, to make it take longer and put more distance between them and the killing."

Realizing he was right, her mind cleared enough to think about how she could prove it was Lije without needing to take plaster casts. Closing her eyes, she saw his fingers waggling at her. Of course there was no jewelry on them; Lije didn't wear any and Moshel would have had Liat take it with them if he did. But what about his wedding ring? With the thrill of discovery, she ran over to Kapdan, shouting "I can identify him! I can identify him!"

He blinked at her exuberance. "How can you be so sure?"

"His wedding ring!"

"Rachel, I already told you, there was no jewelry on his hands."

Rachel smiled. "I know, but Lije didn't wear his wedding ring when he wasn't around me; he only put it on for me, to make me happy."

Kapdan was puzzled. "But then how are we going to find it?"

"Well, he lost the first ring I got him within three weeks of our wedding, so I made him promise that whenever he wasn't wearing it, he'd put it in his shoe. That way, he wouldn't lose it, a mugger wouldn't steal it, and with every step, he'd remember me. So take off his boot—which they would do for the real burial anyway, right?" As she asked the question, her internal observer wondered why she was so concerned at not disturbing the body any more than absolutely necessary. Kapdan nodded.

"Anyway, if you take off his right boot," those stupid hiking boots she had always hated, but that Lije had favored above all other footwear, "I think you'll find a ring."

Skeptical, he did as she said, and, to her relief and (almost) joy, a gold band fell to the ground. Kapdan picked it up. "Very impressive, but I confess I don't know whether that will be enough for full identification. We'll have to ask the rabbis in Jerusalem."

She wasn't worried. "It gets better. If you look inside the ring, it's inscribed to Elijah b. David Zeale from Rachel b. Shoshana Tucker. It cost me a fortune to get them to write that small, but it was a joke, my way of making fun of the names on our marriage document. Which I still have at home, in case..." She had been about to say in case Lije comes back, but choked on the words as it once again hit her that they were now proving that he was never coming back.

She blinked away the largest of the tears and managed to get out, "well, anyway, that should do it, shouldn't it?"

Kapdan wasn't going to argue with her. "We'll still have to ask, but I suspect so. Meanwhile, this has been a very rough day, so let's pack it in. The investigation will take a couple of more days, to see if the Moshels left behind any evidence, but that need not concern you. The body certainly won't arrive in Jerusalem before the weekend, so you can plan the funeral for next week sometime."

It took ten minutes for Kapdan's associate to get there, a young, determined looking woman, whose hair was cut short but stylishly, fitting so well under her police cap that you could barely see it. Her brief conversation with Kapdan was littered with references to God, and, when she was introduced to Rachel, she shook her hand and said, "May He who takes vengeance for widows and orphans take full vengeance for your loss and pain and bring you the comfort you deserve and need in the coming months." Which was touching, but felt like a little much from someone she had just met.

Still nervous as to whether Kapdan could accurately tell the good guys from the bad, she got in the car, settling into a dense fog of grief. She had known that Lije wasn't alive but seeing his unrecognizable body brought out layers of hurt she had hidden from these past months. She spent most of the ride in a sea of memories, disconnected, disorienting, but all focused on Lije, their time together, the things she had hated about him, the things she had loved about him, the things she had both hated and loved. Ah, Lije, we were going to grow old together, remember?

It wasn't until they were five minutes from the house that she thought of all the questions she should have spent the ride home asking. "What happens now?"

He thought a minute before answering. "Well, once the body gets to Jerusalem, it has to be buried that day, bodies don't stay overnight in the city. I'll make sure Traffic Victims calls and gives you an exact day, but I assume it'll be Monday or Tuesday of next week. After the funeral, you and the rest of the family will have to sit a symbolic *shiva*, for an hour or two. Given the delay in the funeral, we should be able to have the neck-breaking ceremony the day after that; do you know what that is?"

Rachel knew she had heard the term before, but didn't know what it meant.

Kapdan explained. "When a body is found on the road, with no known murderer, the surrounding towns have to take responsibility for what happened. The leaders measure the distance from their town to the body, and the closest one has to do a ceremony, part of which involves breaking a heifer's neck. But you should know about this—there's going to be one next week for Shlomit Hami, on Sunday."

That's where she'd heard about it! "I did hear about it, but Sunday? Sunday's the funeral! Although...can I go when I haven't buried my...Lije yet?"

"Because it's been so many years, the family got permission to have the funeral at the ceremony; they think it'll be a larger crowd and be more of an honor to Shlomit. As for you, I think you can, but you might want to check. Do you know any rabbis? I can have someone contact you."

"What about Esther Kevuda, my sponsor?"

"She should do fine, actually, that's a much better idea. In any case, we'll have to do a ceremony for Elijah as well, up Katsrin way, but we need to publicize it fully, because we only do the ceremony if we don't have eyewitness testimony about who committed the crime. So figure maybe late next week, Thursday?"

"But what about the diary? Doesn't our finding the body where the diary said prove that it was Moshel?"

Kapdan paused. "A lot of this stuff isn't so clear in the case law; it hasn't been that long that we've gone back to acting on these laws, you know. But I *think*—and obviously we'll check it out—that it has to be testimony, and a diary doesn't qualify as knowing who killed Lije."

She turned to go, but he held her back. "If I were you, Rachel, I'd focus on healing, physically and psychologically. You've taken quite a beating, which you may not realize. Take the rest of your maternity leave, maybe even some compassionate leave, and be nice to yourself for a while. Get a massage regularly, find a soothing activity, let yourself recover."

Although it was better advice than she cared to admit, her first reaction was panic. The network! She hadn't been getting any footage for Ed, and he'd be furious. She would call him first thing when she got into the house. Finding Lije's body meant that he couldn't be angry with her, and in the coming days, the mourning and heifer ceremonies would provide more than he needed.

As her thoughts about Ed trailed off, Rachel flashed back to when her grandfather had died, a man she knew her mother had revered and adored. He had lived a long life, but the end had come suddenly and shockingly, knifed to death on a subway at the age of ninety-three. By a quirk of physics, his body was left in a sitting position, his head fallen forward as if asleep. It took hours before other passengers realized what had happened.

Heartbroken as her mother was, she had managed to still give instructions on all the usual details she busied herself with, how the house should look, who should wear what, who needed to improve their table manners. Rachel had been annoyed at her concern with such trivia when there was the hard work of mourning to be done. Yet here she was, worrying about the network! Mom would get a kick out of knowing that her daughter, whose entire career was insurance against becoming a housewife like mom, couldn't escape her genes.

"Rachel?" Kapdan was looking at her with some concern.

"I'm sorry, what did you say?"

"I said we're here, but you didn't hear me. Are you ok? Do you want me to come in? Do you want me to send someone over? I know excellent crisis counselors, or I could call one of your friends."

"No, really, I'm ok. I'm going to call my mom when I get in the house, and we'll find something to fight about. That should carry me well into the night." Rachel had intended to sound ironic, but it came out bitter, perhaps a symptom of the awkwardness she was feeling with Shomer Kapdan right now.

She didn't know him all that well, nor did she feel any great warmth for him, yet he had helped her find Lije's body, a debt that would never go away, and that she couldn't properly articulate. "I appreciate your help; I'll never forget that it was you who brought a painful chapter in my life to a close and helped me move on to the next one." There was probably more to say, but she didn't know what it was.

He seemed to understand. "It's my privilege. But don't talk as if this is good-bye; Moshel will certainly find out about this, which heightens the danger to him considerably. I suspect, though, that he knows we don't have any real evidence tying him to that, what with Liat dead, so I don't think he'll do anything rash just yet. In case I'm wrong, though, call me, day or night." He offered her another copy of his card.

She put it in her purse, nodded to him, and started up the stairs. Thank God that she had asked Esther to call a nighttime babysitter she knew. She didn't know if she'd sleep much, but she desperately needed somebody else to take care of Atid during the night. She steeled herself, opened her door, and walked into her future as a widow.

CHAPTER TWENTY-EIGHT

As if to balance her life, the next several days treated her more gently than she would have ever guessed. When she walked in that first night, Atid was a pleasure, no a comfort, for about two hours—smiling, sitting happily, looking at his mommy and his mobile—and slept for the next ten.

Her mother, who had often made known her disappointment with Rachel's having "settled" for Lije and even more so for having stayed married to him when he insisted on moving to Israel, immediately offered to come help indefinitely. And, lest Rachel fear that she planned on intruding on her space, she made it clear that she intended to stay in a hotel on those nights when she wasn't needed to care for the baby. Who was this generous, sensitive woman and where was the imperious and judgmental one she'd grown up with?

Ed Appleby, also not someone whose empathy she would have bet on, ignored the lack of footage, and also offered to make it to Israel for the funeral. When she protested that he needn't trouble himself (she suspected he'd find a way to get her to pay him back), he suggested sending a cameraperson to take care of the filming, to relieve her burden, to get the upcoming ceremonies properly filmed for her series, and to include her co-workers in the mourning/comforting process.

By the time she got off the phone with Ed, it was 11:30. She had to call Lije's parents, but they were certainly already asleep, and there was no need to wake them up to get final notice of bad news they half-expected, especially at a time when there was nothing productive to be done til at least morning, when they could start making phone calls about the funeral.

She knew she should get to bed herself, but she couldn't get rid of the gnawing feeling—false, if past experience was a guide—that she should be doing something else. She would call Reuven. Idly, she dialed the number and asked for his room, expecting to be told that he was sleeping. Instead, they connected her, which she regretted as soon as she heard his sleep-filled voice.

"I'm sorry, Reuven, it's Rachel. I wanted to say good night, but I'll talk to you tomorrow."

He mumbled a bit, but was obviously trying to keep her on the phone, his voice slowly getting clearer as he woke up. "No, no, talk to me. I heard you found Lije."

Rachel was a little surprised by how raw the nerve still was; some part of her had expected that when he was finally found, she'd grieve a little and be done with it. She knew he was trying to express his sorrow for her loss, but it washed over her like a flood of grief. She had looked forward to speaking to him one more time before sleep, to have a smile on her face as she went to bed, and now wished she hadn't called at all. She didn't want him to know that, though, because he'd apologize, which would only make it worse.

"Yes, they did. I haven't heard details, but I think burial and the neck-breaking will happen early to middle of next week. Will you be around?"

Reuven sensed that he had misstepped, and had woken up enough to speak more carefully. "They tell me they'll let me out tomorrow, and from then on, I am hoping to be wherever you need me to be, whenever you need it, and however you need it. I'm just sorry I wasn't there with you at the moment; I know how hard it is to lose someone."

And then more tears came, tears she dreaded and craved. She hung up as quickly as she could without being rude, and threw herself on her bed where racking sobs took control for what seemed like hours but turned out to be thirty-seven minutes. She couldn't remember ever crying that long before, but now she cried, for Lije, for herself, a widow at thirty-four, for Atid never having the chance to know him, for the Messiah not having prevented his death, for everything that was not yet perfect in the world.

Eventually she ran down, got up from the bed, a little shakily, and went to the bathroom to wash away the tears. Weak from her spent emotions, she lay back down in her clothes, and closed her eyes, planning on going to sleep. Except, of course, that the rush of planning was upon her, with her mind bringing up lists of the various people she had to call about the funeral. Friends of hers, friends of Lije's, relatives, co-workers (Ed had promised to spread the word at the network, but there were Lije's co-workers, and other friends and acquaintances who would feel left out if she didn't call herself). Sleep no longer an immediate possibility, she got a pad of paper and started to write.

CHAPTER TWENTY-NINE

When she woke, in her bed, she had no memory of how she had gotten there. Her mind didn't give her a chance to ponder that, as it automatically shifted to planning time with the baby, to make up for her absences of the last few days. She'd make a few of the central phone calls and then she'd take him to the park and for a walk. After assuaging some mother-guilt, she'd be ready to continue the phone calls and planning.

Back in her usual race to both stay calm and keep track of the several tasks set for the next twelve hours, she went to get the baby; it didn't go so well. Seeing him reminded her that he'd grow up an orphan, a fact she'd mostly managed to avoid thinking about until now. Not for the last time, she heard a little voice in her head say, "This grieving thing really sucks."

She had never paid attention before to how blessed she'd been by the nearly total absence of young death in her close circle. Lije's was working its way into her system, but too slowly. She tried to remind herself that grieving for a husband can easily take years, even if she included the months he was missing and only presumed dead, when she had vented anger and grief whenever she was alone, it could easily be another year before she'd be back to herself.

After feeding him breakfast, making goo-goo faces, taking him to the park, and putting him down for a nap, she felt a little better, and sat down to make her phone calls. First, Shomer Kapdan to get the number for Traffic Victims, to plan the funeral. He wasn't there, but the secretary gave her the number. Traffic Victims took not one phone call, but six, although she finally found out that Lije's body could be released as early as Monday, and then the ceremony in Katsrin could be on Tuesday. She was a little worried about putting them so close to Shlomit's ceremonies—Esther's comments about it being helpful to attend those now seemed even more prescient—but she also liked the idea of getting it over, since she dreaded each part of the process more than the next.

She spent the baby's nap making phone calls, and when he woke up, took him and a tape recorder to the park. After he was walked around and held for a bit, he settled down to watch other kids play, and she took out her recorder and began to talk. She figured she'd go stream of consciousness, edit later.

"The first feeling is of knowing that your world will never be the same. Although I suppose it might be true of losing any relative, when a husband goes, even if he's already been out of your life for several months, even if the marriage had tensions in it yet to be resolved, a part of yourself is gone forever. Lije Zeale was a good man, who didn't deserve to be buried in a poorly marked grave by the side of a rarely traveled road in the north of Israel. I say this not as his wife, although I would, or as a reporter, but as a human being."

"Police have yet to announce any suspects or leads," how were they going to handle this; wouldn't Moshel have to hear about it at some point? "capturing the man, men, woman, or women who did this will not change the crime, will not wipe it away, will not make it better. I hope he or they are caught, get the punishment they deserve, whatever that is, but it won't change the horror of what happened to Lije Zeale."

"Or to Shlomit Hami, either. Viewers will know about Lije Zeale because he was married to a public figure. Shlomit Hami was a young woman who had the misfortune of being accidentally killed by a man who couldn't stand the thought of being sent to a city of refuge. Her family, too, suffered for years before authorities, by happenstance, found out where the body was buried."

"The New Israeli society has adopted a practice to deal with this kind of circumstance. Sunday, this reporter will be attending an odd ceremony that expresses this society's determination to avoid what happened to Shlomit Hami and Lije Zeale. As far as I understand it, major communal leaders will gather in an unused riverbed with a calf that has never been used as a beast of burden. In front of a large public, they will declare that they knew nothing about the circumstances of Shlomit's death, were not negligent in protecting her life, and will call on God to atone for whatever crimes of omission or commission that they bear liability for. I'll have more on that from the scene; until then, this is Rachel Tucker, ABC News."

As she turned off the recorder, she wondered whether the ceremony would change anything. Making a big deal was always helpful; it broadcast society's values, which would be enough for a high percentage of the people in that society. But would it stop future killings or bring their killers to justice?

CHAPTER THIRTY

Over the weekend, its crowning moment, Atid smiled for the first time. She knew that it was probably gas, but it was a welcome relief from having to infer his interest by whether his eyes focused on her or not. She made a strict practice of lying down to rest whenever he did, so that by Sunday morning she felt much more herself than she had in a long time.

Sunday dawned cloudy and gray, matching her mood. She always felt uncomfortable when she didn't quite understand her place, and Shlomit's neck-breaking would be such an occasion. Reuven had had some fever the hospital had been monitoring, so he wasn't sure he'd get out of the hospital in time to make it, her mom had decided she was too freaked out (her words) to join her, and Rachel didn't relish the thought of attending with Esther and Shomer Kapdan. As she stirred coffee she wasn't drinking, the phone rang.

"Hi, Rachel?"

"Who is this, please?"

"It's Brian Fortnought from ABC News? Ed Appleby sent me to film with you for this week? Well, anyway, I'm through customs, and wanted to know where you wanted me to go now."

An *American*, a real-live ordinary person, to stand next to her! She could barely restrain her excitement when she answered him. "Hey, Brian, great to hear from you! Listen, there's this thing this morning between Jerusalem and the airport; I was going to leave for it in 15 minutes. Are you too wiped out from the flight, or could you meet me there? After that, you'll have plenty of time to get to the hotel, unpack, unwind, all that."

"No problem; I flew business, so I'm good to go. Tell me how to get there."

"Well, actually, it's going to be just off the main highway at mile marker 27, but if you have the cabdriver listen to the radio, they're broadcasting it like crazy; it's kind of a due diligence thing, the mayor has to make sure that as many people as possible hear about it."

"Ok, I'll go straight there and get some background footage. Oh, and wait, here's the number for the cell phone I rented." He read it off as Rachel wrote it down, a little bemused at his thinking she'd need to call to find him, since they'd be two of maybe fifty people at the thing, and he'd be the one holding a professional-size videocamera.

A mile before she got there, when she saw the authorities turning cars off the highway into makeshift parking lots, with shuttle buses running to the ceremony site, she began to think she might have been wrong. When she finally arrived at the dais, where the various members of Shlomit's family were waiting for the ceremony to begin, she looked out on a crowd of at least fifteen thousand people. She picked up the phone, and called Brian's cell number.

"Brian Fortnought."

"Hi, Brian, it's Rachel. I'm standing 20 feet in front of the big dais now; where are you?"

"I'm further back in the crowd; I found out that they're going to start with eulogies, then politicians, the ceremony, and the funeral procession to the family plot in Ashdod. I'll start working my way towards you, and we should have plenty of time to tape an intro before they start."

Soon after she finished filming, mostly the same as what she had said the previous night, making her feel redundant, a man approached the microphone. By this time, the dais had filled with two distinct groups of people, Shlomit's family and local and national politicians. Rachel recognized a few by face and was sure she'd recognize the names of others. Then the man at the mike began to speak.

"Excuse me, ladies and gentlemen, I am Kavul Hami, Shlomit's father. We are honored by the presence of so many important officials, both political and priestly; after the ceremony, we will introduce the dais. For now, we welcome Zecharyah Shakhor, mayor of Zichron Yaakov, who will be conducting. Before we turn the microphone over to him, we wanted you all to meet our Shlomit before we bid her our final farewell."

Rachel was not looking forward to this part of the experience. She had been to many funerals, and knew that constructing a moving eulogy was extremely difficult; unbidden, she thought, who will do it for Lije? Emotion, even honest and deeply felt, was not easily expressed in a way that others could relate to. As she expected, only two presentations were worthwhile. The father gave biographical details that turned Shlomit into a real person, and one of Shlomit's nieces, so movingly that Rachel jotted down her words, planning to excerpt it later for her voice-overs.

Dear Aunt Shlomit,

I've missed you when it's raining and I had no one to stand outside with me, our mouths open wide.

I've missed you when I'm bored and I couldn't just call you and talk about –*whatever*—until I wasn't bored anymore.

I've missed you when I had a nightmare and no one to give me good thoughts to focus on instead.

I've missed you when I had a big project for school and couldn't call to get you to help me cut it up into pieces I could handle.

I've missed going to your wedding, whenever it would have been; I'll miss having you at my wedding, my children's births and celebrations.

I'll miss you, Aunt Shlomit, every time I think of our family, because we'll never be whole again."

The tears Rachel wiped away were for Shlomit, but also for Lije, who she was trying to leave out of her consciousness, to give the deceased the respect she deserved. She had barely finished wiping her tears, when Shlomit's boyfriend got up to speak.

"Shlomit, what is there to say? We were robbed of the chance to get to know each other, the chance to find out where our future lay, the chance to walk together in the park, to stare deeply into each other's eyes, to bask in the knowledge that someone else in the world thinks we're the best. I have not had you with me for a long time already, Shlomit, but I always have, and always will have, the endless possibilities of what might have been, and for that, Shlomit, I thank you."

It was as he was speaking—perfectly, in Rachel's mind; simple, heartfelt, direct—that she fully registered that people would expect her to speak at Lije's ceremony. As accustomed as she was to public speaking, she very much didn't want to. Lije's death was personal, and she didn't want to share it with thousands of people.

The mayor convinced her otherwise, though. In the polished delivery of the veteran politician, he spoke of the town's efforts to insure the security of residents and visitors; they had already installed guardrails on all of the highways, so that even cars that veered off the road wouldn't hit anybody or fall off a cliff, a travelers' bureau to insure that anyone passing through could find a place for the night, free accompaniment for those who had to travel in the dark, and a significant public relations program emphasizing citizens' responsibility to report inappropriate activity. Although not as emotional as the other speeches, it was moving in its own way, since he made it clear that the town was determined to never again be the scene of a tragedy like Shlomit's.

Rachel's mind wandered a bit, because the mayor was not one to use two words when ten could be found, but she came back in time to hear him close by saying,

"The society we build depends on each and every one of us. We today tell the Hami family that we recognize that this should never have happened, that we accept, as individuals and as a community, the responsibility to insure that this never happens again. We cannot bring Shlomit back although, with God's help, the time of the Resurrection should come soon, but we assure everyone here that the terrible tragedy we have gathered to mourn will make Zichron Yaakov and its surroundings safer, for its residents, for its visitors, and for its passers-through. And every time someone avoids danger or finds a helping hand in Zichron, they will know that Shlomit is the reason they are being so well taken care of."

"The calf we will kill we hope will appropriately commemorate Shlomit's death. We hope that we will convert her senseless tragedy into an event that will bring greater safety and security to so many others."

And then it was the priests' turn. Since the circumstances of death were pretty well known—Zeke was telling and selling his story to everyone who would listen and buy it—they skipped the usual call for information and went straight to the ritual. They priests brought out a young calf, and had the assembled dignitaries step forward and place their hands on its head. The priests then led them in a recitation of verses, declaring that they had had no knowledge of this woman's situation, and no complicity in her death. Then, they brought the calf down from the dais, to the designated spot in the riverbed, and...well, when Rachel had heard about this part, she had wondered whether watching priests break a calf's neck would itself be so horrible as to overwhelm all the other parts of the ceremony.

It was pretty bad, but the aftermath was equally so. At the crack of the neck, the entire crowd gasped; some people fainted, vomited, or retched. Most hung their heads. Listening to the calf low pathetically as the life slipped away from it brought home the horror of death in a way that reading, hearing, even covering as a reporter, had not. She had stood outside burning buildings as firefighters carried out small dead children, she had sat with terminal cancer patients a few hours before they departed, but watching a healthy large animal slowly die, all because of a lack of care by a thoughtless human being, powerfully reminded Rachel and, she assumed, everybody else present, of the importance of protecting life, animal or human.

When the animal finally died, the Hami family and friends moved off for the drive to Ashdod and final burial. As the rest of the crowd dispersed, with a few hushed conversations about safety improvements other locales could introduce, Rachel tried to find reasons not to leave.

As soon as she walked out of here, she'd go with Brian to Jerusalem, get him settled, look at the pre-edited footage, come up with a voice over, go home to the baby, go to sleep, and wake to go to Lije's funeral, burial, and then, the next day, *his* heifer ceremony. Moving as it was, she didn't know what a second one within 72 hours would accomplish. Pushing those thoughts aside, she walked out with Brian, to begin what she assumed would be the worst time of her life.

CHAPTER THIRTY-ONE

Reuven's showing up at her doorstep soon after she put Atid to bed did wonders for her mood, although the day's ceremony and her anticipation of tomorrow's funeral had pretty much sapped any energy she had for human interaction. He himself looked every ounce of the fatigue that pushing to get out of the hospital in time for the funeral had caused. They mostly sat on her couch, he closing his eyes—the fever wasn't gone, but he had convinced the doctors that he could monitor himself—snippets of conversation peppering the amiable silence.

The most important was his advice about the eulogy.

"I have to figure out what to say tomorrow, and I feel like it's going to take me the whole night to come up with anything."

"Why not go to sleep now, wake up in six hours, and do it then?"

"I'm afraid I won't wake up."

"Maybe don't speak, then? You've got Lije's parents and good friends already speaking, so it's not like he'll go uneulogized; a lot of people think it's a bad idea for spouses to speak at funerals anyway. After all, the best of marriages are so complicated that it's difficult to step back and give the purely positive picture a eulogy is supposed to be. Besides, you've gone through a lot, people won't expect you to speak."

"I know, and ordinarily I'd do that, but—and I don't mean this the wrong way—I'm Rachel Tucker. I speak very publicly for a very nice living. It was my money that helped Lije move to Israel, but also my money that kept us in America for longer than he wanted. I just feel that it's the least I can do to use these talents to honor his memory."

"Sure, but as a news anchor, you have other people write the news for you. I know, I know," she had been about to protest, "you do a lot of your own reporting, and write your live copy. But your day to day newscasts have a team of writers putting them together."

Which, of course, was the answer; she almost kissed him, she was so relieved. "Reuven, you're a genius! I'll call my copywriter back in the States, tell her what I want to say, and she can write it for me, fax it here, I can review and edit it, and it'll be great! Oh my God, what a weight off my shoulders."

Twenty minutes later, flushed with the excitement of having jumped an insurmountable hurdle, she came back in the room, saying, "Well, in an hour from now, I should have a fax of my eulogy to review and revise. I'm going to lie down in my room; the fax'll wake me when it comes in. Reuven?" Temporarily finished rambling, she finally looked and saw that he was sound asleep.

In repose, a wounded, tired man whose face softened in sleep, much of the worry erased. Not handsome of face, Rachel thought, but the strength and caring made up for that in spades. She covered him with a blanket, air kissed his forehead, went into her room, closed the door, and went to sleep.

Waking up to edit three drafts of a eulogy—mental note, send flowers to Karen in New York—made sleep less restful than it could have been, but it was enough to get her through the day. Her morning review of upcoming events focused first on the visitations people made before the funeral. While ordinarily frowned upon because mourning didn't start until after burial, Lije's extended absence before the body was discovered helped the rabbi in charge decide it could be condoned in this case (with a lot of help from Reuven, who was clearly more comfortable being creative than this rabbi, a bureaucratic functionary left over from before).

After *that* ordeal—she hated two minute conversations in which sincere and inarticulate people tried to convey their sympathies— there would be the funeral itself. She'd asked both of Lije's parents to speak, but, in character for them, only his mother would. Each of his siblings wanted a chance, as did his oldest nephew, whom Lije had practically raised, since he'd been single when the boy was young.

And then it would be her turn, but she wasn't nearly as nervous as yesterday. Subconsciously, she patted the speech in her pocket, to give herself the confidence that it was still there. Her mind, however, had gone on to the funeral, to watching the pallbearers carry the stretcher to the grave, to imagining what it would be like to see him lowered into the ground, to start shoveling the dirt on him and watch others complete the job. Certainly she needn't worry that she wouldn't recognize the finality of the moment.

Pausing her tape of the day to come, she put her feet on the floor and went into the bathroom to shower. In what felt like barely an instant, she found herself at the podium, the pages of her speech on the lectern in front of her. She looked out at the crowd. Numerous people from ABC were there, local staff, coworkers from the States, a bunch from the European bureaus, her parents, Esther, Kapdan. But, in massive numbers, the funeral was populated by Lije's family, friends, and other people she had never met at all.

Many of them had spent the hour before the funeral telling her of how Lije had affected their lives, how his generosity of spirit and presence had given them more than he would ever have admitted. The responsibility to capture his wonderful qualities and disregard his failings, to give them some sense of the Lije she knew and loved, overwhelmed her once again, and she almost fled. Then she looked at Reuven, cradling Atid in his massive arms and looking up at her expectantly, encouragingly, and endearingly, and she was ready to go on.

"I mourn you, Elijah Zeale, for the man you were and would have been, the husband you were and would have been, and the father we will never know." The beginning, so powerful in her mind when she went over it with Karen, was even more so as she said it, so that she recited most of the eulogy from memory, her eyes too filled with tears to read the pages in front of her, flowing too freely to wipe away.

"I mourn you for the idealism that led you to bring me to this remarkable and infuriating country, to cast our lots, as a couple, with the future of history, with the center of a new era of peace and prosperity for all human beings. I mourn you for the gentle way you interacted with all the people you met, respecting each for who he or she was, and yet making clear how much more they could become. The mourners here today, from the various areas of your life, testify to how much you did in how little time."

"I mourn the husband who was the hand of God in my life in so many ways." She'd hesitated greatly before writing these words, as this had been a bone of contention between them. Lije had always been trying to interpret events as signs from God, and Rachel had absolutely hated that. Over time, but mostly in retrospect, she had come to see some of what he meant. Promotions she could have taken but for his lifestyle and needs, promotions she got because he happened to make a clever comment at a cocktail party, their having been living in Israel when he disappeared, forcing her to keep returning there, all of these had, every so often, made her, too, feel a guiding hand, and it always appeared in the form of Lije's needs sending their lives in the direction that later turned out to be where they needed to be.

"I mourn the husband who challenged me, loved me, and fought with me..." She couldn't let even a eulogy pass with the impression that anything was perfect. For too long, she had suffered from hearing eulogies that spoke of the wonderful marriage of the deceased, making her think her own relationships and eventually marriage must be in some way defective. She had, when she was still single, broken up with perfectly acceptable men, and had worried each time she argued with Lije because of that, and she wouldn't be part of perpetuating that myth.

She hoped nobody walked away from this funeral thinking that she hadn't loved him or enjoyed being married to him, but she intended to be absolutely certain that all here would know of their fights, would know that she loved him in spite of, or maybe even all the more because of, the fights they had, "as an equal, who respected my independence, my thoughts, my right to differ from his views. I mourn the husband who made me feel whole, made me feel like I didn't need any companion other than him. I mourn the years we will never have together."

"You know, on our anniversaries, Lije would each year give me a plaque—once in wood, once in pottery, once in silver, whatever material he thought was pretty that year—that read 'Come grow old with me, the best is yet to come.' I mourn the plaques I will never get, and the years that would have brought the plaques with them."

"Most of all, I mourn on behalf of our son, Atid. I mourn the father he will never have the chance to know, the silly faces and games he will never have the chance to enjoy with his dad, the walks they will never take where Lije could pass his knowledge and perspective of the world on to his little boy. I mourn not having him by my side as I grow into motherhood, not having the opportunity to be married to the wonderful father I know he would have been."

"I mourn the mode of your passing, Lije, as much as the passing itself. Would that you would have had the blessing of a bedridden death, your loved ones at your side, a stream of visitors reminding you daily and hourly of how much you had contributed to the world. Would that you had not died on the side of a road, struck by an unknown car, buried by unknown hands in a barely marked grave, with none to stop and say, here lies a man who lived his life seeking to improve the world."

"Now at least you can rest, Lije, you can rest with the words we have all heard today accompanying you in that next world you always spoke of. You can wear our love and admiration as a garland around your neck, as a crown upon your head, as a badge of the honor your life earned you."

"I mourn you, Lije Zeale, in private and in public; I will mourn you in sickness and in health, in happy times and in sad; and I will mourn you as I build the rest of my life with our son, until death reunites us. May your soul be bound up in the bond of life, may your repose be peace, and let us look forward to the day that the Prophet speaks of, the conclusion to history you repeated to me endlessly, "Death will be swallowed up forever, and the Lord God will wipe away tears from all faces. Amen."

She had been so focused on saying the words clearly and audibly, so busy crying her way through her speech, that she had not paid attention to how people were reacting. When she left the podium to go back to her seat, she sat with head bowed, too emotionally spent to engage in eye contact with anyone else. As the silence continued for long minutes, she looked up wondering what had gone wrong, and realized that people were silently absorbing the tragedy, joining her in mourning Lije. Many were crying, and the empathy of their tears went far in easing the burden of grief she bore.

When she stood for the memorial prayer, the rabbi referring to Eliyahu b. David haLevi, she felt a closing. At the cemetery, when the stretcher had been placed in a makeshift cement grave in the ground and covered over with earth, she again felt the finality of the farewell. She recited the *kaddish* prayer with the rabbi and Lije's other relatives, and turned away to walk through the line of those who had come to offer condolences. They all went back to her house, where she and his family sat on the floor for a ceremonial few minutes and accepted condolences, after which they rose, embracing life even while still mourning death.

But people stayed long into the night, telling her stories she had never known, introducing her to parts of Lije's life she had never been aware of, deepening even further her appreciation of the man he had been. She went to bed that night spent but enriched, almost ready to face the next day. It was only as she was falling asleep, and too late to reawaken herself to think about it, that she noticed that Reuven hadn't come back to the house after the burial.

CHAPTER THIRTY-TWO

It was not yet a complete disaster. Certainly Tucker knew, since she otherwise couldn't have found the body. Presumably that meant that others knew, but he was pretty sure they had no proof. When word leaked of her accusations, he would have to spend a few days on damage control, convincing those under and above him that she didn't know what she was talking about, that he would certainly continue in his various functions, that the stability of the Mikdash would be unharmed.

It was a very close thing, though. Tucker was a sympathetic figure, a young mother, an *agunah*, and no one knew of any reason she would lie about him. Should he bring up her obsession with Liat, her attempted murder of Harvey?

Her claims would strike deep, and he didn't know how much longer he could keep it together. There would come a point, maybe soon, that a lack of proof wouldn't be enough to save him and them all from what she was unwittingly doing.

The day of the funeral passed more slowly, and less cathartically, for Pinhas Moshel than for Rachel. The next day would be a problem; any more evidence against him and it was all over. He went to sleep trying to be sure that he had bought off all those who might have relevant evidence.

CHAPTER THIRTY-THREE

Rachel woke to light streaming through her window, the remnants of a dream in her head. Lije was fighting with Reuven, except that he kept shouting, "Let me go and I'll walk away!" For some reason, Reuven wouldn't, even though he was getting clobbered. Despite being shorter and smaller, Lije kept landing punishing blows, although never enough to be able to run away. A few times, he managed to get a few steps, but Reuven would pull him back, almost as if he wanted to get beat up some more.

Rachel thought about the dream during her shower, breakfast, and brief prayers. The prayers were a chore, but she knew that when all of this cleared up, she still needed to be making progress towards becoming a *haverah* or the authorities would expel her. She had no idea whether she wanted to stay, but she wanted to leave the option open. All the thinking about the dream brought her no greater insight than when she had started, but did remind her of Reuven's absence the previous night.

She called the Temple Grounds, to be told that Reuven had taken the week off, on doctor's orders. When she called his apartment, he answered groggily, as if he had been sleeping. Rachel looked at her watch; 8:45. "Reuven, are you still asleep?"

"No, again. I was up on and off all night with pain, but I kept telling myself that I could get through this without the medication, so I'm still trying to get a night's sleep. What can I do for you, Rachel?"

Rachel didn't like his tone; it was more professional than personal, more the public Reuven than the complex private individual she'd gotten to know over the past two weeks.

"I just called to find out if everything's ok. I was surprised

I didn't see you at my apartment last night" then, not wanting to sound accusatory, hastily added, "although you obviously had no responsibility to come, and then when I heard you had taken the week off, I wanted to check that you're ok. And, of course, I wanted to find out if you're feeling up to being at the neck-breaking today; it's almost time to leave if we're going to make it up North by 11:30."

"I'm fine, just a little tired, and I'll be at the ceremony in a professional capacity; I've been asked to recite the call for God to atone for this blood among us. But I'm sure I'll see you around afterwards."

Something odd was going on, but she couldn't figure out what it was. "See me around? Reuven, did something happen between us that I don't know about?"

He thought before answering. "I think we should have this conversation in person, and I don't think today or right now is a good time to do it. How about if, after the ceremony, we go somewhere and talk?"

"Fine, but promise me you'll sit next to me for the beginning part of the ceremony, so you can explain what's going on. I got some idea from Shlomit's, but I want to get a better understanding- so I can be a better *haverah*." She added that last part just to annoy him, since they both knew of her continuing skepticism about the process and the religion.

He wasn't rising to the bait, at least not today. "You know what, I'm sure Esther will be there; as your sponsor, she can do a fine job telling you what's going on," and hung up.

Wondering what was bothering Reuven successfully insulated her from considering how hard the ceremony would be. It had been challenging enough when it was just a garden variety tragedy, where everyone really knew how Shlomit had died, whether or not confessions were admissible as evidence, but this was Lije, and while *she* knew what had happened, everyone there would be assuming they had no idea of what had occurred.

In the end, it went nothing like she had expected. It started smoothly at noon, and proceeded just like at Shlomit's, except that here, as they were about to break the calf's neck, they asked one last time whether anyone had direct knowledge of the killing; whoever did should step forward and make themselves known.

After pausing, the priest lifted the meat cleaver, but as his hand started coming down, a man came running up to the dais, shouting, "Wait, I know the killer!" throwing the whole proceeding into an uproar. The man, wearing a dirty uniform and with grease-stained hands, was about to continue, when police officers surrounded him and escorted him away from the podium.

The priest addressed the audience. "Ladies and gentlemen, with all due apologies, we need to hold off on the ceremony until we check out this man's story, and we must do that in private, so as not to allow for the possible slander of an innocent man. Please excuse us."

As soon as Rachel saw the man who had come forward, she slapped her forehead hard in exasperation. Esther, misunderstanding her reaction, tried to soothe her, "It's all right, Rachel, it's probably a mistake and they'll come back in a minute to finish."

She said, "No, I think you're wrong. I bet that's the man from the garage they took the car to after hitting Elijah. I slapped myself because I should have thought of that. Moshel's car would need repairs, so they had to take it to a garage! If I only had managed to figure that out, we could have avoided this whole thing. I *hate* when I do that. All right, let's go."

Esther looked puzzled. "Go where?"

"To hear what he has to say."

"We can't go; didn't you just hear? They do this in private, so as not to slander an innocent man. If there's any validity to his story, they'll come out and tell us, and then we'll find out what's going on. Meanwhile, maybe we should catch up on other areas of your progress."

She knew Esther meant religiously, but her conversation with Reuven was still on her mind. Since he had done more to spark her interest in religion than anyone else, including Lije, she figured that telling Esther about it half-qualified as progress.

"You know what? I know this isn't directly about religion, but

I don't know what's going on with me and Reuven and its bugging me. I can't pray, not like when I was at the group, I can't focus on my reporting. It's not even like I'm sure of my feelings for him, but after his tone on the phone…"

Esther seemed puzzled. "What are you talking about? What did Reuven do on the phone? Are the two of you in a relationship? Don't worry about the prayer thing, it's always up and down kind of thing and with a group is almost always, if not always, better than alone, so I wouldn't worry about that part of it, I'd just come back to group ASAP. But what about Reuven?"

So she caught her up, explaining that they had never spoken about "them," but she had always assumed that if Lije's death were confirmed, they would try things out at some point thereafter. But now, he was acting really weird.

Esther smiled understandingly. "Rachel, you have to give the man a break. Yesterday, he heard a beautiful set of eulogies, yours in particular, showing the depth of people's feelings for a special man. Even if he hopes the two of you will test out your relationship one day, I bet he's nervous about stepping on your time of grief, about making a move too quickly, about taking advantage of what is often a vulnerable time. Especially as a priest, misconduct is deeply discouraged and might have serious consequences; plus, as a nice guy, he probably doesn't want to make any missteps. Give him clear signals—saying it straight out would be even better—as to what you want from him, and I'll bet he'll return to himself."

She was surprised by Esther's words, because, as true as they sounded, she never would have thought of that herself. Did Reuven (and Esther, for that matter) really not know her at all? Did he not know how much she had come to enjoy his company, just for ordinary things like walking with Atid, like having a cup of coffee, like laughing at some conceited politician's windy speech? Did he really think of her as a vulnerable female who couldn't control herself from falling in love with the first man who cared for her after her husband's disappearance and death? And, for that matter, did he really think that she hadn't had any men trying to step into Lije's void these past several months?

She didn't get the chance to say any of that, though, because just then, a youngish priest went to the podium and said, "Ladies and gentlemen, we apologize for the inconvenience, but it seems that we have a preliminary identification of the killer, rendering this ceremony superfluous. Thank you for coming and congratulations to Katsrin on no longer having to worry about its role in this horrible tragedy."

The priest left the podium, came directly to Rachel and Esther and asked them to join him, leading them to one of the tents where the organizers had coordinated the logistics of a large gathering of people. Hurrying to catch up, Esther asked, "What's going on?"

"I don't know anything; I was told to make that announcement and to bring you back to my superiors. Sorry." With that, they walked the fifty meters to the tent in silence. Once under the roof, it was easy to see where they were heading, as all eyes were focused on a closed-off area, the staging area for the event. At the entranceway, the priest opened the door, gave a little bow, and walked away.

They went in, certainly not expecting what they found, which was Shomer Kapdan, Gaavtan Yoshor, Reuven, and several other priests sitting with the scruffy man who had interrupted the proceedings earlier. Kapdan rose when they entered.

"Ah, Ms. Tucker, how nice to see you. And you are Esther Kevuda, if I'm not mistaken? I've heard wonderful things about your prayer services; I keep meaning to make the time to attend, but… well, anyway, let me introduce you to my colleague Gaavtan Yoshor, police chief of Nitzots haYeshuah, as well as some local priests, Mah Ichpat, Shlumiel Geulah, and Balshan HaKohanim, who were planning on overseeing the pre-neck-breaking investigation. Ms. Kevuda," he said, turning to Yoshor and the others, "is one of the most popular prayer-service leaders in Jerusalem, as well as Ms. Tucker's sponsor for *haverah* training."

Esther and Yoshor shook hands hello while Kapdan continued, pointing to the man still sitting down. "Joseph Metaken here has a most interesting story for us, which we are currently sharing only with those whose discretion we can trust. It seems that around the date that your husband disappeared, Ms. Tucker, Pinhas Moshel— Mr. Metaken recognized him from his pilgrimages to the Temple, and from various news reports—and a woman, whom he has since identified from photographs as Mr. Moshel's late ex-wife, Liat, came into Mr. Metaken's garage here in Katsrin to get their fender fixed. It had been bent all out of shape and needed to be replaced. Mr. Metaken fixed it and put the matter out of his head."

"Now here's the interesting thing. Mr. Metaken is a junk collector, so when he fixes a car, he keeps the parts he removes, hoping that someday he will need it for another repair, and will be able to charge less than other used parts vendors. When the news went out about your husband's body, he got to thinking, went to his pile of used fenders, and took out the one in question. Looking at it more carefully, he found that there was in fact some dried material on the bottom. We're heading over there in a few minutes to see if we can get a blood sample, which would connect Moshel directly to Lije's death."

Rachel had to consciously remind herself to breathe. Getting Moshel was almost too good to be true; she worried that it was in fact too good to be true. "But even if Lije's blood is on it, couldn't Moshel claim that Liat had been driving the car? What would be the consequences if he were only an accessory to covering up an accidental killing?"

Kapdan smiled. "An interesting and perceptive question, Ms. Tucker, but one we need not worry about, because…"

Reuven interrupted. "Because Liat had a broken ankle at the time, so she couldn't have been driving!"

Rachel wheeled on him. "How the hell did you know that?"

He smiled, pleased with himself. "Because I remembered the diary. Liat mentioned that she had broken her right ankle three weeks before the accident, and only got the cast off two or three weeks afterwards. When you first pointed out that we couldn't prove Moshel was driving, I didn't think of it. But when Metaken was telling us about the fender, something in my head clicked. She only sought you out after the cast was off, wanting to wait until you had gotten over the initial shock before trying to steer you towards finding the body."

"But we don't have the diary, so we can't prove that!"

Kapdan answered this time. "Not from the diary, but with a proper warrant we can open medical records for deceased people. We called and verified that Liat Moshel was treated for a broken ankle 17 days before your husband disappeared, and had the cast removed 25 days after. Those records, combined with Mr. Metaken's testimony, this fender, and yours and Reuven's claims about the contents of the diary, are enough, I'm pretty sure, to establish that Pinhas Moshel drove the car that killed Elijah Zeale."

The words she had hoped to hear since Reuven had first linked Harvey to Moshel for her. "And what will that mean for Moshel? Will he be permanently disqualified from Temple service? Will he have to go to a city of refuge?"

Gaavtan Yoshor stepped in. "If I may, Ms. Tucker, as this is sort of my jurisdiction. We are in the process of asking that question to the relevant authorities; it is clear that it is good enough to suspend him from Temple service. I suspect it will be enough to land him in a city of refuge, unless a blood-avenger gets him first."

Reuven jumped up, struck by a thought. "Temple service! I'll bet that...that...." He controlled his next words with some effort, but the underlying hatred came through, "murderer is there now, offering sacrifices with all the other priests, as if nothing had happened. We've got to stop him, now! Kapdan, can we get a police escort?"

Kapdan stood up as well. "It would be my pleasure to drive you; I assure you, you will not find a faster ride back to Jerusalem."

Reuven looked to Rachel and Esther. "You two coming?"

CHAPTER THIRTY-FOUR

Kapdan, Esther, and Reuven all seemed to understand why they were driving at—she checked the speedometer on Kapdan's police cruiser—over 140 kilometers per hour (her mind automatically started calculating, "let's see, 140 times 5/8ths, 8 into 140 is 1 remainder 6, 8 into 60 is 7½, 17 ½ times 5 is 87½ miles per hour;" she had tried to convince herself to just live in metrics when in Israel, but it was another one of those life-tasks easier said than done), but she didn't.

In explanation, Reuven, looking back from the front passenger seat, pointed out that it was already 1:00 and sunset was around 4:45. That meant that they would start slaughtering and preparing the last sacrifice of the day at 1:45, planning to offer it by about 2:30. Depending on how fast Kapdan could drive, they still had an outside shot at preventing Moshel from taking part in the actual offering.

She knew she was missing something. "I don't understand; what if you don't catch him until after sunset? Is he going to run away?"

Esther smiled, apparently aware how incongruous the whole thing seemed to someone not yet used to it. Before she could answer, though, Reuven burst out, "Rachel, it's the Temple service! It's what Jews waited thousands of years to have back, and now this man is defiling it by his very participation! Imagine if I had hidden my deformity and continued to serve. That would mean all the sacrifices I ever offered were improper; the owners would have to buy *another* animal, and go through the ritual again. Aside from that, though, it would invalidate sacrifices that *can't* be redone, such as this one, on behalf of the whole nation."

She wasn't convinced, but here Esther came to her rescue.

"Sure, but Reuven, you haven't explained why we need to get there in person to keep Moshel away from the sacrifice. Why didn't we just call in?" A question she hadn't thought of, but a good one.

Shomer Kapdan spoke without taking his face off the curving road. "That actually comes up often in my line of work. The Temple is a completely independent jurisdiction, and its laws are administered by the priests on-site. They do not accept phone testimony, regardless of the circumstances, so that until we appear there in person, our words and information are irrelevant. To get Moshel out of the Temple will require personal testimony as to what Joseph Metaken told us and the state of the investigation."

Since Kapdan felt comfortable joining the conversation even when speeding around turns, and to take her mind off her own discomfort with same, Rachel asked him, "So what happens once we take him off the Mount?"

To her horror, he turned his head around to answer; she braced herself for a crash, only barely able to focus on his words. "We'll take him into protective custody until a court decides whether there's enough evidence to require him to flee to a city of refuge. If they do, we'll let him go so he can run. Either way, suspending him from service will end his career as a power broker, since that is the source of his influence."

Zeke Long had scared Rachel enough to be glad that he was confined to a city of refuge, but she hadn't spent much time thinking about whether she thought it was sufficient or appropriate punishment. Now that it was more personal, she knew it wasn't, especially since he seemed like he wouldn't have to move. "And that's it? He kills my husband, hides his body, leaves me an *agunah* throughout a pregnancy and childbirth, kills his own wife, and all we can do is remove him from the Temple?"

Reuven put up his hands placatingly. "Rachel, Rachel, you're not thinking about how authorities have to handle situations. What we can prove is different than what we know, and, by the way, you don't *know* half of what you just said—you don't *know* Pinhas was behind Liat's death."

"Oh, sure, then why wasn't she just shot—he gave her

something that would look natural and that he wouldn't be in the room for, so he wouldn't have to stop being in the Mikdash. You know that as well as I do!"

"I agree with you that I strongly suspect it, but I don't know it. And that's true of lots of the other stuff. But more important, you're not thinking of who he is. Losing the Temple service, and the perks of his position, is just about a death sentence for him."

"He'll adapt. I know his type. He'll hit rock bottom, and then carve out some kind of life, and people will end up admiring him for having made something of himself after such a dramatic and public downfall. Twenty years from now, some eager journalist, the next version of myself or the version after that, will do a prime time interview with him, celebrating his new life. And Lije and Liat will still be dead."

Esther joined the conversation. "I don't usually play the *haverah*-sponsor card, but you're ignoring our belief in God and His ultimate control of the system. We don't pretend to catch all the criminals, right all the wrongs, protect all the innocents; we do our best. The evidence we have now lets us get Moshel out of the Temple, lets us embarrass him publicly and destroy his reputation and his powerbase. If more evidence comes up in the future, we'll get him for other wrongs he's perpetrated; maybe this will encourage others to report his other crimes, who knows? The important thing is that we do what we can; the rest, we leave to God."

The image of Moshel living out his life with what she could only describe as a slap on the wrist got the better of her, and she said, bitterly, "Some Messiah!"

Reuven shook his head, frustrated that he couldn't get her to agree with him. "Rachel, don't blame him for other people's flaws. He sets a standard every day that the rest of us try to follow. Sure, we're not there yet, but here's a statistic I find interesting. A recent survey showed that 65% of this country feels more engaged with God and religion than before the Arrival. Now, that leaves 35% the same or less, which is an awful lot of people, but change takes time, and 65% is also a lot of people."

"You're paying attention to Moshel, one guy, who may have

a few hundred helpers. So you're right that less than .01% of the population can muck up the system pretty good and create a lot of misery. Sure, we need to get rid of him and his type, and that'll happen, but it doesn't take a day or a week. I think we're making good progress, and this whole incident—Lije and Liat's deaths, our finding Shlomit Hami, Moshel's being taken away from Temple service—is going to be a giant step in that direction."

His being right did nothing for Rachel's mood. She turned her face to the window and watched the road whiz past the rest of the way to Jerusalem.

CHAPTER THIRTY-FIVE

Kapdan drove miraculously, and they pulled up at the car park, the last place they could take a vehicle, at 2:15, the four of them piling out to the nearest entry gate. As they ran, Kapdan said, "Rachel, remember that you and I touched Lije's body, so we can't go onto the Temple grounds."

She flashed her badge. "I can't even go onto the Mount for another couple of days, so don't worry about me." Sure enough as they came to checkpoint to get onto the Mount, they were stopped by, of all people, Yedidya Gross.

He smiled at them, nodding at Esther, Reuven, and Rachel, saying, "Nice to see you again, Ms. Tucker, but you know I can't let you onto the Mount yet." She nodded in turn, about to step back and let the others continue on, when something about the coincidence of seeing Yedidya again, at a different entrance, on the day she happened to come once again, struck her as too fortuitous to ignore.

Even afterwards, she couldn't explain it other than to say that the serendipity of Yedidya's presence made her sure that she was supposed to be the one pointing the finger at Moshel. It was important—to her? the Jewish people? God?—that news reports about the arrest include the notation that Moshel's ex-wife's friendship with Rachel Tucker led to his defrocking. The thought, welling up out of her being, turned her back to Yedidya.

"Do you have a kind of intercom or phone system to the Temple floor, where they are actually offering the sacrifice? You know, for emergencies?"

"We do, but it has to really be an emergency, or I'll be severely punished."

"Well, pull it out, because we've got a murderer serving up there right now."

Yedidya was suspicious. "Another murderer, Ms. Tucker?"

She smiled, remembering her hysteria about Harvey. "Actually, I was wrong about that guy. This time, I've found the murderer I was looking for, and I've got better proof. You know Captain Kapdan, right?" He nodded.

"He is here to take Pinhas Moshel into protective custody for the accidental murder of my husband, Elijah Tucker. Reuven HaOzer can corroborate." Yedidya looked over at Kapdan, who agreed, and at Reuven, who smiled encouragingly. Uncertainly, he picked up a phone and dialed. When the phone was picked up on the other end, he explained the situation. Looking at his watch, he listened, said, "OK" and hung up.

Turning back to them, he said, "Given the time pressures, the higher-ups over there decided to just ask Moshel to come down and meet with you. As it happened, he had not yet participated in the sacrifice, so they can do it with a minimum of fanfare and embarrassment. He'll be here in a moment."

She was disappointed, only now realizing that she had been daydreaming about this moment on the ride back to Jerusalem, but had thought there would be a loud alarm, heard over the whole Mount, and an automated voice ringing out "Murderer! Murderer in the Mikdash!" with a human voice chiming in, "This is not a drill! This is not a drill! Pinhas Moshel has been identified as a murderer and is to be removed from the Temple *immediately*!"

Maybe he'd have run, and there'd have been a brief chase, before he was tackled by several other priests (or maybe the Levis would be the ones to do it, they were the Temple police, weren't they?). And then he'd have been escorted off in disgrace.

But of course it didn't work like that in real life, as her mother would have said. They'd have to verify her story, check the evidence, give him time for a reply, and so on. Yet again, life got in the way of the kind of satisfying black-and-white good-and-evil moments of good drama. For a journalist that was good, since it meant his story would dominate the news for weeks to come, with debate about the justice of the arrest, whether he was really guilty, whether the system should give him another chance.

She winced anticipating it. And then Kapdan was taking them to the police station, to give their statements against Moshel, to start the process of bringing him to justice.

CHAPTER THIRTY-SIX

The mechanic!!! Moshel could confess, although only to himself, that he had had a nagging feeling he had missed something. He thought he had covered the diary, even once Tucker found it. The shooting on the road was just stupid, as he had tried to tell them. It had stopped him from sending two people to quietly move the body to a different resting place. Even once it had been found, though, he had felt sure they couldn't pin it on him. Not that he had thought of it, but what mechanic keeps a blood-stained fender without even washing it?

Ah, well, he was where he was. As he closed the lights in his office, carefully watched by security guards, he wondered bitterly if HaOzer, Kapdan, and the rest of their crew knew what they had done. Would whoever replaced him be able to keep the operation afloat, negotiate the supply and financing issues he had struggled with? He doubted it, but it was out of his hands. Surely now they'd find out about his other compromises over the years. Some reformer would make hay out of improving on his work, further besmirching his name.

And it all started with Rachel Tucker, who Moshel had come to respect more than he had thought he would, although that didn't mean he'd fail to take the necessary action. Squaring his shoulders, leaving everything where it lay, he walked out of the office, past the security guards, into the next, even more dangerous, stage of his life.

CHAPTER THIRTY-SEVEN

Rachel assumed a night would come where she didn't drag herself into bed completely spent from the day's happenings, but this wasn't it. She managed to take Atid for a walk, narrating to him the little she knew about the streets of Jerusalem, swearing to herself for the umpteenth time that she'd buy and memorize a guidebook. When he got cranky, she gave him a bath, spoke to him about her day while she fed him (she figured she could talk about murder for a while longer before worrying about him understanding; for now, as long as she spoke soothingly, she could say what she wanted).

Once he was in bed, fatigue really hit. She needed to pay bills, record voice diary for the footage she was sure Brian had been collecting that day. She had seen him at the funeral, today's ceremony, and she assumed he'd secure some footage of Moshel being escorted from the Mount.

All that would have to wait until tomorrow; right now, she wasn't getting out of bed, especially since she could only bet on five uninterrupted hours. If she went to sleep *right now*, she could probably be rested by his second waking of the night and do her chores then. She dropped off into a deep and restful sleep, so deep that when Moshel woke her three hours later, it took her a few moments to realize what was going on.

"Pinhas! What are you doing here?" Even as she put a name to the face standing over her, terror invaded every part of her body, and, wildly, her thoughts, turned to the baby. Had he hurt Atid?

"The court decided, a few moments ago, that there was enough evidence for Liat's blood-avenger to kill me, so I'm on my way. I just wanted to stop by for a moment and let you know what you've done.

You probably think of yourself as some kind of hero, as the woman who brought down a great priest."

Even cloudy-headed from sleep, she knew that wasn't right. "I couldn't care less about your priesthood; I only cared about Liat and Lije."

Moshel gaped at her. "Couldn't care less? Don't you understand? It was always *about* the priesthood and the Temple; that was what got between Liat and me; that was why I couldn't let anyone know about your husband. Temple, first, last, and always!"

As her mind regained its sharpness and she began to take stock of her situation, she decided Moshel hadn't come to kill her. If not, she might as well argue. Maybe, if she kept him here long enough, she could herself be Lije's blood-avenger.

"And why, pray tell, are you so important to the Temple?"

The question distressed him, good! Now he'd keep talking. "Nobody ever stops to think about these things. Do you think it's easy keeping an institution like that going? Do you know how much the gold and silver utensils cost, how easily they can become overused or defiled? Do you know how hard it is to reeducate people to give money to yet another cause, one which many of them had stopped caring about? Think about yourself—have you ever donated to the Temple?"

"Of course not; I give to the poor, or some other worthy cause."

"Exactly. Do you know how many Jews think like you? 66% in the last poll. In fact, when I took over, we got more donations from non-Jews than from Jews. And even that wasn't enough to balance our budget! Without me, the whole thing would have gone kaput before it ever really got off the ground. We're only just beginning to see financial stability. So do you think exiling me is going to be worth the cost?"

Rachel was shocked that he could actually believe what he was saying. "Do you mean that you should be immune to prosecution because of your importance?"

He shook his head vigorously up and down. "I know how it

sounds, but at this juncture in history, yes. I made myself a deal when I…hit your husband; you can check this out. I placed a full, handwritten confession in a safe-deposit box, with orders to deliver it to the High Court in Jerusalem five years from the day I opened it. I figured by that time, I'd have been able to get the Temple on a secure footing. But, of course, you've ruined all that. I hope when it goes under that you are very happy with yourself."

He turned to leave, but Rachel wasn't done with him. "Wait a minute! What about all the other abuses—the fake blemishes, the extortion of extra donations, the maiming of priests you felt you couldn't control?"

He winced. "All necessary evils, I assure you. New projects are always difficult, Ms. Tucker, and the first few years require painful choices, choices I made because I could and nobody else would. I assure you that I took no relish in any of that side of the business, but I did what I had to do to allow the service to continue. Maybe one day you will understand that success often requires sacrificing some ideals for others."

He turned to go, only to see Gaavtan Yoshor standing in the doorway. In the heat of their discussion, neither of them had heard her appear. She pointed her gun steadily at them, and spoke with a steel that had been absent earlier.

"How unfortunate for you, Ms. Tucker, that Moshel here felt the need to unburden himself to you before fleeing. We might have been able to rid ourselves only of him; now I have to take care of you as well."

She was confused enough by Moshel's weird mix of commitment and corruption, but Yoshor's words were beyond her. She said, "What are you talking about?" at the same time as Moshel said, pleadingly, "I didn't tell her anything, I swear! She has a newborn; just leave her alone! I knew you'd try to find me, but leave her out of this!"

Yoshor shook her head disapprovingly, as she came forward into the room. "Do you really think I have the luxury of believing that? This operation generates *waay* too much money for us to take the word of a dead man, especially one as fundamentally idealistic as you, Pinhas. May I call you Pinhas? I hate being formal with someone I'm about to kill."

Dimly, Rachel remembered that in situations like these the goal was to keep everybody talking, to give events a chance to unfold with the least violence possible, and, she hoped, leaving her alive to tell the tale. Right now it was no effort, since she had no idea of what was going on. "I'm sorry, but I really do not know what you're talking about. Before you kill me, as you apparently intend to, could you just clue me in to why? Why," she added bitterly, "my child is going to have to grow up as a complete orphan?"

Yoshor seemed surprised but not at all put out. "You mean you really don't know? Now that's a pity, a truly unnecessary death. Tell me, Ms. Tucker, who did you think was running the operation Moshel was telling you about?"

She didn't even have to think. "Why, he was!"

Yoshor snorted. "Let me tell you this, Ms. Tucker, idealists do not run the real world, because they are too caught up in their dreams. Pinhas Moshel would have dithered every time we had to bend the rules a bit. Each blemish, each priest moved out of the way, each action we took to make the Temple stronger, and to make ourselves a little money, would have been weighed, thought about, put aside, and only then put into action. We didn't have time, nor did we care enough. His ideals were a luxury we could not afford."

"Isn't that another form of idealism, where putting ideals into practice overrides other considerations, where the ends justify the means?"

Yoshor laughed. "I wish I could dignify my position so well. My ideals pretty much end at getting myself extra money and a better job than police chief of Nowheresville. Once I take care of this unpleasant business, I'll be promoted to a real city, with salary and prestige to match. Because, Ms. Tucker, many of us don't care about Arrivals or anything like that. What's in it for me, that's what I say."

Rachel saw only part of what happened next; when she retold

the story afterward, her mind filled in the blanks. She did see Reuven come barreling through the doorway, slamming into Yoshor before the policewoman had a chance to fully turn around. Instead of tackling her, though, he knocked her over, assuming, Rachel supposed, that that would knock the gun out of her hand or stun her enough that he could immobilize her.

It did neither. Yoshor fell to the floor but quickly turned over, raising the gun to shoot. Rachel closed her eyes, unwilling to watch Reuven die. Instead of a single shot at close range, killing Reuven, there were two, coming almost simultaneously with a window being smashed into the apartment. At the window was Shomer Kapdan, which sort of made sense, but seeing Harvey Keiter at her door was a complete surprise. Each of them was holding a newly fired weapon in his hand; after registering that fact, she looked down at Yoshor, who had dropped the gun and was holding her hand, bleeding profusely.

Kapdan carefully removed the rest of the glass from the window, and climbed into the room. "Don't worry, Ms. Tucker, the government will pay for the window." He walked over to Yoshor, kicked the gun further away from her, bent down and said, "Gaavtan Yoshor, you are under arrest for the attempted murders of Pinhas Moshel and Rachel Tucker. You have the right to remain silent, the right to..."

Yoshor interrupted. "Yeah, yeah, I know my rights. I'll call my lawyer from the station, but you can bet I'll be cutting a deal. For now, get me a doctor, you idiot!"

Kapdan was in no hurry. "I've seen many wounds like that, we've got plenty of time. But why aren't you wounded elsewhere? I know I shot you in the hand; Harvey, it's not like you to miss!"

Harvey laughed. "With my record, even in these circumstances, I wasn't going to shoot anyone; I shot the gun itself."

Rachel found her voice. "Wait a minute! I don't understand why you're all here. Did everyone but me know I was going to be attacked tonight?"

Reuven answered first, his breath still coming in rasps from the adrenaline of bursting into the room. "I thought Moshel would come to kill you. I wanted to give him time to hang himself with his confession," he pulled a tape recorder out of his pocket, "but when Yoshor showed up, I figured I'd get two for the price of one."

Kapdan said, "For my part, I began suspecting Yoshor after those two officers she sent attacked us at the gravesite, but I got even more sure when she didn't ask to come apprehend Moshel. She worried, what with the jig being up, that he'd identify her. I made a few calls, and decided to have her tailed. When I got the call that she was on her way to Jerusalem, I picked up her trail myself."

Moshel looked at Harvey. "And you?"

Harvey looked uncomfortable. "Well, I knew that being kept out of the Temple would be a big blow to you, and I worried you might do something stupid, so I was hoping to talk to you, let you find another way of handling it. When you came here, I wasn't sure what to do; I knew Yoshor from the Organization, so I followed her up. When I got up the stairs and saw Reuven here, I dropped back so he wouldn't see me. And then, once he went in, I jumped in to see what happened."

Moshel turned to Kapdan. "Captain, Harvey here originally connected me to the Organization; we had a serious money problem in the Temple, and I was desperate. For a long time, he was my liaison and errand boy.But since he was given The Choice, he took his *haver*-training more seriously than I could have imagined. He still did me favors occasionally because I forced him to, but none criminal. Anyway, I'd like to speak in his favor; his Organization activities are a thing of the past, and I hope this will not count against him."

Kapdan looked at Moshel witheringly, and said, "Right now, I don't think standing up for others should be the first thing on your mind. You still have to get to a city of refuge before a blood avenger gets you, and I see one such avenger right here."

Rachel dimly realized that he was talking about her, that there were guns available in the room, and that she should be trying to kill Moshel. But she couldn't do it; she knew that the court was going to find the death accidental, and to take advantage of a loophole that gave her an opportunity for revenge just because Moshel felt the need to warn her about the Organization didn't seem right. She picked up a gun, but lowered it.

"Thank you, captain, but I think someone else will have to do that job; maybe someone from Liat's family will get him one day. Or maybe we'll leave it to God."

Then, Moshel got upset. "Look, I admit I was driving the car when your husband got killed, but I had nothing to do with Liat's death. Sure, we'd gotten divorced, and she was going to eventually reveal what I had done, but I wouldn't kill for that!"

Harvey nodded. "It wasn't him; the Organization knew they could control Moshel and preferred the devil they knew—especially with the Temple becoming more fiscally sound, they didn't trust whoever would replace him. So they had someone kill Liat, in a way that would seem natural. It both saved Moshel and sent a warning."

Kapdan looked at him. "So who did that?"

Harvey shook his head. "Sorry, I don't know. I had already begun negotiating my exit at that time, and since they believe that once you're in, you're in for life, it's been kind of a tense negotiation, one I think will end with me having to disappear completely, I had hoped to move up North, but I'm thinking I'll have to leave the country. They insisted I go to Liat's to confirm the "kill," but already didn't trust me with doing the actual killing."

"The same goes, by the way, for whoever sent HaOzer and Tucker off the road; I knew it happened, but I have no idea who actually did it. In any case, the longer I stay, the more dangerous my situation becomes, so, with your permission, Captain?"

Kapdan hesitated, struggling with himself, but then nodded. Rachel had gotten so used to trailing Harvey that when he turned and left the room, she had the urge to go, too.

Moshel's speaking up stopped her. "I don't know who killed Liat, but the name of the operative who ran Ms. Tucker and HaOzer—and, incidentally, who had your toe cut off; I know you blame me, but I strongly advised against it—goes by code names, but I have his contact information here, in my PDA," he handed it to Kapdan, "although I suspect he has disappeared or is well on the way to doing so."

"Truth to tell, I need to do a little disappearing myself. Getting to a city of refuge will be kind of a blessing, since the Organization has yet to penetrate there. If you'll excuse me.... I'll be one of the few residents praying for long life for the High Priest. Which is kind of funny, because until now, I'd have given anything to get him out of the way. Ah, well, life." He looked to Kapdan to be sure he was allowed to go, and then headed out the same door as Harvey.

At the door, Reuven was standing in his way. They eyed each other for a long moment, and then Reuven stuck out his hand. As they shook, Reuven said, "It might be hard for both of us at first, but if you need a sponsor, and you're ready to work, I'm available." Moshel nodded briefly and ran out of the room.

CHAPTER THIRTY- EIGHT

For what she hoped was the last time ever, she spent the night navigating a police presence in her home. Although they all knew what had happened, it took a while for Internal Affairs to verify the various stories, especially as Yoshor had stopped talking, saving any information for when she was making her plea bargain. After several hours, including Atid waking up for a feeding, she collapsed into bed and stayed there, bringing the baby to her when he woke up for the morning, until the sitter came.

Acting impulsively but confidently, she gave the woman the day off, apologizing for not having called before she left her house. She couldn't have explained why, but she needed a day with her son; she could get her errands done with him just as well as without, although probably a little more slowly. She could do her voice over diaries while he napped. Most of all, she needed to have him close.

It was a melancholy morning, the kind she enjoyed from time to time. She wandered around the city, stopping at some parks to watch kids playing, shedding a few tears when she saw families walking together, even as she wondered who these people were who had the time to be wandering around in the middle of the day, and cuddling the baby a lot. Had it been gray and drizzling, it would have been perfect.

As they sat at a café having a late lunch (well, Rachel was having a late lunch; the baby had needed lunch earlier and gotten fed in a bathroom stall in the mall, the most discreet place she could find), she lifted herself out of her funk enough to wonder what had put her in it in the first place.

Finding out that Moshel wasn't the monster she had thought he was should have made her happy. Finding out that Harvey wasn't a bad guy or was no longer a bad guy was sort of a happy ending. And they had apprehended Gaavtan Yoshor, a valuable asset to the Organization.

That word, though, brought her thoughts out into the open. She had once reported a Mafia story and spent the year after with police protection, as inconvenient and (she thought) useless as that was. A determined assassin would get to her, protection or no. It was only later, during a major sweep of organized crime that New York's Finest found papers that mentioned that the Family had decided to ignore her offense, putting her back in the clear.

Was the Organization like that? Did her role here, in losing them Moshel, getting Yoshor arrested, sparking an investigation and (she hoped) reform of the workings of the Mikdash, mean they'd try to remove her?

A younger Rachel Tucker, still somewhere inside of her, thrust out her jaw, refusing to be intimidated. She hadn't let the Mafia bother her; she'd broken three more major stories that year. She almost felt like staying in Israel, investigating the Organization, and showing Reuven and the others that the media could be a force for positive change.

Which, she now realized, was why her newest persona, mother, had sent the babysitter away. In the adrenaline rush that had started with chasing Harvey and continued almost unabated until this moment, she had been in grave danger at least four times. She ticked them off in her head; there was the guy who warned her to put the diary back (well, maybe that shouldn't count, since she now realized it was Harvey and he wouldn't have hurt her unless she threatened him directly), the man who took the diary the next day, who had also shot at Reuven and run them off the road, and then Yoshor from last night.

Her mental jaw still jutting way out, one side of her argued that she had done vastly more dangerous things many times before. Never as a mother, shot back a side of her she wasn't used to seeing, and especially not as mother of an orphan. Important work needs to get done, the younger side said; nothing is more important than helping Atid grow up as happily, normally, and healthily as possible.

As the internal conversation continued, she paid her lunch tab, and started walking, still aimlessly as far as she could tell. Her mood had lifted as the internal debate clarified itself. When she looked up to see that her legs had taken her on the familiar route to the Temple Grounds, she knew what she had to do. It took twice the ordinary time to ready herself; when she had, she opened the door and went in.

CHAPTER THIRTY-NINE

"**M**y work on this series has combined a personal journey with a professional task and, I hope, resulted in a pleasurable and informative experience for you, our viewers. While the rest of my reports have dealt with facts of life in Israeli society, I wanted to close tonight with a more subjective summary of what I learned about this experiment in Utopianism and to explain, as much to myself as to anyone else, why I have returned to America, to continue my regular work here with ABC News."

"Before there was an Arrival on the scene, the word Messiah always seemed to indicate a future that couldn't really happen or could only come about miraculously. When a man convinced the Jews in the State of Israel (and many worldwide, including my late husband) that he was that long-awaited figure, I was subconsciously offended by how naturally it all occurred, and how little had changed in the New Israel. Viewers of this series have been offered ample evidence that there is still theft, murder, infidelity, and even organized crime in the country. Israelis will tell you that the highly unlikely takes some time to achieve, the impossible just a little longer."

"I didn't want that; if there was going to be a Messiah who was going to change my whole life, I needed the change to be clear and obvious and immediate. Is the current King of Israel the Messiah? I can't tell you; even after all of this reporting, the only conclusions I can draw are purely factual: crime is down, the economy is up, and the percentage of Israelis who describe themselves as "working hard" to build a better relationship with God is at its highest level ever. For many, those are clear signs of the Messiah. For me, Pinhas Moshel, Gaavtan Yoshor and their ilk proved that my husband wasted his life on a dream that he still didn't get to see in his lifetime."

"Early letters responding to our reports have asked why I didn't just stay in Israel, some even asking straight out whether Reuven HaOzer and I have secretly married and are waiting until the end of this series to announce it. I suppose these are the questions I wanted to answer tonight. I decided to stay in America because I wanted what this country is best at giving: freedom to guide my own religious development without having it overseen and judged by someone else, freedom to decide when I was ready for what, and the freedom to raise my son with the beliefs and views that I chose."

"Reuven and I discussed these issues, and recognized that our acquaintance will have to remain that, as we each feel the ties of different countries and beliefs too strongly to work out more of a relationship. My time in Israel changed me in profound ways, as anyone who views tapes of me before and after Atid's birth will be able to see. For now, though, my place is here, raising my son safely. I hope and pray that thirty years from now, when I look back on this decision, I will feel that it was the right one. Until tomorrow, this is Rachel Tucker, ABC News. Good night."

Ed Appleby was waiting just off-camera, holding flowers and offering a big hug. "Rachel, the numbers are *excellent*. Great job! And, we're all thrilled to have you staying with us!" Applause rang throughout the studio as she walked through, mostly in a fog of her own. Not in the mood just then for the socializing she knew she'd have to do at the victory party planned for the next night, Rachel walked through the crowd of well-wishers as politely as she could, went to the daycare in the studio building, picked up her son, and left to face her future.

.

64943